THE
FOURTH WATCH

H. A. CODY

AUTHOR OF THE FRONTIERSMAN, UNDER SEALED
ORDERS, THE LONG PATROL, ETC.

1st WORLD
LIBRARY
Literary Society

The Fourth Watch

H. A. Cody

© 1st World Library – Literary Society, 2004
PO Box 2211
Fairfield, IA 52556
www.1stworldlibrary.org
First Edition

LCCN: 2004091189

Softcover ISBN: 1-59540-635-2
eBook ISBN: 1-59540-735-9

Purchase *"The Fourth Watch"*
as a traditional bound book at:
www.1stWorldLibrary.org/purchase.asp?ISBN=1-59540-635-2

The Fourth Watch
contributed by the Mahaney Family
in support of
1st World Library Literary Society

TO ALL

"Messengers, Watchmen and Stewards of the Lord," who have faithfully toiled through Life's long night, and now in their Fourth Watch and Last Watch behold the dawn of a new Life breaking, this book is affectionately dedicated by one but yet in the Second Watch.

Contents

Chapter I

The Awakening

The boy plied his hoe in a listless manner, for his thoughts were elsewhere. Several hundred yards to the right stood the forest, glorious in its brilliant autumn hues. There among those trees the wary partridges were feeding or perching temptingly upon bough, fallen log or ragged stump. To the left the waters of the noble River St. John rippled and sparkled beneath the glowing sun. Over there amidst that long stretch of marshland, in many a cove and reedy creek, the wild ducks were securely hidden. What connection had a rugged, stirring lad with a brown sombre potato patch when the strong insistent voice of the wild was calling him to fields afar? There was no inspiration here - among these straggling rows. Nothing to thrill a boy's heart, or to send the blood surging and tingling through his body. But there - ! He sighed as he leaned upon his hoe and looked yearningly around. Down on the shore; in a sheltered cove among the trees, the *Scud*, a small boat, was idly flapping her dirty patched sail.

"Wonder what dad left it up for?" thought the boy.

"Maybe he's going after more ducks. Wish to goodness he'd help with these potatoes so I could get off, too."

Then his eyes roamed out over the water until they rested upon a whitesail away in the distance, bearing steadily down-stream. He watched it carelessly for some time, but noticing the manner in which it drooped under an occasional squall his interest became aroused.

"There's too much canvas, that's sure!" he ejaculated. "Some idiot, I s'pose, who doesn't know 'bout these squalls. Guess he'll learn soon if he isn't careful. Now the *Scud*, she's all right. I'd risk her any time - My - !" and he almost held his breath as the white sail, much nearer now, swooped to the water like the wing of a gigantic bird. The boat righted herself, however, and sped gracefully forward. Again and again she dipped and careened under each successive squall, winning the lad's unstinted admiration. But even as he looked and wondered, a furious gust caught the white sail as it listed heavily, and drove it with one sweep to the water, overturning the boat as it did so. With a cry of fear the boy dropped his hoe, stared for an instant at the overturned craft, and then sped across the potato field sloping to the shore. He did not wait to go by the path, which led straight up to a little cabin in the valley, but, making a short cut to the left, leaped into a tangled thicket beyond. He crashed his way through the branches and underbrush, not heeding the numerous scratches upon face and hands.

He reached the *Scud*, tore, rather than untied the painter from an old oak root, and sent the boat reeling backwards from its moorings. The sail flapped wildly in the breeze, which was now growing stronger, and the craft began to drift. Catching up the centre-board, lying near, the boy drove it down into its narrow groove with a resounding thud. Seizing the sheet-line with one hand, and squatting well astern he grasped the tiller with the other. Nobly the boat obeyed her little determined commander. The sail filled, she listed to the left and darted forward, bearing bravely up the wind. Straight ahead the boy could see the distressed boat sinking lower and lower in the water, with a man and a woman clinging desperately to the upturned side. The wind was now whistling around him, and at times threatening to rip away the patched sail. The water was rough, and the angry white-caps were dashing their cold spray over his clothes. But not for an instant did he swerve from his course until quite near the wreck. Then letting go the sheet-line he permitted the boat to fall away a little to the left. In this manner he was able to swing gradually in a half-circle, and by the time he was up again to the teeth of the wind the *Scud* was lying close to the overturned boat.

So preoccupied had been the boy up to this moment that he had no time to observe closely the shipwrecked pair. Now, however, he cast a curious glance in their direction, as he let go the rudder and sheet-line, and threw out the painter to the man. Eagerly the latter seized the rope, and managed to hold the two boats together.

"Give us yer hand," shouted the boy, "and let her come out first. Be careful now," he continued as the crafts bumped against each other. "There, that's good."

With considerable difficulty the two strangers were rescued from their perilous position, and then the *Scud* dropped away from the wreck.

"Where do you want to go?" asked the boy, as once again he brought the boat to the wind.

"Over there," responded the man, pointing to the opposite shore. "We can land on that point and get driven home."

Almost mechanically the boy swung the *Scud* around, and headed her for the place indicated. From the moment he had caught a glimpse of the woman clinging to the boat he had found it hard to turn away his eyes. Her hat was gone, and the wind was blowing her dark-brown hair about her face, which was white as death. But when she turned her large blue eyes filled with gratitude and fear upon her rescuer, a strange feeling of embarrassment swept suddenly over him. Women he had seen before, but none such as this. How quiet she was, too - not a cry or complaint did she make. Her clothes were wet; the water cold, and the wind raw. But she sat there in the boat watching him with those big eyes as he guided the *Scud* steadily forward.

He looked at her dress, how neat and clean it was. Then he glanced at his own rough togs. How coarse, worn and dirty were they, while his shoes were heavy grey brogans. A flush mantled his sun-browned face. He shifted uneasily, gripped the tiller more firmly, and drove the *Scud* a point nearer to the wind. What must she think of him? he wondered. Was she comparing him with the well-dressed man at her side, who was looking thoughtfully out over the blue water? A feeling of jealousy stole into his heart. He had never known such a thing before. He knew what it was to be angry - to stamp and shout in his rage. He had engaged in several pitched battles with the boys in the neighbourhood who had made fun of him. But his life - a life of freedom - had satisfied him. To hunt, to trap, to wander over hill, valley and forest was all that he

H. A. Cody

asked for. He had never thought of anything higher, never dreamed of any life but the one his father led, hunting, and trapping in season and making a slight pretence of farming. Now, however, something was stirring within him. He longed to show this woman that though his clothes and shoes were rough, he was almost a man and could do great things.

"What is your name, my boy?"

The words startled him, and he glanced quickly up. The woman was looking at him still, but now she was smiling. Was she laughing at him?

"My name's Dan," was the reply.

"Dan, Dan what?"

"Oh, just old Jim's boy."

"Old Jim, Old Jim!" repeated the woman. "Do you mean Jim Flitter, the trapper?"

"Yep, that's him."

"And do you live over there?"

"Yep. In that shanty up the valley, Dad and I live there alone."

"Have you no mother, Dan?" and the woman's voice was soft and low.

"None now."

She was about to question further, but noticing the

look upon the boy's face she desisted.

"Do you know you've saved our lives?" she remarked after a short silence. "I can never thank you enough for what you have done for us to-day. I don't think I could have clung to that boat much longer."

"I ain't done nuthin'," Dan replied. "But next time you go out don't carry so much sail, specially when it's squally. I mayn't always be handy like I was to-day. But come, we're at the pint, so I'll land you here." Saying which, Dan let the sail go free, and ran the boat gently up the pebbly shore.

"Now, my boy," asked the man, "how much do I owe you?" Dan had stooped and was about to push the *Scud* from the beach. He looked up quickly at the question, but made no reply.

"How much?" demanded the man, somewhat impatiently.

"What do you mean?" asked the boy.

"What do I mean? Simply this. You've done us a great service, saved us from death, and how much money do you want? How much shall I pay you?"

"Nuthin'."

Dan was standing erect now. His dark eyes fixed full upon the man's face, flashed with anger, while his heart thumped tumultuously beneath his little checkered shirt.

"What! won't take any pay!"

"No!"

"And why not?"

"Cause I won't. You've no right to ask me. It ain't fair!"

That was all Dan could utter. He could not express his feelings; repugnance filled his heart at the thought of taking money for what he had done. He felt the woman's eyes fixed upon him. What would she think, of him, Dan Flitter, taking money for saving people's lives? He gave one quick glance in her direction, turned, and pushing the boat from the shore, sprang in, leaving the man and the woman upon the beach gazing wonderingly after him.

Chapter II

The Vision

"Danny, what's the meaning of this?"

Mr. Flitter laid down his paper, took his pipe from his mouth, and looked inquiringly at his son.

Dan was seated at the farther end of the table, cleaning his beloved shot-gun. It had done good work that day, and a fine string of partridges hung in an outer room, ready to go to the store early the next morning. A week had now passed since the rescue on the river, and during the whole of that time he had said nothing about it to his father. There was a reason for this. The latter had been much away from home during the day, only coming in late at night when his son was in bed, so they had little chance for conversation. It was a busy season, and they must make the most of it. So while the one scoured the forest for partridges, the other searched the river for ducks and geese. But Dan did not feel inclined to say anything to his father about what he had done. To him it was not worth mentioning. That he had picked up two shipwrecked people, and set them ashore, in his eyes was a very simple thing. It was made less so by the thought of that woman with the large eyes, beautiful face and sunny smile. How could he describe to his father the new feeling which

H. A. Cody

had come into his breast, the longing for something more than the life he was leading, and the desire to show that woman what he really could do?

His father's sudden question startled him. The mail was carried but once a week to this place, and by the time the paper arrived from the post office it was several days old. Mr. Flitter had come home earlier than usual, having had a fine day's shooting on the river, and was in excellent spirits. Game was in great demand, and he looked hopefully for good sales on the morrow. After their scanty meal he picked up the paper and began to read. Silence reigned in the little dingy shanty for some time, broken only by the short, sharp question.

"Don't you know anything about it, Danny?" insisted Mr. Flitter, noticing the startled and puzzled look upon his son's face.

"What do you mean, dad?"

"Why, about that wreck on the river. This paper says that you saved two people from drowning right off here over a week ago."

Dan's face flushed and his heart beat fast. What! was his name in the paper? Would the people in the big city see it? What would the boys in the neighbourhood think? Would they make fun of him any more? He could show them now that he was somebody, for his name was in the paper! These thoughts drove surgingly through his brain. He rose from his place and stood by his father's side.

"Show me, dad," he whispered; "let me see it."

"There, Danny, look at the heading: -

"'A Boy's Brave Deed.'"

"And is that long piece all about me, dad?"

"Yes, and it states what you did. Why didn't you tell me about it, son?"

"Where's my name, dad?" asked Dan, unheeding his father's question.

"There," and Mr. Flitter, pointing with his finger, spelled out the words, "Daniel Flitter."

"Does it say, dad, who those people were that got swamped?"

"No, their names are not given. It only says that the young man lives in the city. But why didn't you tell me about it, Dan?"

"Thought it wasn't worth while," replied the boy. "But I don't see how they know about it down there to put it in the paper."

"How did it happen, son. Let's have the whole story." Mr. Flitter pulled off his boots, lighted his pipe afresh, and leaned back to listen.

"I wonder who that woman is," he remarked, when Dan had finished his brief account. "I know most people for miles around, and it's strange I don't know her from your description. However, I shall make inquiries and find out."

During the days that followed, Dan lived in a new world. His feet trod the earth, and he trudged for miles the woodland ways. But his mind was in fairyland.

It was an enchanted world through which he moved, and he was master of all. The trees on every side were crowds of admiring people, and the branches were so many outstretched hands pointing to him. His breast swelled with pride. He walked erect, his head held high, while his eyes flashed with a triumphant light. The birds sang his praises; the squirrels chattered one to another, and every brook babbled "Daniel Flitter, Daniel Flitter." His name had appeared in the paper! He was no longer an obscure person, but a hero - a wonder! He kept the clipping carefully wrapped up in his pocket. Often he would sit down in some quiet forest spot, unfold his treasure and look long and proudly upon those two magic words. One day as he sat studying the paper a desire came into his heart to know all of those wonderful words before and after his name. He could not read, never having gone to school. In fact he never wanted to do so. His one aim was to be a mighty hunter and trapper like his father. But now, a longing had entered his soul; a spark from the mysterious fire of life had found a lodging which needed only a little fanning to produce a bright and fervent flame.

"Dad," said he, that night, while eating his supper, "I wish I knew how to read. All the boys in this settlement can read and write. Ain't I old enough to begin?"

"You're old enough, lad, but we live a long way from the schoolhouse, and when you were little it was too far for you to walk. You might go this winter, when there's spare time, if you don't mind the distance."

"I don't mind that, dad, but all the rest will know so much that they'll make fun of me. I only know a few of my letters, and mother taught me them before she died."

"She did, lad, she did, God bless her," and a huskiness came into Mr. Flitter's voice as he spoke. "If she were alive now you would know as much as any boy of your age, for your mother was a smart one, and I guess you take after her, Dan.

"I wish I had her now," and the boy gave a deep eigh. "She'd help me every night, and I wouldn't be stupid any more."

Mr. Flitter made no reply to these words. He finished his supper in silence, and while Dan washed the few dishes he sat thoughtfully smoking his old clay pipe.

"Laddie," he remarked as they were preparing for bed, "I've been having deep thoughts to-night, and I've come to the conclusion that I haven't done right by you. I've neglected you too much."

"In what way, dad?" questioned the boy.

"Oh, in many ways. I've fed and clothed you, though I guess you've earned it all. But I've not thought enough about your mind - your education, I mean. Besides, there are deeper and more serious things in life of which I've told you nothing. I do feel mighty guilty when I think about it all."

"You've been good to me, though," and Dan looked inquiringly into his father's face.

"Yes, in a way. But, then, haven't I been good to our old mare, Queen? I feed and blanket her. But what more have I done for you - and you are my own son? Now look here," he added, after a pause, "I'm willing to teach you at nights how to read, and see if we can't make up for my past neglect."

"Dad! D'you mean it?"

"There now, that'll do. No more talking. Let's off to bed, and we'll have the first lesson to-morrow night."

The days that followed were busy ones for Dan. The shooting season closed, but there was other work to do. The rabbits had to be snared and his regular rounds made to the traps set for the wiry mink, lumbering raccoon, and the wily fox. Each night, the animals brought in during the day had to be skinned, and the pelts carefully stretched. Then when this had been accomplished to his satisfaction he would turn his attention to his studies.

His father was cutting cord-wood for a neighbour, and was able to get home at night. Then the two pored over the mysterious letters and words in the little cabin, the elder doing his best to impart his scanty knowledge to the younger. They were happy times for Dan. He had something to live for now, and throughout the day, as he wandered from trap to trap, the words he had studied the night before kept ringing in his ears.

But, alas! such scenes were to be dispelled all too soon. They were too good to last long. One evening Dan returned home to find an unusual commotion about the place. Men and women were there who had never before entered the building. And the doctor, whom he had often met on the road, what was he doing there? What were they whispering about? and why did they look at him in that way, when he entered the house? Where was his father? Who was that lying on the bed so very still? Could it be dad? He had never seen him like that before. Then the thought flashed upon him: something was wrong! His father was hurt! and with a cry he rushed forward, and bent over the prostrate form. But no word of welcome, no sign of recognition did he receive. Nothing but that vacant stare met his ardent gaze.

Slowly, very slowly, he grasped the meaning of it all, as the sympathetic watchers told the brief story. His father had met with a serious accident. A large birch tree in falling had lodged against another, a sturdy maple. While cutting at the latter the birch had suddenly turned over and swooping to the ground with a resounding crash had buried Mr. Flitter beneath the branches ere he had had time to escape. He had been carried home bruised, broken, and unconscious. The doctor had been hurriedly summoned, and had done all in his power for the injured man. But in vain, for in a short time he had breathed his last.

Dan uttered not a word when the tale had been told. He asked no questions, neither did he make any outcry. He stood like one stricken dumb, dry-eyed and motionless, gazing upon that quiet form lying upon the bed. Gently they led him away, and tried to speak to him. He did not heed them. A weight such as he had never known before pressed upon his heart. He wished to be alone, somewhere in the woods, out there where no one could gaze upon him. His father was dead! For him there was no consolation from the words of the Man of Sorrows. The life beyond had no meaning for him. His mother had taught him to say the little prayer, "Now I lay me down to sleep," but that seemed so long ago, and he had not repeated it after her death. He had seen the birds and animals lying dead, but had thought nothing about it then. Now his father was just like them, would never look at him again, would never speak to him any more.

He watched in a dazed manner what took place on the two following days. Neighbours came, spoke to him, stayed awhile and then departed. The day of the funeral arrived. He stood with the rest at the graveside. It was cold, and the wind laden with snow whistled about him. He heard the grey-headed, white-bearded clergyman read the Burial Service. The words of hope had no meaning for him. An awful feeling of desolation filled his heart as he watched the earth thrown into the grave. A shiver passed through his body, caused not by the coldness alone. Several came to speak to him. He did not want to see them. He turned and fled down across the field over the fence to the humble cabin in the valley. This he entered, now so quiet and desolate. He reached the bed - his father's bed - and throwing himself upon it gave vent to his grief. His pent-up feelings at last found an outlet and tears coursed down his tanned cheeks, moistening the pillow beneath his little curly head.

Chapter III

Glendow Rectory

"Are you cold, lad?"

"No," was the brief reply.

Parson John, Rector of Glendow, glanced down at the little muffled figure at his side. He reached over, tucked in the robes more closely about their feet, and spoke one word to Midnight. The horse, noble animal that she was, bounded forward. The ice, glassy and firm, stretched out far ahead. It was a raw, midwinter day and the wind drifting in from the north-east presaged a storm. But the magnificent beast, black as a raven's wing, did not mind it. With head low, tail almost touching the dash-board, and eyes sparkling with animation, she clipped along with great strides.

The parson gave a half-audible chuckle as he settled back in the seat and gripped the reins more firmly.

"What will Nellie say," he thought, "when she sees the lad? Won't she be surprised! She's never tired of talking about that rescue on the river."

Dan thoroughly enjoyed the drive as he nestled by the parson's side. It was very strange to be speeding along

H. A. Cody

in such a luxurious manner, with a horse travelling like the wind, and a big jolly man holding the reins. He said nothing, but kept his eye fixed upon Midnight, his admiration steadily increasing. He would like to own a horse like that, and down in his heart he determined to have one some day - his very own.

"What do you think of Midnight, lad?" asked the parson, noticing Dan's admiring gaze.

"Great!" was the reply.

"Wish to have one like her, eh?"

"Y'bet."

"You will some day, boy; you will. But get a good one or none at all, and here's a safe rule:

"Round-hoof'd, short-jointed, fetlocks shag and long,
Broad breast, full eye, small head and nostrils wide,
High crest, short ears, straight legs and passing strong.
Thin, mane, thick tail, broad buttock, tender hide.

"Now the man who said that, knew what he was talking about."

"What's his name?" asked Dan. "Does he live here?"

"Ho, ho!" and the parson's hearty laugh rang out over the snow. "'Does he live here?' I'm afraid not. Very few in Glendow know old Will Shakespeare, more's the pity."

"I should like to meet him, though," remarked Dan. "He must know a lot about horses."

"Ay, ay, lad, he knows a lot about most things, and you shall know him some day, Dan, when you get older. But here we are right at home. We've made great time."

After Midnight had been carefully stabled and fed, Parson John led his little charge into the Rectory. Scarcely had they crossed the threshold into a brightly-lighted room ere the sound of a sweet voice humming an old familiar tune fell gently upon their ears. Then a heavy tapestry curtain was drawn aside, and a slender girlish form stood before them. Beholding the lad, she gave a start of surprise, while her face, of more than ordinary beauty, flushed with pleasure.

"Ha, ha, Nellie," laughed her father, giving her an affectionate kiss, "I have captured your young hero at last, and I'm glad you recognize him. He's to live with us, to be your honourable bodyguard, your Fidus Achates, in fact."

What a picture this venerable man presented as he stood there. Wrapped in a great-coat, with fur mittens in his hands; a long grey beard sweeping his breast; hair abundant and white, crowning a face of singular strength and refinement, he seemed the very embodiment of health and hearty cheer. No ascetic this, but a man in whose veins flowed the fire of youth, and whose eyes twinkled with quiet, honest laughter as they looked into his daughter's puzzled face.

"I don't exactly understand," Nellie remarked, glancing first at her father and then at Dan.

"No, I know you don't, dear, but I'll tell you all about it later. It's enough now to know that I found him, and we are to give him a home here. So if you'll let us have something to eat, we'll be very glad, won't we, laddie?"

Dan stood as if in a dream during this conversation. His eyes remained fixed upon Nellie's face. Could it be possible that this was the woman he had rescued, and who had spoken so kindly to him? It was the same, there could be no mistake, only now she seemed more beautiful than ever. He felt her soft hand pressing his rough, brown one, and heard her hearty welcome. Words would not come to his lips. He was like a dumb person. But his eyes noted much, especially the dining-room, with the table spread, the white cloth and wonderful dishes. He had never seen anything like them before.

And good reason was there for Dan's wonder. Others too would have looked with admiration upon that scene had they been present. Everything in the room bespoke Nellie's gentle care, from the spotless table-linen to the well-polished, old-fashioned sideboard, a relic of the stirring Loyalist days. Several portraits of distinguished divines adorned the walls, while here and there nature scenes, done in water-colours, by whose hand it was easy to guess, were artistically arranged.

Nellie's devotion to her father was beautiful to behold. Her eyes sparkled with delight as he related several amusing incidents of his visit to a sick parishioner in an outlying district.

"And how did you find Mr. Stickles?" she inquired.

"'Simply joggin', parson, simply joggin,'" came the

reply, at which the fair hostess laughed heartily.

"And I suppose Mrs. Stickles is as jolly as ever?"

"Oh, yes. She is just the same. Poor soul! she has her hands full with her sick husband, and a houseful of little ones. Yet she keeps remarkably bright and cheerful. She was much concerned about my welfare, and while she sent Sammy to look after Midnight she bustled around to make me as comfortable as possible."

"'Poor dear man,' she said, 'ye ain't as young as ye used to be, an' I often say to John that the work's tellin' on ye. Ye've got too large a circus, parson, too large a circus.'"

"Dear soul," laughed Nellie. "There isn't a more real person in Glendow than Mrs. Stickles. She's a friend to everyone, and knows everybody's business for miles around."

"Indeed, she does," replied her father. "It was she who told me about our young friend here, and I started off post-haste to capture him. So we have to thank Mrs. Stickles for it all."

Supper ended, Parson John and Dan went into the study, while Nellie cleared away the dishes. A bright fire burned in the large fire-place, giving the room a most genial appearance. The parson brought down a long church-warden pipe, filled and lighted it. Next he drew up a comfortable chair and proceeded to read his mail which had arrived during his absence. Dan, in the meantime, had taken up his position in a cosy-corner nearby. A large picture-book had been given to him, and eagerly his eyes wandered over the wonderful things he found therein. After a while he closed the book and leaned back against the cushions. How comfortable it was. What luxury! He had never experienced anything like it in his life. It seemed like a dream. He watched Parson John for a time as he read his letters and papers. Then he looked about the room, admiring the many things he there beheld. Gradually his eyes closed. He forgot his surroundings, and was soon fast asleep, far away in dreamland.

When Nellie had finished with the dishes, she came into the study, and, seeing Dan, she paused to look upon him. Then she crossed to where her father was sitting, and touched him gently on the shoulder and pointed to the sleeping lad. Together they watched him and in their hearts there welled up a deep love for the orphan boy.

"Poor little fellow," remarked Nellie, in a low voice, taking a seat by her father's side. "I am so glad he is with us to-night. He seemed to be tired out."

"Yes, dear," her father replied, laying down the paper. "We are fortunate in getting him. I wanted a boy for some time. I understand he has a fine character."

"And you said that Mrs. Stickles told you about him?"

"Yes. And what she said was quite true. I found Dan living with the Tragen family. Mr. Tragen has seven children of his own, and could not very well keep another for any length of time. He told me that the day of the funeral he went to the Flitter house, and found Dan all alone, lying on his father's bed, weeping as if his heart would break. With difficulty he had persuaded him to leave and go with him. That was over a week ago and Dan has been with him ever since. Mrs. Tragen, worthy woman that she is, took good care of him and treated him like one of her own. Truly the Lord will reward her. By the way, she told me an interesting thing about the boy."

"What is it?" questioned Nellie.

"It seems he has never been at school, and cannot read or write. He is very anxious to learn, and his father, before his death, was giving him some lessons. We must see that he has every chance to learn while with us."

"But, father, there's no school in the district this winter, a most unusual thing."

"Why not teach him at home, dearie?" and the parson looked into his daughter's face. "Why not have a school here? We can give him a start anyway, and he will not be too far behind the rest when next the public school opens."

"Oh, that will be splendid!" exclaimed Nellie, "and may I be the teacher? I always wanted to do something in that line, and may we begin to-morrow?"

"Any time you like, dearie, and may God bless you, child, for your interest in the boy. You remind me more and more of your dear mother."

"And why should I not take an interest in him, father? He saved my life, and, though I can never repay him, I should like to feel that I am doing something. You know I read to Nora whenever I can, but this need not

H. A. Cody

interfere with that. And, oh, father, Stephen was here this afternoon, and he's in great trouble."

"What's wrong, dearie?" questioned the parson, as Nellie paused and a deep flush suffused her face.

"The Frenelle homestead is to be sold."

"What! do I understand you aright? Peter Frenelle's farm, that fine property which he left free of debt when he died?"

"Yes, it's only too true. You know there has been a heavy mortgage on it for several years, and as the interest has not been paid for some time the mortgage has been foreclosed, and the place is to be sold."

"Dear me, dear me," and the parson leaned back in his chair and closed his eyes, as he always did when in deep thought. "It's bad management, that's what it is. Stephen has had a splendid start, and through careless-ness he has let everything go to ruin."

"Father, don't blame Stephen too much. He's only young, and had a great responsibility placed upon his shoulders after his father's death."

"Blame him! Blame him! Why should I blame anyone?" and the parson placed his hand to his forehead. "Stephen is as dear to me as my own son - and I love him. But, oh, it is hard to see my old friend's farm go to others. I have talked with Stephen time and time again. But he has not taken the right grip of life. Poor Mrs. Frenelle, her heart must be broken. And Nora, that dear invalid girl, how hard for her."

Nellie made no reply to her father's words. She sat looking into the fire. Tears were in her eyes and her heart was heavy. Everything had seemed so bright but a short time before, and now this dark cloud had arisen. Oh, if Stephen would only bestir himself. They had known each other from childhood. He had always been her hero. As a child her day-dreams and fancies were woven about him. And as years advanced their love for each other had increased. It was the natural blending of two souls which had gradually and silently grown together in the bright sunshine of happy youth.

A knock upon the door at the side of the house startled her. At once she arose to ascertain its meaning, and shortly returned.

"Father," she said, "Billy Fletcher is very sick, and wishes to see you."

"Who brought word, my dear?"

"Hugh Peters. He called to see the old man as he was coming down the road, and found him quite ill."

The effect of this message was quite magical. No longer was Parson John the quiet fireside reader, but the true sympathetic pastor. He laid aside his pipe, and at once arose from his comfortable chair. An expression of loving concern overspread Nellie's face as she assisted him on with his storm coat, and procured his cap, mittens and overshoes. But no word of remonstrance came from her lips, no urging him to put off his visit until the morning. From a child she had been accustomed to these sudden calls to the side of departing parishioners, to read the Word of life and at times to administer the Holy Communion.

Her father's step was slow as of one much wearied, though his voice was cheery and strong as he bade his daughter good-bye, seized the small lantern she had lighted for him, and stepped out into the cold night on his mission of love.

Chapter IV

The Warder of the Night

After her father's departure, Nellie sat before the fire engaged upon some needlework. Occasionally her hands rested in her lap, while she gazed thoughtfully into the bright blaze. The soft light from the shaded lamp fell athwart her wealth of dark-brown hair and fair face. Her long lashes drooped as she leaned back in an easy-chair, and let her mind wander to the days when she and Stephen played together as happy children. What bright dreams were theirs, and how many fairy palaces they erected in the far unknown future.

A movement in the cosy-corner roused her from her reverie. She glanced quickly in that direction and saw Dan sitting bolt upright, gazing intently upon her. Nellie smiled as she saw his look of wonder mingled with embarrassment.

"Have you had a nice sleep?" she asked.

"Guess so," came the slow reply. "I dreamed that you and my father were right by my side, but when I woke he was gone and only you are with me."

"I hope you will like it here," Nellie remarked, hardly

knowing what to say. "We want to make you happy, and love you just like our own little boy."

"I'm almost a man now," and Dan straightened up his shoulders and proudly threw back his head. "I can hunt and work. See how strong I am," and he placed his right hand upon the muscle of his doubled-up left arm.

"Some day you will be as big as my father, won't you?" replied Nellie, much amused at the sturdy lad.

"Was that your father who brought me here?"

"Yes."

"And what's his name?"

"Mr. Westmore. But most people call him 'Parson John.' You'll call him that, too, won't you? He likes it better."

"Yes; if you want me to, I will. But, say, what's your name?"

"Oh, mine's just Nellie, Nellie Westmore. Not very pretty, is it?"

"I think it is. Do you know that was my mother's name - Nellie, I mean, not the other one."

"And do you remember your mother, Dan?"

"Only a little. She was good and pretty, just like you."

"Tell me about her, will you? I should like to hear."

And there in the quietness of that room Dan's tongue was unloosed, and in his own simple way he told about his mother, her death, and how he and his father had lived together in the little log shanty. Half an hour passed in this quiet talk, and when at length Dan ceased Nellie glanced at the clock.

"Why, I didn't think it was so late! It is time you were in bed. You must be tired. Come, I will show you where you are to sleep to-night, and to-morrow we will fix up a room for your very own."

Going to the kitchen Nellie lighted a small lamp, and with this in her hand she and Dan went up the small winding stairway.

"This is the place," and she opened a door leading to a room at the north of the house. "The pipe from the hall stove comes up there, so it's always quite warm. I do hope you will sleep well."

She went to the window to draw down the blind and as she did so a light fell upon her eyes which gave her a distinct start. It was not from the moon, for the night was dark, but from a burning building, a short distance up the road. The flames were leaping and curling through the roof, sending up blazing cinders in every direction.

Nellie's heart almost stopped beating as she gazed upon the scene. It was Billy Fletcher's house! and what of her father? Was he amidst those flames, or had he escaped?

"Dan, Dan!" she cried, turning to the lad, "Come, quick! I'm afraid that something terrible has happened!

Get on your coat and cap as quickly as possible and let's make haste!"

It did not take them long to throw on their wraps, and to hurry forth into the night.

To Nellie the distance seemed never-ending. Would they ever reach the house? How the road had lengthened! and her breath came hard and fast as she staggered forward, trying to keep pace with the more hardy lad. The light of the fire illumined the road for some distance around, and guided their steps. Drawing near they could discover no one about the place. What did it all mean? Here Nellie paused and with wildly beating heart looked at the seething mass before her, and listened to the roar of the flames as they sent up their wild flamboyant tongues into the air. Had her father been entrapped in that terrible furnace? She glanced towards a barn on her right and as she did so her eyes fell upon a sight never to be forgotten. Someone was there, kneeling in the snow with bent head gazing intently upon some object before him. It was her father! and with a cry of joy Nellie rushed forward. She found he was kneeling by Billy Fletcher's side, supporting his head, and carefully wrapping around him his own great-coat. He looked up and an expression of relief came into his face as he saw his daughter standing there.

"I am so glad you have come," he exclaimed. "Poor Billy's in a bad way. We need help. He must be taken to some house. I wish you would hurry up the road for assistance. Dan will go with you. Get his nephew Tom as quickly as possible."

Waiting to hear no more, Nellie, fatigued though she

was, started at once for assistance, Dan following close behind. They had gone only a short distance, however, when they met Tom himself running along the road.

"What's wrong?" he gasped.

"Don't you see?" Nellie replied. "The house is burning down."

"And Uncle Billy; is he safe?"

"Yes, he's safe, but almost dead."

"And the box, what about it?"

"What box?"

"The money box; the iron one, where he keeps his papers and gold."

"I know nothing about the box," replied Nellie, while a feeling of great repugnance welled up within her at the heartlessness of the man. He cared little for his uncle, the feeble old body, but only for what he possessed.

By this time they had reached the place where the sick man was lying.

"Is he living?" shouted his nephew.

"Yes," replied the parson, "though I doubt if he can last long. We must get him away to your house as soon as possible."

"But the box, Parson; did you save it?" questioned Tom.

"No, I never thought about it, and, besides, I did not know where it was."

At this Billy opened his faded eyes, and fixed them upon his nephew's face. He tried to speak, but his voice was thick and his words were unintelligible.

"Where's the box?" shouted Tom.

Again the old man endeavoured to say something. Failing in this he made an effort to rise. The struggle was too much for him, and with a cry he sank back upon the snow, dead.

By this time several neighbours had arrived, and stood near with a look of awe upon their rugged faces. Nellie drew her father aside, knowing full well that his care was needed no longer.

"Come," she said, "we had better go home, These men will do the rest. You have done your part."

He followed her along the little path leading to the main road. Reaching this she took him by the arm and supported his steps, which were now over-feeble. Slowly and feelingly, he told the story of the night. He had found the old man in a bad condition, and cold from the lack of a good fire. Filling the stove with a liberal supply of wood, and making Billy as comfortable as the circumstances would permit, he had sat down to watch his charge. Ere long the sick man grew much worse. Then the chimney had caught fire. The bricks must have been loose somewhere, which allowed the flames to pour through into the dry woodwork overhead, which was soon converted into a blazing mass. Seeing that nothing could be done to save the building Mr. Westmore was forced to carry Billy, sick though he was, out of the house. He tried to reach the barn, but his strength failed, so he was forced to lay his burden upon the snow, and wrap his greatcoat around the helpless man.

"Poor Billy! poor Billy!" said the parson in conclusion. "He was careless about higher things. I hope the good Lord will not judge him too harshly."

"But he was not always like that, father," Nellie remarked.

"No, no, thank God. He had a happy home when I first came to this parish, long before you were born. I have often told you about the sweet, God-fearing wife he had then. But after she was laid to rest a great change took place in Billy's life. He became very rebellious and never darkened the church door. He acquired a great passion for money, and grew to be most miserly. As the years passed his harshness increased. He waxed sullen and disagreeable. His neighbours shunned him and he looked upon them all with a suspicious eye. His money he never placed in a bank, but kept it in his house in gold coin, in a strong, iron box, so I have been told, and would count it over and over again with feverish delight."

"But, father," remonstrated Nellie, "there must have been something good in poor old Billy. You know how fond he was of Tony Stickles."

"True, very true, dear. I have often wondered about the affection between the two. No one else could live with the old man, except Tony, and he served him like a faithful dog. It is generally believed that Billy confided many things to Tony. He is a peculiar lad, and people have tried in vain to find out what he knew. He will certainly feel badly when he comes out of the woods, where he is now working, and hears about Billy's death. But here we are at home. Oh dear, the journey has greatly tired me," and the parson panted heavily as he entered the house.

During the homeward walk Dan trudged along close by Nellie's side, busy with his own thoughts. He longed for something to happen that he might show her what a man he was. If a robber or a wolf, or some frightful monster, would spring out from the roadside, he would meet it single-handed, kill or drive it away. Then to behold the look of gratitude and admiration upon the woman's face as she looked at him, what bliss that would be! Little did the father and daughter realize, as they slowly walked and conversed, what thoughts and feelings were thrilling the little lad by their side, feelings which in all ages have electrified clods of humanity into heroes, and illuminated life's dull commonplaces with the golden romance of chivalry.

Chapter V

The Breath of Slander

"When a man dies he kicks the dust." Thus pithily wrote Henry Thoreau, the quaint philosopher, in his little shack by the beautiful Walden pool. The truth of this saying was certainly verified in old Billy Fletcher's death, and the people of Glendow were destined to see the dust stirred by his departure, rise in a dense cloud and centre around the venerable parson of Glendow.

The day after the fire was clear and fine. Not a breath of wind stirred the crisp air, and the sun-kissed snow lying smooth and white over all the land sparkled like millions of diamonds.

Near the window in her little cottage, not far from the Rectory, sat Mrs. Larkins, busily knitting. She was a woman of superior qualities and had seen better days. Her toil-worn hands and care-marked face could not disguise the gentle, refined spirit within, which expressed itself in her every word and action. Two little graves in the Churchyard, lying side by side, and marked by a small cross of white marble, told how the silent messenger had entered that home. Often the husband and wife were seen standing by those little mounds, while tears coursed down their rugged, honest cheeks.

H. A. Cody

"No father could have been kinder than Parson John," she had frequently remarked when speaking about their loss, "and no sister more sympathetic than dear Nellie. They loved our little ones as if they were their very own. On that bright summer day when we laid our lambs to rest the parson's voice faltered as he read the Burial Service, and tears glistened in his eyes."

Since then whatever happened of joy or sorrow at the Rectory was of the deepest interest to the lonely two over the way. So on this bright afternoon as Mrs. Larkins sat by the window her thoughts were busy with the events of the past night.

A knock upon the door broke her reverie. Opening it, what was her surprise to find there a woman, with an old-fashioned shawl about her shoulders, and a bright, jolly face peering forth from a capacious grey hood.

"Mrs. Stickles!" she exclaimed. "Is it really you? Why, I haven't seen you for such a long time! Come in at once, and lay off your wraps, while I make you a cup of tea, for you must be chilled through and through."

"Indeed, I am," Mrs. Stickles replied, bustling into the room, and untying her hood. "Sammy hed to bring the old mare to the blacksmith shop to git shod, an' John, my man, sez to me, 'Mother,' sez he, 'ye jist put on yer duds, an' go along, too. It'll do ye a world o' good.' I hated to leave John, poor soul, he's so poorly. But I couldn't resist the temptation, an' so I come. My, that's good tea!" she ejaculated, leaning back in a big, cosy chair. "Ain't that tumble about old Billy Fletcher, an' him sich a man!"

"You've heard about his death, then?" Mrs. Larkins replied.

"Should think I hed. We stopped fer a minute at the store. I wanted to git some calicer fer the girls, an' while I was thar I heerd Tom Flinders an' Pete Robie talkin' about it. Why, it was awful! An' to think the dear old parson was thar all alone! When Pete told me that I jist held up me hands in horror. 'Him thar with that dyin' man!' sez I. 'Jist think of it!'

"'I guess he didn't mind it,' sez Si Farrington, who was awaitin' upon me. 'He likes jobs of that nater.' I don't know what in the world he meant. I s'pose ye've heerd all about it, Mrs. Larkins?"

"Yes," came the somewhat slow reply. "I've heard too much."

"Ye don't say so now!" and Mrs. Stickles laid down her cup, and brought forth the knitting which she had with her. "Anything serious?"

"Well, you can judge for yourself. John helped to carry Billy to his nephew's house, and then assisted the others in putting out the fire. But search as they might they could not find the box."

"Ye don't say so! Well, I declare."

"No, they searched every portion of the rubbish, ashes and all, but could find no trace of it. That's what's troubling me. I do hope they will find it for the parson's sake."

"Indeed! Ye surprise me," and Mrs. Stickles laid down

her knitting. "Wot the parson has to do with that box is more'n I kin understand."

"No, perhaps you don't. But you see after the men had made a thorough search and could not find the box, Tom Fletcher became much excited. He swore like a trooper, declared that there had been foul play, and hinted that the parson had something to do with it. You know that the Fletchers have been waiting a long time for Billy to die in order to get his gold, property and - "

"Yes, yes, I know Tom Fletcher," broke in Mrs. Stickles. "Don't I know 'im, an' wot a mean sneak he is. He's suspicious of everybody, an' is always lookin' fer trouble. An' as to meanness, why he hasn't a heart as big as the smallest chicken. Ye could take a thousand hearts sich as his'n an' stick 'em all to the wall with one tiny pin, an' then they wouldn't be half way up to the head. Mean! Why didn't he once put a twenty-five cent piece inter the kerlection plate by mistake, an' come back the next day to git it, an' gave a cent in its place. If that ain't mean I'd like to know whar ye'd find it," and Mrs. Stickles sniffed contemptuously as her needles whirled and rattled between her nimble fingers.

"Yes," Mrs. Larkins replied, "he carries his meanness into everything. If he even imagines that it was the parson's fault that the house burned down, and the will was destroyed, his anger will burn like fire. He's very revengeful, too, and has an old grudge to pay back. The parson, you know, was the means of making him close up his liquor business some years ago, and he has been waiting ever since for a chance to hit back. I tell you this, Mrs. Stickles, that a man who tries to do his duty is bound to stir up opposition, and sometimes I wonder why such a good man should have to bear with vindictive enemies. I suppose it's for some purpose."

"Indeed it is, Mrs. Larkins. Indeed it is," and Mrs. Stickles' needles clicked faster than ever. "It was only last night I was talkin' to my man John about this very thing. 'John,' sez I, 'd'ye remember them two apple trees in the orchard down by the fence?'

"'Well,' sez he.

"'An' ye recollect,' sez I, 'how one was loaded down with apples, while t'other had nuthin' but leaves?'

"I remember," sez he.

"'Well, then,' sez I, 'One was pelted with sticks an' stones all summer, an' even hed some of its branches broken, while t'other was not teched. Why was that?

"'Cause it hed plenty of good fruit on it,' sez he.

"'Jist so,' sez I. 'Cause it hed good fruit. An' that's why so often the Lord's good people er pelted with vile words cause they're loaded down with good deeds. If they never did nuthin' the devil 'ud leave 'em alone, but jist 'cause they bear good fruit is the reason they're pelted.' John reckoned I was right, an' he's got a purty level head, if I do say it."

"I only hope most of the people in the parish will stand by the parson," replied Mrs. Larkins. "I know some will, but there are others who are easily led, and Tom Fletcher's got a sharp tongue."

"Why wouldn't they stan' by 'im, Mrs. Larkins? Wot

hev they agin 'im? Tell me that."

Mrs. Larkins did not answer for a while, but sat gazing out of the window as if she did not hear the remark.

"I'm thinking of the parson's son, Philip," Mrs. Larkins at length replied. "You know about him, of course?"

"Sartin' I do. I've knowed Phillie sense he was a baby, an' held 'im in me arms, too. He was a sweet lamb, that's wot he was. I understan' he's a minin' ingineer out in British Columbia, an' doin' fine from the last account I heerd."

"That was some time ago, Mrs. Stickles, was it not?"

"I believe it was last summer."

"Well, it seems that Philip's in trouble."

"Lan' sake, ye don't tell me!" and Mrs. Stickles dropped her knitting and held up her hands in horror. "I was afeered of it, Mrs. Larkins. It's no place fer man or beast out thar. Hev the Injins hurt 'im, or the bears clawed 'im? I understan' they're thick as flies in summer."

"Oh, no, not that," replied Mrs. Larkins. "You see over a year ago Philip invested in some mining property out there, and the prospects looked so bright that he induced his father to join him in the enterprise. Though the parson's salary has always been small, with strict economy he had laid something by each year for his old age. The whole of this he gave to Philip to be invested. For a time things looked very bright and it seemed as if the mines would produce handsome profits. Unfortunately several claimants for the property suddenly turned up, with the result that the whole affair is now in litigation. The case is to be decided in a few months, and should it go against Philip he and his father will be ruined. Philip manages the matter, and the parson advances what money he can scrape together. Just lately the whole affair has leaked out, and some people, knowing how the parson needs money, may not be slow to impute to him things of which he is entirely ignorant."

Mrs. Stickles was about to speak, when a jingle of bells sounded outside. "Well, I declare!" she exclaimed, "Sammy's back already!" With that, she rose to her feet, and the conversation ended.

The church was crowded the day old Billy was buried, for a funeral in Glendow was always an important event. Parson John was clad in his simple robes of office and read the Burial Service in a resonant, well-modulated voice. Beholding such nobleness, gentleness and dignity of his face and bearing, only the most suspicious could associate him with any underhanded dealing. What connection had such a man with the base things of life? Mounting the pulpit, he gave a short, impressive address. There was no sentiment, or flowery language. He glossed nothing over, but in a few words sketched Billy Fletcher's life, and pointed him out as a warning to those who become careless and indifferent to higher things.

"The parson talked mighty plain to-day," said one man in a low voice to another, as they wended their way to the graveyard. "He didn't put poor Billy in Heaven, that's certain, and perhaps he's right. I guess he hit the Fletchers pretty hard."

H. A. Cody

"Oh, yes," the other replied. "The parson got his say from the pulpit, hut the Fletchers will have theirs later."

"Why, what have they to say?"

"Oh, you'll see."

"About that box?"

"Yes."

"Tut, tut, man. Why, they haven't a leg to stand on in that matter."

"But they'll make legs. Surely you know Tom Fletcher by this time. He'll stop at nothing when once he gets started, and though he may not be able to do anything definitely, he'll do a lot of talking, and talk tells in Glendow, mark my word."

And this proved only too true. Talk did begin to tell both in the homes and at the stores. One man, who had met the parson on a hurried trip to the city, declared that he was driving like mad, and hardly spoke in passing. Another related that when Tom Fletcher asked Billy about the box, the dying man pointed to the parson, and tried to speak. Though some of the more sensible scoffed at such stories as ridiculous, it made little difference, for they passed from mouth to mouth, increasing in interest and importance according to the imagination of the narrator.

Although this slander with malignant breath was spreading through the parish, it did not for a time reach the Rectory. All unconscious of impending trouble, father and daughter lived their quiet life happy in each other's company.

H. A. Cody

Chapter VI

The Auction

The day of the auction of the Frenelle homestead dawned mild and clear.

"Don't give Dan too many lessons," laughed Parson John, as he kissed his daughter good-bye and tucked in the robes about his feet.

"No fear, father," was the laughing reply. "Perhaps he will turn the tables upon me. He knows so much about the woods, wild animals and birds that I like to learn from him."

Midnight strode along the road, glad of the run in the fresh air. The sleigh bells sent forth their sweet music, echoing and re-echoing from the neighbouring hills and forest. Everything spoke of peace, and in Parson John's heart dwelt a deeper peace, as he guided Midnight through the gateway and reined her up before the Frenelle door.

Though he was somewhat early, others were earlier still, and a group of men, hardy sons of toil, were standing near the house engaged in earnest conversation. They had come a long distance, for an auction such as this was a most unusual occurrence in

Glendow. The Frenelle homestead had belonged to the family from the early Loyalist days, descending from father to son for several generations. Each had contributed something to the improvement of the land, but it remained for Peter Frenelle, Stephen's father, to bring it under an excellent state of cultivation. A clear-headed, hard-working man, he had brought his scientific knowledge, acquired by careful study, to bear upon the soil, until his broad, rich acres, free from stone, became the envy and admiration of the parish.

One quiet evening he was strolling around the farm with Parson John, his firm and faithful counsellor from childhood. Looking across the fields of waving grain, and down upon the long straight rows of corn, standing golden in the setting sun, he paused in his walk, and remained for some time in deep thought. "John," he at length remarked, placing his hand affectionately upon his companion's shoulder, "the Lord has been very good to me all of these years. He has blessed me in house and field; He has given me health and strength, and now in my latter days peace and light at eventide."

His companion was not surprised at these words, for often before had Mr. Frenelle talked in this manner. But early the next morning when he was summoned to his friend's bedside, to receive his final message, and to hold the hand outstretched to him till it was still and cold, the solemn utterance of the previous evening came forcibly to his mind.

For several years after her husband's sudden death, Mrs. Frenelle managed the farm and exhibited remarkable skill in directing the various hired labourers.

But as Stephen, her only son, advanced to manhood

she relinquished the responsibility and devoted her time almost entirely to her household affairs. This change was so gradual as to be almost imperceptible. Stephen disliked the drudgery of farm life and left the work to the hired men. So long as he could draw upon his father's careful savings to pay the wages and supply his own needs, he did not worry. The neighbours shook their heads and prophesied trouble as they saw the land producing less each year, and its acres, formerly rich with grain, covered with bushes. Parson John reasoned and remonstrated, though all in vain. Stephen always promised to do better, but in the end continued the same as before. At last the awakening came, sudden and terrible. The bank account had been overdrawn to a considerable extent, and payment was demanded. The only thing to do was to mortgage the farm, and with a heavy heart Mrs. Frenelle signed the pledge of death to the dear homestead. For a time Stephen tried to settle down to steady work, but the old habit of carelessness was too strong upon him, and ere long he drifted back to his former ways. The interest on the mortgage remained unpaid. Foreclosure was the inevitable result, and the farm was accordingly advertised for sale.

At last the day of doom had arrived.

Parson John found Mrs. Frenelle in the cosy sitting-room with her invalid daughter, Nora. The latter was endeavouring to comfort her mother. The girl's face, although worn with care and suffering, was sweet to look upon. She was not what one would call pretty, but it was impossible to be long in her presence without feeling the influence of her strong buoyant disposition. The angel of pain had purged away much of the dross of her nature, leaving the pure gold undimmed. She inherited, too, much of her father's strength of character which seemed to be lacking in her brother.

"What are we to do?" sobbed poor Mrs. Frenelle, as the parson entered the room. "We will be driven from our dear old home, where we have spent so many happy years! We will be penniless!"

"Hush, mother dear," remonstrated her daughter. "Don't get so discouraged. The place may bring more than will cover the mortgage. We will have that to start with again, and in a few years we may be able to pay everything off. Stephen may settle down to hard, steady work and all will be well."

"Nora is right," replied the parson. "The purchaser, whoever he is, will no doubt let you remain here, and give you a fair chance to redeem the place. Our Glendow people, you know, have big hearts."

"Oh, I wish I could see it in that light," and Mrs. Frenelle glanced at the clergyman through her tears. "It is Mr. Farrington I fear. His mind is set upon having this place. He has looked upon it with greedy eyes for a number of years. He has only a little land in connection with his store, and his wife is always complaining that they have not enough room. She has said on several occasions that they would own this farm some day. Then, you see, Farrington is a candidate for the next Councillor election. He has large ambitions, and hopes eventually to run for the Local House. He thinks a place such as this with its fine, old-fashioned house will give him a certain standing which he now lacks. He wants to pose as a country gentleman, and his wife wishes to have the house in which to entertain her distinguished guests, who, as she imagines, will visit them. Oh, to think of Mrs. Farrington living here!" and the poor woman buried her face in her hands.

"But perhaps someone else will outbid him," suggested Mr. Westmore. "I would not lose heart yet."

"There is no one in Glendow able to bid successfully against Mr. Farrington," Nora replied. "We have learned, however, that Mr. Turpin, a real estate man, arrived from the city last night. He wishes to buy the place merely as a speculation, hoping to turn it over to some rich people who wish to come to Canada to settle. But there is the bell!" and she half-started from her invalid's chair, but sank back with a little cry at the pain caused by the sudden movement.

As the day was mild the auction took place in the open where the auctioneer, surrounded by some two dozen men, was mounted on a large box. At first the bidding was general and brisk. Gradually, however, it dwindled down to three or four, and finally to Farrington and Turpin, the real estate man. The former was standing a little apart from the rest, with his eyes intent upon the auctioneer, and unable to repress the eagerness which shone in his face. As the bidding advanced and drew near the three thousand dollar mark, Turpin showed signs of weakening, while his bids came slower and slower. Farrington, noticing this, could not control his pleasure, and when he at length offered the round sum of three thousand dollars Turpin gave up the struggle and, moving back a little, perched himself upon a barrel, and seemed to take no interest in the affair.

A triumphant light gleamed in Farrington's eyes as he observed his vanquished opponent. He glanced towards the house, and, seeing Mrs. Frenelle standing in the doorway, his lips parted in a cruel smile. It was that smile more than anything else which revealed the real nature of the man.

The breathless silence which for a time ensued at this crisis was broken by the harsh cry of the auctioneer:

"Three thousand dollars!" he called. "Going at three thousand dollars! Any advance on three thousand dollars. Going at three thousand dollars. Once - twice - third - and - "

"Three thousand one hundred," came suddenly from Parson John.

An earthquake shock could hardly have startled the men more than this bid from such an unexpected quarter.

Farrington's face reddened, and he moved a step nearer to be sure that he had not been mistaken.

"Did I hear aright?" he gasped. "Did the parson add one hundred to my bid?"

"Three thousand one hundred dollars from Parson Westmore," shouted the auctioneer. "Any advance on three thousand one hundred dollars?"

"Another hundred, then, damn it," and Farrington thrust his hands deeper into his pockets, while his eyes gleamed with an angry light.

"Three thousand five hundred," came the quiet response.

Silence followed this last bid, which plainly proved that Farrington, too, was weakening. He looked around as if uncertain what to do, and his eyes rested upon Mrs. Frenelle. In her eagerness she had moved from the door, and was standing near the group of men with her eyes fixed full upon the clergyman. The expression upon her face was that of a drowning person, who, when all hope has been abandoned, sees a rescuer suddenly at hand. It was this look more than the half-suppressed laugh that passed among the men, which caused him to fling another one hundred dollars at the auctioneer.

"Four thousand," again came strong and clear from Parson John without the slightest hesitation.

The auctioneer waited for Farrington to increase his bid. The men almost held their breath in the excitement of the moment, and Mrs. Frenelle moved a step nearer with her hands firmly clasped before her.

"Four thousand dollars," the auctioneer spoke slowly and impressively now. "Any - advance - on four thousand dollars? Going at four thousand dollars - Once - twice - third - and - last call - , and sold to Parson Westmore for four thousand dollars."

As these words fell from the speaker's lips a deep sigh broke the tense feeling of the little company. They had been stirred more than was their wont by the scene that they had just witnessed. These men knew but little of the rise and fall of ancient kingdoms, the strife of modern nations, the deeds of statesmen, and the affairs of the financial world. And yet in the sale of this farm in an obscure country place the secret springs of life, even though on a small scale, were laid bare. The pathos of a happy home on the verge of destruction, with a loving mother and an invalid child in danger of being cast out upon the cold world, and to see this tragedy so narrowly averted through one staunch champion successfully beating back pride and greed as represented in the person of Silas Farrington - truly it was a miniature of the world's history, which may be found in every town, village or home.

"I trust you understand the conditions of the sale, sir," and the auctioneer looked curiously at the clergyman, who was standing somewhat by himself. "One-third of the amount down, and the balance in half-yearly payments. I only mention this in case you may not know it."

"I understand perfectly well," was the reply. "The *whole* amount shall be paid at once, and the matter settled without delay."

"Guess the ministry must be a payin' job," sneered Farrington, "when a poor country parson kin fork out four thousand dollars at one slap. I see now why ye're allus dunnin' us fer money. Mebbe ye've got a hot sermon all ready on the subject fer us next Sunday."

Mr. Westmore looked intently at the man for an instant, and his lips parted as if to reply. Instead, however, he turned without a word and moved slowly towards the house.

He reached Nora's side, and took her outstretched hand in his. Tears of joy were in her eyes as she lifted them to her Rector's face, and endeavoured to find adequate words in which to express her gratitude.

H. A. Cody

"I know we are safe now!" she said. "But we never thought of you buying the place! I cannot understand it at all. Four thousand dollars! What a lot of money!"

"No, my child, you cannot understand it now, but you will some day," and as Mr. Westmore turned his face towards the window a tear might have been detected stealing slowly down his furrowed cheek.

Chapter VII

The Farringtons

Silas Farrington flung himself out of his sleigh and handed the reins to a young man who had come forth from the store.

"What are ye so slow about?" he snarled. "Here I've been callin' fer the last five minutes. Why don't ye hustle when I call?"

"I was running molasses," came the surly reply, "and how could I leave - "

"There now, no back talk; I never allow it. Put up the horse, an' don't spend all day about it, either."

With these words Farrington made his way to the house, leaving the young man inwardly cursing his unjust master.

"Ye're late, Si," a voice exclaimed, as he opened the door and entered. "We've been waitin' fer ye a full hour or more."

"I couldn't help it," Farrington replied. "I was delayed."

"An' how much did ye pay fer the farm, Si?"

"Farm be - be - hanged! I'm sick of it."

"But didn't ye git it, Si?" his wife persisted.

"Git it? No!"

"What!"

"I said no!"

"But who did, then?"

"The parson."

"What! Parson John?"

"Certainly. Who else would he fool enough to interfere with me?"

"Well, well!" ejaculated Mrs. Farrington. "Do tell us about it, Si?"

"No, not a word more about it," snapped her husband, "till we git down to dinner. I'm most starved. Is it ready?"

"Dear me, yes. I'd clean fergot about it," and Mrs. Farrington bustled off to the kitchen.

Everything in the dining-room betokened care and industry, from the nicely-papered walls, adorned with pictures, to the large sideboard, with its display of old china and glassware. The table-linen was spotlessly clean, and the food served up was well cooked. But, notwithstanding this, something seemed wrong. An indefinable atmosphere pervaded the place which spoiled the effect of it all. It was not the corrupted English falling from the lips of these people which grated so harshly upon the senses. It was the spirit of pretence which overshadowed everything - the effort to be what they were not. Had old Titbottom been there with his magic spectacles, he would have beheld in Farrington little more than a roll of bills; in his wife the very essence of pretence and ambition; while the daughter Eudora and their son Dick would be labelled "exact samples" of the parents.

Farrington told of the auction in no measured terms. He was annoyed at the unexpected outcome and did not try to conceal his anger. The inserted exclamations of the family told their own tale. They were much disappointed, especially Mrs. Farrington.

"Only think!" she cried, when her husband had ended, "that the parson above all men should interfere in this matter! Him that's allus talkin' about lovin' our neighbours as ourselves, standin' a-tween us an' our natral rights. I hev often told Eudora, heven't I, dear? that we need a better place than this. Now, that Frenelle homestead is jist what we want, an' it seemed as if the Lord intended we should hev it, too. It is so included from all pryin' eyes, an' away from them country people who are so uncongenial. Their manners are so rough an' they know so little about proper equity. The parson knows very well that we are city bred, an' that our descendants hev allus had good blood in their veins, an' that we try to follow their Example by givin' a tone to the community ever sense we came from the city. He knows what we are a-tryin' to do, an' yit he'll serve us in this mean fashion."

"I wonder where he got the spondulicks," broke in her

son Richard.

"Richard, Richard! you must not use sech a word as that," and Mrs. Farrington cast a reproving glance at her son. "Ye must hev heerd it from Tom Jones; ye know ye never hear it at home, fer we are allus very pertickeler about our language."

"Well, money, then, ma. I don't care what ye call it."

"Oh, I guess that'll not be hard to account fer," replied Farrington with a knowing laugh. "Tom Fletcher may be able to throw some light upon the subject. It seems to me that the parson has come to the end of his rope. We've borne with 'im fer years, an' it's about time he was makin' a move. He's too old fer the ministry. We need a young man, with fire an' vim. Anyway, the rest may do as they please, but as fer me not another cent do I pay as long as he is in charge."

"Ye've allus paid well, Si," remarked his wife, "an' the parson is not one bit grateful."

"Yes, I reckon I hev," and Farrington gulped down, his tea. "I used to contribute heavily; eight dollars a year, an' a bag of oats at Christmas. Now I give only four sense I've enlarged my bizness an' can't afford so much. Besides, the parson doesn't deal with me as much as he should. He gits too many of his supplies in the city. If he expects me to paternise 'im he must deal with me. I've told 'im so very plainly on several occasions."

"Ye certainly did yer part, Si," Mrs. Farrington replied. "If all in the parish 'ud do as well there'd be no trouble. It is disgraceful that these country people do not pay more to support the Church. It throws sich a burden upon us. Only think of Mrs. Jimmy Brown buyin' a new Bristles carpet, when the old one was quite good enough. An' her last year's hat could hev been made over as well as not. But, no, it would not do. She had to hev another, which cost quite a penny, so I understand."

"An' Vivien Nelson's fur-lined coat, ma," chimed in Eudora, "I know it didn't cost one cent less than seventy-five dollars!"

"These country people are so extravagant, ye know," returned her mother. "They are allus tryin' to imitate their sufferiors. To think of Vivien Nelson, a farmer's daughter, hevin' a fur-lined coat which cost almost as much as Eudora's! It is really disgraceful! I'm sure her father could give more to the Church than he does, an' yit he'll let us hear the brunt of the burden."

"Guess he'll hev to bear mor'n ever now," replied her husband as he rose from the table. "I'm done with the whole bizness, an' I'm mighty glad I heven't paid fer the last year, an' don't intend to now."

As Farrington passed out of the dining-room into the store, his clerk, a young man new to the business, was serving a middle-aged woman at the counter.

"I'm sorry, Mrs. Sturgis," the former was saying, "but we are entirely out of it just now. We can order it for you, though, and have it in a few days."

Farrington turned angrily upon his heel as these words fell upon his ears.

"What does she want?" he demanded.

"Number forty, white thread; but we're out of it."

"You stupid blockhead, we're not out of it! We're never out! If you'd use yer eyes half as much as yer tongue ye'd be all right."

"But I can't find it. I've looked everywhere," and the clerk's eyes flashed danger as he turned them upon his master.

"Well, look again. Don't stand thar starin' like an ijut!"

The young man did as he was commanded. He searched and rummaged, but all in vain.

"Oh, come out of that, an' let me thar," and Farrington shoved his way past the clerk, and fumbled excitedly in the box.

"Ah-yes-no-fifty-sixty-Well, I declare! Not thar! Confound it! Why didn't ye tell me we were out before? Why did ye wait till the last spool was gone afore sayin' a word about it?"

"I've only been here a week," replied the clerk, "and how could I know you were out. No one has called for number forty thread since I've been here."

Farrington was beaten, and was forced to swallow his anger as best he could. It was most aggravating to be thus humiliated in the presence of this woman. He strode across the room, and stood with his back to the stove, wondering how he could get even with his clerk. He would discharge him. "No, that wouldn't do. It was hard to get a man to stay with him, and this was a good worker. Anyway, he must be taught his place, and not answer back. He would let him know that he owned the store.

"Give me my mail, please."

Farrington started, and turning, beheld a little lad standing by his side.

"Mail! whose mail?" he demanded, glad of an excuse to give vent to his anger. "What's yer name? I don't know anything about *my* mail."

"I want Parson John's mail," persisted the boy. Don't you know him?"

"Know 'im! Well, I guess! I know 'im too d - n well. But who are you, and what do ye want with the parson's mail?"

"Oh, I live with him now. I'm Dan, old Jim's boy. Didn't you know I was there?"

"Ha, ha, that's a good one! To think that I should know every brat who comes to the place."

"I'm not a brat! I'm almost a man," and Dan straightened himself up. "Give me my mail, please; Parson John's waiting for it."

"Let 'im wait. I'm not supposed to give out mail to all the riff-raff who comes fer it. Why doesn't he come 'imself?"

"He's busy."

"Busy! busy! Yes, I s'pose he is busy, plannin' mischief; wonderin' what to do with Billy Fletcher's gold. How much did he git? I s'pose he gave you some to hold yer tongue."

Farrington had no intention of uttering these last words, but his heart was so full of anger that he hardly knew what he was saying.

Dan's eyes flashed, and his little hands suddenly doubled at his side. He did not comprehend the meaning of these words, but he felt that his friend, the white-headed old man, was being insulted. With him to think was to act, and many a boy larger than himself had felt the lightning blows of those little tense knuckles.

"What do ye mean?" he demanded, looking up into Farrington's face.

"What do I mean? Well, if ye want to know, I mean that Parson John is a rogue, an' that you are nuthin' but a young sucker, an impudent outcast, spongin' fer yer livin' upon others."

Hardly had the words left Farrington's lips, when, with a cry as of a wild animal, Dan leaped full upon him, caught him by the hair with one hand, and with the other rained blow after blow upon his face.

With a howl of mingled pain and rage, Farrington endeavoured to free himself from this human wild-cat. He struggled and fought, and at length succeeded in tearing away that writhing, battering form. With one hand he held him at arm's length and shook him as a terrier shakes a rat. Dan struggled, squirmed and bit, but all in vain; he was held as in a vice. Not satisfied with shaking the lad, Farrington reached over and, seizing a broken barrel stave from the wood-box, brought it down over the lad's shoulder and back with a resounding thud. A cry of pain, the first that he had uttered, fell from Dan's lips, and with a mighty effort he tried to escape. The stick was raised again. It was about to fall, when suddenly it flew into the air, the grip of the boy relaxed, and Farrington staggered back from a furious blow dealt him by the young clerk. Farrington tried to recover, but each time he was hurled to the floor by the stalwart athlete standing before him, his eyes blazing with anger.

"Get up, you coward!" he cried, when at length Farrington remained sprawling upon the floor. "Get up if you can, and dare!"

"Curse you!" snarled the defeated man. "Ye'll pay fer this!"

"We'll see about that later," calmly replied the clerk. "There's to be no more bullying while I'm here, and I won't be here long, for I'm done with you and your outfit."

"Go, go at once, d - n you, or I'll kick ye out!" shouted Farrington.

"Kick me out, if you can," came the reply. "Get up and do it," and the young man laughed scornfully. "No, you know you can't. Now, look here; just a word before we part. I've stood your insolent abuse for a week, without retaliating. But when you laid hands upon that boy it was a different matter."

"But he flew at me like a wild-cat," Farrington growled.

"Yes, and wouldn't anyone with a spark of life in him at all, after he had been insulted by such a thing as you. You like to get a chap such as that in your claws and torture him. You've done it before, I understand. But it's not been such fun this time. No, no, the worm has turned at last. I'm going now - so do what you like. I've no fear of such a thing as you."

He turned, put on his heavy coat and left the building. As he did so Dan slipped out ahead of him, and started up the road as fast as his little feet would carry him.

Chapter VIII

The Golden Key

"Why, Dan, what's the matter?"

Nellie was sitting before the open fire busily engaged with her needle as the lad entered the room. He stared at her for an instant, and then a sheepish grin crossed his face. His clothes were torn, and his hair tossed in the wildest confusion, while marks of blood spotted his cheeks.

"What in the world have you been doing?" Nellie insisted.

"Nuthin' much," came the slow reply,

"Well, you don't look like it. Have you been fighting?"

"Y'bet!" and Dan smacked his lips. "I swatted him good and hard, that's what I did."

"Did what?"

"Swatted him - punched his face, and dug out some of his hair."

"Punched his face and dug out his hair!" Nellie

exclaimed. "I don't understand. Sit down, and tell me about it."

Perched upon a chair Dan gave a brief though vivid description of the scene in the store, to which Nellie listened with almost breathless interest.

"And did he say that father took old Billy's gold?" she asked. "Are you sure?"

"Sure's I'm livin'. He said it, and he called him a rogue and me a - a - bad name!" Dan was about to tell what that name was, but the word stuck in his throat, and he found it impossible to bring it forth. "Sucker and sponger!" how those words stung him. How contemptuously his father had always spoken of such people. They rankled in his heart as he sped up the road. A squirrel in an old fir-tree had shouted them at him, while a forlorn crow soaring overhead had looked down and given its hoarse croak of contempt. He was a sucker - a sponger! living upon others! What was he doing to earn his living? Nothing. What would his father think were he alive?

"Dan, I'm sorry you did that," and as Nellie looked into those big brown eyes a deep love for this little lad welled up in her heart.

"Why. I thought you'd be glad," came the astonished reply. "If anybody called my dad bad names when he was alive I'd been glad if someone swatted him."

Nellie remained silent for a while, steadily working away at her sewing.

"Dan," she said at length, "I want you to promise me

something, will you?"

"Y'bet. What is it?"

"I want you to promise that you will say nothing about this to my father."

"Why? Wouldn't he like to know how I punched that man?"

"No, no. And besides I don't want him to know what has been said about him. It's a cruel lie, and if father hears of it, it will worry him so much. Will you keep the secret with me?"

"Yes, if you want me to. I'll not say a word, but, oh, I think Parson John would like to know how I punched him," and Dan gave a deep sigh at the thought of losing such pleasure.

"Thank you," Nellie replied. "I know I can trust you. Run away now, change your clothes, and wash your face; then get the wood in, before father comes home."

Long and silently Nellie remained before the fire with her hands resting upon her lap. Her brain was in a tumult, and her heart ached. What else was being said about her father? To whom should she go for information? She thought of Mrs. Larkins, but then she was over at the Hall getting ready for a church sale to be given that very evening by the Ladies' Aid Society. Stephen was coming for her early, as she was to have charge of one of the fancy booths. Afterwards there was to be a quiet dance by the young people, and she had promised Stephen that she would stay for a while, and have her first dance with him.

At length she aroused from her reverie and prepared her father's supper. How weary he looked, she thought, as she sat and watched him, and listened to his casual talk about his afternoon visit and the auction in the morning. A feeling of resentment filled her heart as she recalled what Farrington had said. To think that he should say such things about her father, who was always so patient and loving; who was ever trying to help others, no matter who they were. Tears came to her eyes at the thought. Suddenly she rose, and going to where her father was sitting put her arms around him, and gave him a loving kiss.

"Ho, ho!" came the delighted exclamation. "What ails my little girl to-night? What does she want now?"

"I want you, daddy," she replied. "I want to love you more, and be more help to you."

"Help me more! What could you do more than you do now? There, run away and get ready. I hear bells; Stephen must be coming, and I'm afraid you'll be late. Dan and I will look after the dishes."

That evening in the church hall, when the sale had ended, the fiddler tuned up his instrument, and several made ready for the dance. It was truly a pleasant sight which met the eyes of a number of the older ones as they sat back near the wall. Grouped around the large room the flower and strength of the neighbourhood chatted with one another, while waiting for the dance to begin. They seemed like one large family, these youths and maidens, who had known one another from childhood. Bright and happy were their faces, glowing with health, and the active exercise of daily life.

Somewhat apart from the rest stood Nellie Westmore, engaged in earnest conversation with Vivien Nelson. Presently the former turned partly around and her eyes rested upon Mrs. Larkins sitting quietly in one corner of the room. A bright smile illumined her face as she crossed over and sat down by her side.

"I am glad you stayed, Mrs. Larkins," she began. "I did not think you would care to remain."

"I like to see the young people enjoying themselves," Mrs. Larkins replied, "and I hope you will have a pleasant time, Nellie."

"I generally do," came the slow response; "but to-night my conscience troubles me."

"And in what way?"

"Oh, about my father."

"Why, is he sick?"

"No, not that. He is troubled somewhat in his mind, and I feel I should have stayed at home to cheer him up. I know he needs me to-night, and it was just his love which made him forget himself. He is always like that; thinking about others all the time."

"Don't worry, Nellie. Your father will have his books to occupy his mind."

"Yes, I know that. But he is feeling rather down-cast to-night after that auction this morning. Some cruel things were said about him, and I always know when he is in trouble, though he seldom complains."

Nellie paused, and gazed for a time upon the group in the centre of the room, as if intent on what was taking place there. Then her dark eyes, filled with a questioning look, turned full upon Mrs. Larkins' face.

"I am glad to be with you for a few moments," she whispered, "for I wish to ask you something. I have only spoken of it to Vivien, for she is so true and noble. Have you heard these stories about my father, Mrs. Larkins?"

"In connection with Billy Fletcher's gold?" was the reply.

"Yes, yes, that is what I mean. Oh, it troubles me so much."

"Yes, I have heard some of them, Nellie. But do not give yourself unnecessary concern. Evil-minded people will talk. I said nothing to you, hoping the matter would soon die down. Has your father heard anything?"

"No, not yet, and I trust no one will tell him. He has enough worry now without these. He has that trouble with the mine in British Columbia; then, this morning's annoyance. Oh, he must not know what people are saying!"

"I have heard but little lately," Mrs. Larkins responded in an effort to comfort her. "Let us trust that the talk will not amount to much."

"But Vivien tells me that it is not so. Since the auction the stories have started up again stronger than ever. People cannot understand where father got so much money to pay for the farm. I don't even know myself, for father never told me. Tom Fletcher and others are saying all sorts of things. What shall we do?"

Her bosom heaved as she uttered these words, which somewhat expressed the agitated state of her mind. Before Mrs. Larkins could further reply, the music struck up, and Stephen came for Nellie to claim her for the opening dance.

"How worthy," thought Mrs. Larkins as her eyes followed Nellie as she went forward, "is she of a true man's love. What nobleness and strength of character are there. But what of Stephen? If he would only get the right grip. Such a face as his is surely meant for higher things than a life of carelessness."

She was aroused by Farrington, who had taken the seat by her side which Nellie had recently vacated.

"They're hevin' a good time," he began, nodding towards the dancers. "Dick's in his element to-night."

"Rhoda Gadsby makes him a good partner," replied Mrs. Larkins.

"Only fair, Mrs. Larkins, only fair. She's not a bad girl, but no real pardner fer my son Dick. I'm sorry her father is my opponent at the comin' election. He'll never win, mark my word. Gadsby's too full of notions. He wants to set the world on fire, an' has all kinds of new-fangled idees. He will never do fer a Councillor-never. What Glendow wants is a real practical man, one who understands human nater."

"But Mr. Gadsby is a superior man," replied Mrs.

Larkins. "He reads much, and is trying to farm along scientific lines."

"Tryin' to farm! Yes, yer right thar, Mrs. Larkins. But that's about as fer as he's got. He has big idees, an' is allus talkin' about this parish bein' behint the times."

"And in what way?"

"Oh, as regards the schools. They don't teach enough branches, sich as botany, drawin' an' sich like. What do the childern of Glendow want with botany stuck into their brains? Let 'em learn to read, write an' cipher. Them things will pay. But as fer botany, who ever heerd of it helpin' a man to manage a farm, or a woman to sew, cook or make butter? Now, look at me, Mrs. Larkins. I never studied botany, an' behold my bizness. I don't know a bit about botany, an' here I'm runnin' fer a Councillor, an' lookin' forred to the Local House. No, no, this botany bizness is all nonsense."

"But," remonstrated Mrs. Larkins, "do you not enjoy the beautiful? Life should be more than the mere grubbing through dust and heat, grinding out our little day, wearing out the body and cramping up the soul in field, factory, office or behind the counter. Life is meant to be enjoyed, and whatever tends to enlarge our children's perspective, which will give them a love for the beautiful, will lessen the drudgery of life, and develop their characters. The Creator who made human beings in His own image, and endowed them with powers above the brute creation, surely intended that these divine faculties should be used and not allowed to lie dormant."

Mrs. Larkins spoke more strongly than was her wont.

She was naturally a quiet woman. But this man's narrowness and ignorance nettled her. Farrington, however, was not in the least affected by such words; in fact he rather pitied anyone who did not see eye to eye with him.

"What ye say, Mrs. Larkins," he replied, "is very fine in theory. But the question is, 'Will it pay?' Fer them as likes sich things they may study 'em to their hearts' content. But what do sich people amount to? I seen the parson once stand fer a long time watchin' the settin' sun, an' when I axed 'im what he saw he looked at me sorter dazed like. 'Mr. Farrington,' sez he, 'I saw wonderful things to-night, past man's understandin'. I've been very near to God, an' beheld the trailin' clouds of His glory!' 'Parson,' sez I, 'What will ye take fer yer knowledge? How much is it worth? While ye've been gazin' out thar at that sunset I've been gazin' at these letters, an' I find I'm better off by twenty-five dollars by gittin' my eggs an' butter to market day afore yesterday, jist when the prices had riz. That's what comes of gazin' at facts sich as price lists an' knowin' how to buy an' sell at the right time. That's of more value than lookin' at all the flowers an' sunsets in the world!' The parson didn't say nuthin', but jist looked at me, while the men in the store haw-hawed right out an' told the joke all round. Xo, you may find music in ripplin' water, an' poetry in flowers, an' sunsets, as Phil Gadsby and the parson sez, but give me the poetry of a price list, an' the music of good solid coin upon my counter. Them's the things which tell, an' them's the things we want taught in our schools."

Just as Farrington finished, cries of fright fell upon their ears. Turning quickly towards the dancers Mrs. Larkins noticed that most of them had fallen back in little groups, leaving Stephen Frenelle and Dick Farrington alone in the middle of the room. The attitude of the two left no doubt as to the cause of the disturbance. With clenched fists they faced each other as if about to engage in a fierce struggle. The former's eyes glowed with an intense light, while his strained, white face betokened the agitated state of his feelings.

"Say that again!" he hissed, looking straight at his opponent. "Say it if you dare!"

Dick stood irresolute with the look of fear blanching his face at sight of the angry form before him. While he hesitated and all held their breath, Nellie Westmore moved swiftly forward, and laid a timid hand upon Stephen's arm.

"Stephen, Stephen!" she pleaded. "Stop! don't go any further! Be a man! Come, let us go home!"

Quickly he turned and looked into her eyes, and at that look the pallor fled his face, leaving it flushed and abashed. His clenched hands relaxed, and without a word he followed her to the door. As they donned their wraps and passed out into the night, sighs of relief at the termination of this startling incident were plainly heard. Dick gave a sarcastic laugh, and the dance continued as if nothing unusual had happened.

For a while neither Nellie nor Stephen spoke as they sped along the road, drawn by a magnificent chestnut mare. The night was clear, and the crescent moon rose high in the heavens. Not a breath of wind stirred the trees, and the only sound which broke the silence was the jingling bells keeping time to the horse's nimble feet.

"He called me a fool and a pauper!" Stephen at length exclaimed. "Did you hear him?"

"Certainly," came the reply. "How could any one help hearing him?"

"I'd have knocked him down if it hadn't been for you, Nellie."

"I'm glad you didn't, Stephen."

"But I'll show him a thing or two. I'll get even with him yet. I'll teach him to call me a fool and a pauper!"

"Why not get more than even with him? You can do it without any trouble."

Nellie spoke very impressively, and Stephen looked at her in surprise.

"I know I can do that, for he's nothing but a clown. But what else can I do?"

"I didn't mean that, Stephen. That is only getting even with your opponent in brute fashion. You will only be putting yourself on an equality with him. You want to get more than even, not by hitting back and returning abuse for abuse. No, not that way, but by rising above him in manhood."

"How? In what way, Nellie?"

"Settle down to steady work. Redeem your home. Show Dick and the people of Glendow that you are not a fool or a pauper, but a man. Oh, Stephen, we want to be proud of you - and I do, too."

H. A. Cody

"Do you, Nellie, really?"

"Indeed I do, Stephen."

For an instant only their eyes met. For an instant there was silence. But in that instant, that mere atom of time, there opened up to Stephen a new meaning of life. A virile energy rent the old husk of indifference, and a yearning, startling in its intensity, stabbed his heart, to "make good," to recover lost ground and to do something of which Nellie should be proud.

It was love - the golden key which had at last opened to the young man the mystic door of life's great responsibility.

Chapter IX

Beating the Devil

"Father, I am becoming uneasy about Dan."

Parson John and Nellie were walking slowly along the road from the neat little parish church. It was a Sunday morning. Not a breath of wind stirred the balmy and spring-like air. A recent thaw had removed much of the snow, leaving the fields quite bare, the roads slippery, and the ice on the river like one huge gleaming mirror.

"Why, what do you mean?" asked the parson. "What makes you uneasy about Dan?"

"He has been so restless of late."

"Doesn't he mind you?"

"Oh, yes. He is always ready and anxious to do anything I ask him. But there is a far-away look in his eyes, and sometimes he gives such a start when I speak to him. His old life was so rough and stirring, that I fear he misses it, and longs to be back there, again."

"But he is interested in his studies, is he not?"

H. A. Cody

"Yes, to a certain extent. But not as much as formerly. It is hard for him to settle down to steady work. He seems to be thinking and dreaming of something else. I cannot understand him at all. I love the lad, and believe he is much attached to us."

"What do you think we had better do?"

"I hardly know, father. But you might take him with you sometimes on your drives. He is passionately fond of Midnight, and it would liven him up. Why not let him go with you to the funeral at Craig's Corner this afternoon? He would be company for you, too."

"But I'm not coming home until to-morrow. I expect to spend the night there, and in the morning go overland to see the Stickles and take those good things you have been making for the sick man. You will need Dan to stay with you."

"No, I shall be all right. Vivien Nelson has asked me to go there to-night, so I shall get along nicely."

"Very well, dear," her father replied. "You are just like your mother, always planning for someone else, and planning so well, too."

Dan's heart thrilled with pride and delight as he sat by Parson John's side and watched Midnight swinging along at her usual steady jog when there was no special hurry. So intent was the one upon watching the horse, and the other upon his sermon, that neither noticed a man driving a spirited horse dart out from behind a sharp point on the left, and cut straight across the river. It was old Tim Fraser, as big a rogue as existed anywhere in the land. He was very fond of horses, and that winter had purchased a new flier. He was an incessant boaster, and one day swore that he could out-travel anything on the river, Midnight included. He laid a wager to that effect, which was taken up by Dave Morehouse, who imagined the race would never come off, for Mr. Westmore would have nothing to do with such sport. Old Fraser, therefore, set about to meet Parson John, but for some time had failed to make connection. Hearing about the funeral, he was determined that the race should come off that very Sunday, and in the presence of the mourners and their friends at that. He accordingly hid behind Break-Neck Point, and with delight watched the parson drive up the river, and at the right moment he started forth for the fray. As Fraser swung into line and was about to pass, Midnight gave a great bound forward, and it was all that Parson John could do to hold her in check, for she danced and strained at the reins as her rival sped on ahead. At length Fraser slowed down, dropped behind, and, just when Midnight had steadied down, up he clattered again. This he did three times in quick succession, causing Midnight to quiver with excitement, and madly to champ the bit. At length the climax was reached, for the noble beast, hearing again the thud of her opponent's hoofs, became completely unmanageable. With a snort of excitement she laid low her head, took the bit firmly between her teeth, and started up the river like a whirlwind. The more Parson John shouted and tugged at the reins the more determined she became. The ice fairly flew from beneath her feet, and the trailing froth flecked her black hide like driving snow. Neck and neck the horses raced for some time, while Fraser grinned with delight at the success of his scheme.

Before long the funeral procession came into view,

making for the little church near the graveyard on the opposite shore. Parson John was feeling most keenly the position in which he was so unfortunately placed. He could see only one way out of the difficulty, and that was to leave Fraser behind. Therefore, before the first sleigh of the funeral procession was reached he gave Midnight the reins, and thus no longer restrained she drew gradually away from her opponent. On she flew, past the staring, gaping people, and for a mile beyond the church.

By this time Fraser was so far in the rear that he gave up the race. Beaten and crestfallen he turned to the left, made for the shore and disappeared.

At length Parson John was able to bring Midnight under control, when she trotted quietly down the river with a triumphant gleam in her handsome eyes. After the funeral had been conducted, a group at once surrounded the parson and questioned him concerning the strange occurrence on the river. Some were pleased with Fraser's ignominious defeat, and treated it as a huge joke. But others were sorely scandalized. What would the members of the other church in Glendow say when they heard of it? To think that their clergy-man should be racing on the river, and on a Sunday, too, while on his way to attend a funeral - the most solemn of all occasions!

"Well, you see," continued the parson, after he had explained the circumstance, "Fraser is a hard man to deal with, and in some ways I am really glad it happened as it did."

"Why, what do you mean?" gasped several of the most rigid.

"It's just this way," and a twinkle shone in the parson's eyes. "Five and thirty years have I served in the sacred ministry of our Church. During the whole of that time I have endeavoured to do my duty. I have faced the devil on many occasions, and trust that in the encounters I did no discredit to my calling. I have tried never to let him get ahead of me, and I am very thankful he didn't do it this afternoon with Tim Fraser's fast horse."

*   *   *   *   *

Parson John had won the day, and the group dispersed, chuckling with delight, and anxious to pass on the yarn to others.

That same evening Mr. Westmore was seated comfortably in Jim Rickhart's cosy sitting-room. The family gathered around in anticipation of a pleasant chat, for the rector was a good talker, and his visit was always an occasion of considerable interest. A few neighbours had dropped in to hear the news of the parish, and the latest tidings from the world at large. They had not been seated long ere a loud rap sounded upon the door, and when it was opened, a man encased in a heavy coat entered.

"Is Parson John here?" were his first words.

"Yes," Mr. Rickhart replied. "He's in the sitting-room. Do you want to see him? Is it a wedding, Sam? You look excited."

"Should say not. It's more like a funeral. Old Tim Fraser's met with a bad accident."

"What!"

"Yes. He was drivin' home from the river this afternoon, when that new horse of his shied, and then bolted. The sleigh gave a nasty slew on the icy road, and upset. Tim was caught somehow, and dragged quite a piece. He's badly broken up, and wants to see the parson."

By this time Mr. Westmore had crossed the room, and stood before the messenger. A startled look was in his eyes, as he peered keenly into Sam's face.

"Tell me, is it true what I hear," he questioned, "that Fraser has been hurt?"

"Yes, sir, and wants you at once."

"Is he seriously injured?"

"Can't tell. They're goin' fer the doctor, but it'll be some time before he can get there. It's a long way."

"Poor Fraser! Poor Fraser!" murmured the parson. "He was a careless man. I was bitter at him this afternoon, and now he is lying there. Quick, Dan, get on your coat and hat; we must be off at once."

It did not take them long to make ready, and soon Midnight was speeding through the darkness. This time it was no leisurely jog, but the pace she well knew how to set when her master was forth on important business. Across the river she sped, then over hill and valley, which echoed with the merry jingle of the bells. For some time Parson John did not speak, and seemed to be intent solely upon Midnight.

"Dan," he remarked at length, as they wound slowly up

a steep hill, "it's a mean thing, isn't it, to get many, many good things from someone, and never do anything in return, and not even to say 'Thank you?'"

The lad started at these words, and but for the darkness a flush would have been seen upon his face. "What does the parson mean?" he thought. "That was about what Farrington said. To get, and give nothing in return; to be a sucker and a sponger."

But the parson needed no reply. He did not even notice Dan's silence.

"Yes," he continued; "it's a mean thing. But that's just what Tim Fraser's been doing all his life. The good Lord has given him so many blessings of health, home, fine wife and children, and notwithstanding all these blessings, he's been ever against Him. He curses and swears, laughs at religion, and you saw what he did this afternoon."

"'Tis mean, awful mean," Dan replied, as the parson paused, and flicked the snow with his whip. "But maybe he's sorry, now, that he's hurt."

"Maybe he is, Dan. But it's a mean thing to give the best of life to Satan, and to give the dregs, the last few days, when the body is too weak to do anything, to the Lord. And yet I find that is so often done, and I'm afraid it's the case now."

When they reached Fraser's house they found great excitement within. Men and women were moving about the kitchen and sitting-room trying to help, and yet always getting into one another's way. Midnight was taken to the barn, Dan was led into the kitchen to get warm, while the parson went at once to the room where Tim was lying.

Dan shrank back in a corner, for he felt much abashed at the sight of so many strangers. He wanted to be alone - to think about what the parson had said coming along the road. And so Fraser was a sponger, and a sucker too, getting so many good things and giving nothing back. It was mean, and yet what was he himself but a sponger? What was he doing for Nellie and Parson John for what they were doing for him? They gave him a comfortable home, fed, clothed, and taught him, and he was doing nothing to pay them back. How disgusted his father would be if he only knew about it.

For the life of him Dan could not have expressed these feelings to anyone. He only knew that they ran through his mind like lightning, making him feel very miserable. His cheeks flushed, and a slight sigh escaped his lips as he sat crouched there in the corner with one small hand supporting his chin. No one heeded him, for all were too much excited over the accident to take any notice of a little boy.

"I said that horse would be the death of him," he heard a woman exclaim. "Tim's too old a man to drive such a beast as that."

"Oh, the beast's all right," an old man slowly replied, "but it was put to a wrong use, that's where the trouble came."

"Why, what do you mean?"

"Don't you know? Didn't you hear about what

happened on the river this afternoon? Tim went there on purpose to meet the parson, and strike up a race. He's been boasting for some time that he would do it. The Lord has given that man much rope, and has suffered him long. But this was too much, and He's tripped him up at last."

"Peter Brown," and the woman held up her hands in astonishment, "how can you say such a thing about your old neighbour, and in his house, too, with him lying there in that condition?"

"I'm only saying what the rest know and think," was the calm reply. "I've told Tim time and time again right to his face that the Lord would settle with him some day. 'Tim,' said I, and it was not later than last fall that I said it, 'Tim, the Lord has been good to you. He's blessed you in every way. You've health, strength, and a good home. And what have you done for Him? What have you given in return? Nothing. You curse, revile and scorn Him on the slightest pretext. It's not only mean, Tim, but you'll get punished some day, and don't you forget it.' But he only swore at me, and told me to shut up and mind my own business and he would mind his. But my words have come true, and I guess Tim sees it at last."

Dan was sitting bolt upright now, with his hands clenched and eyes staring hard at the speaker. The words had gone straight to his little heart, with terrible, stinging intensity. This man was saying what Farrington and the parson had said. It must be true. But the idea of the punishment was something new. He had never thought of that before.

And even as he looked, a silence spread throughout the

room, for Parson John was standing in the doorway. Upon his face an expression dwelt which awed more than many words, and all at once realized that the venerable man had just stepped from the solemn chamber of Death.

Chapter X

In Camp.

Nestling snugly among large stately trees of pine and spruce, the little log-cabin presented a picturesque appearance. Its one room, lighted by a small window, served as kitchen, living and sleeping apartments combined. It was warm, for the rough logs were well chinked with moss, while the snow lay thick upon the roof and banked up around the sides. This cabin had been recently built, and stood there by the little brook as an outward and visible sign of an inward change in the heart and mind of one of Glendow's sturdy sons.

The night Stephen Frenelle left Nellie at the Rectory after the drive home from the dance, he had fought one of those stern, fierce battles which must come to all at some time in life. As Jacob of old wrestled all night long for the mastery, so did Stephen in the silence of his own room. Sleep fled his eyes as he paced up and down, struggling with the contending thoughts which filled his heart. At times he clenched his hands and ground his teeth together as he pictured Dick Farrington standing in the Hall, hurling forth his taunting remarks. Then he longed for daylight to come that he might go to his house, call him forth, and give him the thrashing he so well deserved. He would drive that impudent, sarcastic smile from his face, and make

H. A. Cody

him take back his words. A voice seemed to say to him, "Do it. *You must* do it if you consider yourself a man. He insulted you to your face, and people will call you a coward if you allow it to pass." But always there came to him that gentle touch on his arm; he heard a voice pleading with him to be a man, and saw Nellie looking at him with those large, beseeching eyes, and his clenched hands would relax. And thus the battle raged; now this way, now that. Which side would win? When at length the first streak of dawn was breaking far off in the eastern sky, and Stephen came forth from the Chamber of Decision, there was no doubt as to the outcome of the fight. His face bore the marks of the struggle, but it also shone with a new light. When his mother and Nora came downstairs they were astonished to see him up so early, the fire in the kitchen stove burning brightly, and the cattle and sheep fed. Usually Stephen was hard to arouse in the morning, and it was nearly noon before the chores were finished, and then always in a half-hearted way. They looked at each other, and wondered at the change which had taken place.

Although Stephen had won a victory over himself, he was yet much puzzled. He wished to redeem the homestead, but how should he set about the task? As he waited that morning while breakfast was being prepared, this was the great thought uppermost in his mind. He knew that when spring came there was the farm to work. In the meantime, however, during the days of winter when the ground was covered with snow, what could he do? Once aroused, it was needful for him to set to work as soon as possible. Mechanically he picked up the weekly paper lying on a chair and glanced carelessly at the headlines set forth in bold type. As he did so his attention was arrested by two words "Logs Wanted." He read the article through which told how the price of lumber had suddenly advanced, and that logs were in great demand. When Stephen laid down the paper and went into breakfast, the puzzle had been solved. What about that heavy timber at the rear of their farm? No axe had as yet rung there, no fire had devastated the place, and the trees stood tall and straight in majestic grandeur. A brook flowed near which would bear the logs down the river.

His mother's and sister's hearts bounded with joy as Stephen unfolded to them his plan. He would hire two choppers; one could go home at night, while the other, old Henry, could live with him in the little camp he would build. They would chop while he hauled the logs to the brook. Mrs. Frenelle and Nora would do most of the cooking at home, and Stephen, would come for it at certain times. Thus a new spirit pervaded the house that day, and Mrs. Frenelle's heart was lighter than it had been for many months. Stephen did not tell her the cause of this sudden change, but with a loving mother's perception she felt that Nellie's gentle influence had much to do with it all.

One week later the cabin was built, the forest ringing with the sturdy blows of axes and the resounding crash of some hoary pine or spruce. Although the work was heavy, Stephen's heart was light. Not only did he feel the zest of one who had grappled with life in the noble effort to do the best be could, but he had Nellie's approbation. He drank in the bracing air of the open as never before, and revelled in the rich perfume of the various trees as he moved along their great cathedral-like aisles, carpeted with the whitest of snow.

The two choppers were kept busy from morning dawn

to sunset. They were skilled craftsmen, trained from early days in woodland lore. One, old Henry, thoroughly enjoyed his work and at times snatches of a familiar song fell from his lips as his axe bit deep into the side of some large tree.

"You did that well, Henry," Stephen one day remarked, as he watched a monster spruce wing its way to earth with a terrific crash.

"It's all in knowin' how," was the deliberate reply, as the old man began to trim the prostrate form. "Now, a greenhorn 'ud rush in, an' hack an' chop any old way, an' afore he knew what he was doin' the tree 'ud be tumblin' down in the wrong place, an' mebbe right a-top of 'im at that. But I size things up a bit afore I hit a clip. Havin' made up me mind as to the best spot to fell her, I swing to, an' whar I pint her thar she goes; that's all thar is about it."

"But doesn't the wind bother you sometimes?" Stephen inquired.

The chopper walked deliberately to the butt-end of the tree, and with the pole of his axe marked off the length of the log. Then he moistened his hands and drove the keen blade through the juicy bark deep into the wood.

"I allow fer the wind, laddie," he replied, "I allow fer that. When the good Lord sends the wind, sometimes from the North, sometimes from the South, I don't go agin it. Why, what's the use of goin' agin His will, an' it's all the same whether yer choppin' down a tree, or runnin' across the sea of Life fer the great Port beyon'. That's what the parson says, an' I guess he knows, though it seems to me that the poor man hisself has head-winds aplenty jist now."

Stephen asked no more questions then, being too busy. But that night, after supper, as the old man was mending his mittens he sat down by his side.

"Henry," he began, "how is it that the parson has head-winds? Do you think it's the Lord's will?"

"'Tain't the Lord's will, laddie," was the slow response. "Oh no, 'tain't His."

"Whose, then?"

"It's the devil's, that's whose it is, an' he's usin' sartin men in Glendow as human bellows to blow his vile wind aginst that man of God. That's what he's doin', an' they can't see it nohow."

"And so you think the parson had nothing to do with Billy Fletcher's gold. You think he is innocent?"

"Think it, laddie? Think it? What's the use of thinkin' it when I know it. Haven't I known Parson John fer forty years now. Can't I well remember when his hair, which is now so white, was as black as the raven's wing. An' why did it become white? I ax ye that. It's not old age which done it, ah no. It's care an' work fer the people of Glendow, that's what's done it. D'ye think I'd believe any yarn about a man that's been mor'n a father to me an' my family? Didn't I see 'im kneelin' by my little Bennie's bed, twenty years ago come next June, with the tears runnin' down his cheeks as he axed the Good Lord to spare the little lad to us a while longer. Mark my word, Stevie, them people who are tellin' sich stories about that man 'ill come to no good. Doesn't the

Lord say in his great Book, 'Touch not Mine anointed, an' do My prophets no harm?' My old woman often reads them words to me, fer she's a fine scholar is Marthy. 'Henry,' says she, 'the parson is the Lord's anointed. He's sot aside fer a holy work, an' it's a risky bizness to interfere with eich a man.'"

Scarcely had the speaker finished when the door of the cabin was pushed suddenly open, and a queer little man entered. A fur cap was pulled down over his ears, while across his left shoulder and fastened around his body several times was a new half-inch rope.

"Hello, Pete," Stephen exclaimed, "You look cold. Come to the stove and get warm."

"Y'bet I'm cold," was the reply. "My fingers and nose are most froze."

"What's brought you away out here this time of the night?" questioned Stephen, "I thought you liked the store too well to travel this far from the fire."

"Bizness, Steve, bizness," and the man rubbed his hands together, at the same time taking a good survey of the cabin.

"You look as if you were going to hang yourself, Pete, with all that rope about your body. Surely you're not tired of living yet."

"No, no, Steve. Not on your life. There'd be no fun in that, an' it's fun I'm after this time."

"But I thought you said you were out on business, and now you say it's fun."

"Bizness an' fun, me boy. Bizness an' fun; that's my motto. My bizness this time is to pinch the Stickles' cow, an' the fun 'ill be to hear Stickles, Mrs. Stickles an' the little Stickles squeal. Ha, ha! Bizness an' fun, Steve. Bizness an' fun."

"What! You're not going to take away the only cow the Stickles have left?" cried Stephen in amazement.

"Sure. It's the boss's orders, an' he doesn't mean fun, either. Nuthin' but bizness with 'im; ah no, nuthin' but bizness."

"Farrington is a mean rascal!" and Stephen leaped to his feet, his fists clenched and his eyes flashing. "Hasn't he any heart at all? To think of him taking the only cow from a poor family when the husband is sick in bed! What does the man mean?"

"Don't git excited, me boy. It's only bizness, boss sez, only bizness. The heart has nuthin' to do with that."

"Business be blowed! It's vile meanness, that's what it is! And will you help him out with such work?"

"It's bizness agin, Steve. I've got to live, an' keep the missus an' kiddies. What else is there fer a feller to do?"

"But why is Farrington taking the cow in the winter time, Pete? Why doesn't he wait until the summer, and give the Stickles a chance?"

"It all on account of a woman's tongue. That's what's the trouble."

H. A. Cody

"A woman's tongue?"

"Yes, a woman's tongue, an' ye know it's Mrs. Stickles' without me tellin' ye. She told Tommy Jones, wot told Betty Sharp, wot told the boss, that she was mighty glad the parson beat 'im at the auction. So the boss got mad as blazes, an' has sent me fer the cow to pay what the Stickles owe 'im. That's all I know about it, lad, so good-bye to yez both, fer I must be off. I'm to stay the night at Tommy Jones', an' in the mornin' will go from there fer the cow. Bizness an' fun, Steve; bizness an' fun; don't fergit that," and the little old man went off chuckling in high glee.

Chapter XI

Guarding the Flock

It was nearing the noon hour, and the sun slanting through the forest lifted into bold relief the trailing shadows of the stately trees. A lively chickadee was cheeping from a tall spruce, and a bold camp-robber was hopping in front of the cabin door picking up morsels of food which were occasionally cast forth. Stephen was preparing dinner, and the appetizing smell drifted out upon the air. Not far away, perched upon the branch of a tree, a sleek squirrel was filling the air with his noisy chattering and scolding. His bright little eyes sparkled with anger at the big strange intruder into his domain, causing him to pour forth all the vitriol of the squirrel vocabulary. Suddenly his noisy commotion ceased, and he lifted his head in a listening attitude. Presently down the trail leading to the main highway the sound of bells could be distinctly heard. As they drew nearer their music filled the air, reverberating from hill to hill and pulsing among the countless reaches of the great sombre forest. Not a child in the parish of Glendow but knew that familiar sound, and would rush eagerly into the house with the welcome tidings, for did it not mean a piece of candy hidden away in most mysterious pockets, which seemed never to be empty? How often in the deep of night tired sleepers in some lonely farm-house had

H. A. Cody

been awakened by their merry jingle, and in the morning husband and wife would discuss the matter and wonder what sick person Parson John had been visiting.

The bells grew more distinct now and brought Stephen to the door. Soon Midnight appeared swinging around a bend in the trail, with her fine neck proudly arched, ears pointed forward, and her large eyes keen with expectancy. The squirrel scurried away in a rage; the chickadee hopped to a safe retreat, and even the saucy camp-robber considered it wise to flap lazily to the top of the cabin.

"I'm glad to see you, Stephen," was Parson John's hearty greeting as he held out his hand. "Dan and I are on our way to visit the Stickles, and called in to see you in passing. What a snug place you have built here. I trust you are getting along nicely."

"Better than I expected," was the reply. "But, say, Parson, you're just in time for dinner. Let me put Midnight in the barn. She won't object, at any rate."

"What! is it that late?" and the worthy man glanced at the sun. "Dear me, how the time does fly! Well, then, if we will not be in the way I shall enjoy it very much, for it has been many a day since I have dined in the woods. But, wait," he cried, as Stephen was leading Midnight to the stable, "There's a basket of stuff, some pies, and I don't know what else, in the sleigh for hardy woodsmen, with Nellie's compliments. No, no, not that basket. It's for the Stickles. The smaller one; I think you'll find it in the back of the sleigh. There, that's it, with the green handle. It takes a large basket for all the little Stickles!" and the parson gave a hearty laugh.

What a dinner they had in the little cabin that day. Never did meat taste so good, and never did pie have such a delicious flavour as that which Nellie had made. The table and stools were rough, the food served on coarse dishes, and each one helped himself. But what did it matter? Their appetites were keen and the parson a most entertaining visitor. He told about the race on the river the day before, and of Tim Fraser's accident and sudden death, to which the choppers listened with almost breathless interest, at times giving vent to ejaculations of surprise.

"I'm sorry we have no milk to offer you," laughed Stephen, passing the parson a cup of black tea. "But at any minute now a cow may be passing this way and we might be able to obtain some."

"A cow passing! I don't understand," and Mr. Westmore stirred the sugar in his tea.

"Yes. The Stickles are losing their only cow. Farrington has sent Pete after her, and he should be along by this time."

"Stephen," and Parson John's face changed from its genial expression to one of severity, "do I understand you aright? Do you mean to tell me that Farrington is taking the Stickles' only cow?"

"Yes, I'm not joking. It's the solid truth. Pete stopped here on his way out last night, and told us all about it."

"Dear me! dear me!" sighed the parson, placing his hand to his head. "When will that man cease to be a thorn in the flesh? The Stickles are as honest as the sun, and Farrington knows it. This business must be stopped. Dan will you please bring out Midnight. We must hurry away at once."

Soon the little cabin was left behind and they were swinging out along the trail. The parson was quiet now. His old jocular spirit had departed, leaving him very thoughtful.

"The poor people! The poor people!" he ejaculated. "When will such things cease? Why will men dressed in a little brief authority try to crush those less fortunate? Dan, my boy, you may be a big man some day. You may get money, but never forget the poor. Be kind to them rather than to the powerful. They need kindness and sympathy, lad, more than others. My parents were poor, and I know how they toiled and slaved to give me an education. I well remember how they worked early and late until their fingers were knotted and their backs bowed. They are the noble ones who live in our midst, and though they may have little of this world's goods, they have great souls and are the real salt of the earth. Never forget that, boy."

Dan did not know how to reply to these words, but sat very still watching Midnight speeding on her way. The road wound for some distance through a wooded region and over several hills. At length it entered upon a settlement where the land was lean and rocks lifted their frowning heads above the surface. The few houses were poor, standing out grey and gaunt in the midst of this weird barrenness. But at every door Midnight was accustomed to stop. Well did she know the little voices which welcomed her, and the tiny hands which stroked her soft nose, or held up some dainty morsel of bread, potatoes or grass. But to-day there was none of this. She knew when the reins throbbed with an energy which meant hurry. Past the gateways she clipped with those long steady strides over the icy road, across a bleak stretch of country, down a valley, up a winding hill, and then away to the right through a long narrow lane to a lone farm-house.

As they approached a commotion was observed near the barn. Soon the cause was clearly manifest. Pete, assisted by someone, who proved to be Tommy Jones, had his rope about the horns of a black and white cow, and was endeavouring to lead her away. Mrs. Stickles and four little Stickles were filling the air with their cries of anger and protest. The cow, frightened by the noise, had become confused, and was trying to bolt towards the barn. Pete was tugging at the rope, while his assistant was belabouring her with a stout stick.

"Ye brutes!" Mrs. Stickles was shouting at the top of her voice. "What d'yez mean by thumpin' me poor Pansy in that way! But here comes the Lord's avengin' angel, praise His holy name! Stop 'em, Parson!" she shrieked, rushing towards the sleigh. "Smite 'em down, Parson, an' pray the Lord to turn His hottest thunderbolt upon Si Farrington's head!"

"Hush, hush, woman," Mr. Westmore remonstrated. "Don't talk that way. 'Vengeance is mine, saith the Lord. I will repay.'"

By this time the refractory cow had been brought to a state of partial subjection, and stood blinking at her captors as if uncertain what course to pursue. Leaving the sleigh, Mr. Westmore strode over to where the three were standing and laid his hand upon the rope.

"What's the meaning of this, Pete?" he asked. "Why

are you troubling this family?"

"It's them that's troublin' me, sir," was the reply. "I'm jist here on bizness, an' it's bizness I mean. If ye'll jist keep that whirlwind of a woman away an' them squaking kids so I kin git this cratur clear of the barn-yard, she'll walk like a daisy."

"But why are you taking the animal? Don't you know it's their only cow, and it's very important that Mr. Stickles, who is sick in bed, should have fresh milk every day?"

"That's not my bizness, Parson. My bizness is to git the cow; so stand clear if ye please, fer I want to git away. I'm late as 'tis."

"Hold a minute, Pete," and the parson laid a firmer hand upon the rope. "Who sent you here after this cow?"

"The boss, of course."

"Mr. Farrington?"

"Sure."

"And he wants the cow in payment of a debt, does he?"

"Guess so. But that ain't none of my bizness. My bizness is to git the cow."

"How much is the debt, anyway?" the parson asked, turning to Mrs. Stickles, who was standing near with arms akimbo.

"Twenty dollars, sir. No mor'n twenty dollars. Not one cent more, an' Tony'll pay every cent when he comes from the woods."

"Well, then, Pete," and the parson turned towards the latter, "unfasten this cow, and go back to your master. Tell him that I will be responsible for the debt, and that he shall have the full amount as soon as I get home."

But Pete shook his head, and began to gather up the loose end of the rope into a little coil in his left hand.

"That ain't the 'boss's order, sir. 'Fetch her, Pete,' sez he, 'an' let nuthin' stop ye. If they hev the money to pay, don't take it. The cow's of more value to me than money.' Them's his very orders."

"Oh, I see, I see," Mr. Westmore remarked, as a stern look crossed his face, and his eyes flashed with indignation. "It's not the money your master wants, but only the pound of flesh."

"Boss didn't say nuthin' 'bout any pound of flesh. He only said 'the cow,' an' the cow he'll git if Pete Davis knows anything."

Quick as a flash Parson John's hand dove deep into his capacious pocket. He whipped out a clasp-knife, opened it, and with one vigorous stroke severed the rope about one foot from the cow's head.

"There!" he cried to the staring, gaping Pete. "Take that rope to your master, and tell him what I have done. Leave the matter to me. I alone will be responsible for this deed."

H. A. Cody

The appearance of Mr. Westmore at this moment was enough to awe even the most careless. His gigantic form was drawn to its fullest height. His flashing eyes, turned full upon Pete's face, caused that obsequious menial to fall back a step or two. Even a blow from the parson's clenched fist just then would not have been a surprise. His spirit at this moment was that of the prophets of old, and even of the Great Master Himself, upholding justice and defending the cause of the poor and down-trodden.

For an instant only they faced each other. Then, Pete's eyes dropped as the eyes of an abashed dog before his master. He stooped for the rope, which had fallen to the ground, and slowly gathered it into a little coil. But still he maintained his ground.

"Are you going?" demanded the parson.

"Yes," came the surly response. "I'm goin', but remember you hev interfered with Si Farrington's lawful bizness, so beware! I'll go an' tell 'im what ye say. Oh, yes, I'll go, but you'll hear from 'im again. Oh, yes, ye'll hear."

"Let 'im come 'imself next time fer the cow," spoke up Mrs. Stickles, who had been silently watching the proceedings. "I'd like fer 'im to come. I'd like to git me fingers into his hair an' across his nasty, scrawny face. That's what I'd like to do."

"Hold yer tongue!" shouted Pete, "an' - "

"There now, no more of that," commanded Mr. Westmore. "We've had too many words already, so take yourself off."

They watched him as he moved down the lane to the road. He was followed by Tommy Jones, who had stood through it all with mouth wide open, and eyes staring with astonishment. When they were at length clear of the place the parson gave a sigh of relief, and across his face flitted a smile - like sunshine after storm.

H. A. Cody

Chapter XII

Light and Shadow

Upon entering the house Mr. Westmore divested himself of his great-coat, and stood warming himself by the kitchen fire, while Mrs. Stickles bustled around, smoothing down the bedclothes and putting the room to rights in which her sick husband lay. The kitchen floor was as white as human hands could make it, and the stove shone like polished ebony. Upon this a kettle steamed, while underneath a sleek Maltese cat was curled, softly purring in calm content.

Dan, assisted by the little Stickles, stabled Midnight, after which he was conducted over to the back of the barn to enjoy the pleasure of coasting down an icy grade. The only sound, therefore, was Mrs. Stickles' voice in the next room as she related to "her man" the wonderful events which had just taken place. A slight smile of pleasure crossed the parson's face as he listened to her words and thought of the big honest heart beneath that marvellous tongue. The sun of the winter day was streaming through the little window and falling athwart the foot of the bed as Mr. Westmore entered the room and grasped the sick man's white, outstretched hand.

"God bless ye, sir," exclaimed Mr. Stickles, "fer what

ye hev done fer me an' mine to-day. It ain't the first time by a long chalk. The Lord will reward ye, even if I can't."

"Tut, tut, man, don't mention it," Mr. Westmore replied as he took a seat by the bed. "And how are you feeling to-day, Mr. Stickles?"

"Only middlin', Parson, only middlin'. Simply joggin', simply joggin'."

Mrs. Stickles seated herself in a splint-bottomed chair, and picked up her knitting which had been hurriedly dropped upon the arrival of Pete Davis. How her fingers did work! It was wonderful to watch them. How hard and worn they were, and yet so nimble. The needles flew with lightning rapidity, clicking against one another with a rhythmical cadence; the music of humble, consecrated work. But when Mr. Westmore began to tell about Tim Fraser, and his sudden death, the knitting dropped into her lap, and she stared at the speaker with open-eyed astonishment.

"An' do ye mean to tell me," she exclaimed, when the parson had finished, "that Tim Fraser is dead?"

"Yes, it's only too true, Mrs. Stickles. Poor man - poor man!"

"Ye may well call 'im poor, Parson, fer I'm thinkin' that's jist what he is at this blessed minute. He's in a bad way now, I reckon."

"Hush, hush, Marthy," her husband remonstrated. "We must not judge too harshly."

H. A. Cody

"I'm not, John, I'm not, an' the parson knows I'm not. But if Tim isn't sizzlin', then the Bible's clean wrong," and the needles clicked harder than ever.

"It teaches us the uncertainty of life," replied Mr. Westmore. "It shows how a man with great strength, and health can be stricken down in an instant. How important it is to be always ready when the call does come."

"Ye're right, Parson, ye're surely right," and Mrs. Stickles stopped to count her stitches. "Wasn't John an' me talkin' about that only last night. I was readin' the Bible to 'im, an' had come to that story about poor old Samson, an' his hard luck."

"'It's very strange,' sez John, sez he to me, 'that when Samson lost his hair he lost his great strength, too. I can't unnerstan' it nohow.'"

"'Why, that's simple enough,' sez I to 'im. 'The Lord when He let Samson's strength rest in his hair jist wanted to teach 'im how unsartin a thing strength is. 'Why, anyone can cut off yer hair,' sez I, 'an' ye know, John,' sez I, 'ye don't allus have to cut it off, either, fer it falls out like yourn, John - fer yer almost bald.' Ain't them the exact words I said, John, an' only last night at that?"

"Yes, Marthy. That's just what ye said, an' we see how true it is. Tim Fraser was a powerful man as fer as strength an' health goes, but what did it all amount to? He lost it as quick as Samson of old. Ah, yes, a man's a mighty weak thing, an' his strength very unsartin, an' hangs by a slender thread. Look at me, parson. Once I was able to stan' almost anything, an' here I be a useless log - a burden to meself an' family."

"Don't say that, John, dear," remonstrated Mrs. Stickles wiping her eyes with her apron. "Ye know ye ain't a bother. Yer as patient as a fly in molasses. The fly is thar an' can't help it, an' so are you, John. It's the Lord's will, an' ye've often said so. He'll look after me an' the little ones. He's never forsaken us yit, an' I guess He won't if we stick to 'im."

"Your children are certainly a credit to you, Mrs. Stickles," remarked Mr. Westmore. "You should be proud of them."

"I am, sir, indeed I am," and the worthy woman's face beamed with pleasure. "But it takes a lot of 'scretion, Parson, to handle a big family. I've often said to John that children are like postage-stamps. They've got to be licked sometimes to do the work they were intended to do. But if ye lick 'em too much, ye spile 'em. Oh, yes, it takes great 'scretion to bring up a family."

"You certainly have used great discretion," replied Parson John, much amused at Mrs. Stickles' words. "I suppose those who are working out are just as dear as the four little ones at home?"

"They're all dear to me, sir, all dear. I kin count 'em all on me ten fingers, no more an' no less. Now some fingers are larger than t'others, and some smaller, an' some more useful than t'others an' do more work, but I couldn't part with one. So as I often tell John our children are jist like me ten fingers. I couldn't do without one of 'em - ah, no, bless their dear hearts."

The sound of little feet and childish voices caused

H. A. Cody

them to look towards the kitchen. There they beheld the four little Stickles, with Dan in the midst, standing in a row by the stove.

"Ho, ho!" exclaimed the parson, rising and going towards them. "So here you are, as fresh and active as ever."

Diving deep into his pocket he brought forth a generous piece of home-made candy.

"Sweets for the sweet," he cried. "Now, who's to have this?"

At once a rush ensued and four little forms surrounded him.

"Wait, wait; not yet!" and the good man held the candy aloft. "Nothing given away here. You must earn every bit. All in a row now. There, that's better," and he lined them up, like a veteran schoolmaster, proud of his little class. "Come, I want your names. You begin," and he tapped the nearest to him on the shoulder.

"John Medley Stickles, sir," came the quick reply.

"A good name, my little man," and the parson patted him on the head. "May you be worthy of your namesake, that noble man of God - the first Bishop of this Diocese. Now next," and he pointed to the second little Stickles.

"Benjamin Alexander Stickles, sir,"

"Ha, ha. Named after your two grandfathers. Fine men they were, too. Now my little maiden, we'll hear from you."

"Martha Trumpit Stickles, sir," came the shy response.

"That's a good name, my dear, after your mother - and with her eyes, too. Just one more left. Come, my dear, what have you to say?"

"Ruth Wethmore Stickles, thir, if you pleath," lisped the little lass, with her eyes upon the floor.

At these words the parson paused, as if uncertain what to say. "Ruth, the gleaner," he at length slowly remarked. "Ruth Westmore. Ah, Mrs. Stickles, I little thought that day my dear wife stood sponsor for your baby here, and gave her her own name, how soon she would be taken from us. Four years - four long years since she went home. But come, but come," he hurriedly continued, noticing Mrs. Stickles about to place her apron to her eyes. "I have a question to ask each little one here, and then something is coming. Look, John, answer me, quick. How many Commandments are there?"

"Ten, sir," came the ready reply.

"What is the fifth one?"

"Honour thy father and mother, that thy days may be long in the land which the Lord thy God giveth thee."

"That's good, that's good. Don't forget that, my little man. The first commandment with promise. I taught your brother Tony that when he was a little lad, and I'm sure he hasn't forgotten it. Now, Bennie, what two things do we learn from these commandments?"

"My duty towards God, an' my duty towards my neighbour."

"Right, right you are. Now, Martha, what were you made at your baptism?"

"A member of Christ, a child of God, and an inheritor of the Kingdom of Heaven."

"Well done. I thought that would stick you, but I see you have learned your lesson well! It's Ruth's turn now. Can you tell me, my dear, what happened on Good Friday?"

"Jesus died, thir, on the Croth."

"And what took place on Easter Day?"

"He roth from the grave, thir."

"Good, good. Always remember that. Good Friday and Easter Day come very near together. 'Earth's saddest day and brightest day are just one day apart.'"

Mrs. Stickles' face beamed with pleasure as the parson praised the little class, and gave a piece of candy to each. Then he drew from his pocket a small package wrapped in white tissue paper tied with a piece of pink ribbon, and held it up before the wondering eyes of the little Stickles.

"From Nellie," he remarked. "Candy she made herself for the one who can best say the verses on the Christian Year she gave you to learn some time ago. Now, who can say them all through without one mistake?"

Instantly four little hands shot up into the air, and four pairs of sparkling eyes were fixed eagerly upon the coveted treasure.

"Well, Bennie, we'll try you," said the parson. "Stand up straight, and don't be afraid to speak out."

"Advent tells us Christ is here,
Christmas tells us Christ is near - "

"Hold, hold!" cried Mr. Westmore. "Try again."

But the second attempt proving worse than the first, it was passed on to Martha. Bravely the little maiden plunged into the intricacies of the two first verses, but became a total wreck upon the third. Try as she might the words would not come, and tears were in her eyes when at length she gave up the attempt and waited for John Medley to conquer where she had failed. But alas! though starting in bravely he mixed Epiphany and Advent so hopelessly that the parson was forced to stop his wild wanderings.

"Dear me! dear me!" Mr. Westmore exclaimed. "What are we to do? Surely Ruth can do better than this."

With hands clasped demurely before her and her eyes fixed upon the floor, slowly the little maiden began to lisp forth the words while the rest listened in almost breathless silence.

"Advent telth uth Christ ith near;
Christmath telth uth Christ ith here;
In Epithany we trath
All the glory of Hith grath."

H. A. Cody

Thus steadily on she lisped through verse after verse, and when the last was completed a sigh of relief was heard from Mrs. Stickles, while the parson clapped his hands with delight. How her eyes did sparkle as he handed her the little package, with a few words of encouragement, and how longingly the three others looked upon the treasure.

"Now," said Mr. Westmore, "we must be away. Nellie will wonder what has become of us."

"Not yet, sir, not yet!" cried Mrs. Stickles. "You must have a cup of tea first.' The water is bilin', an' it'll be ready in a jiffy. Did ye give Midnight any hay?" she demanded, turning to Bennie.

"Oh, ma!" came the reply. "I fergot all about it."

"There now, it's jist like ye. Hurry off this minute and give that poor critter some of that good hay from the nigh loft."

As the little Stickles and Dan scurried out of the room, Ruth still clutching her precious package, Mrs. Stickles turned to Mr. Westmore.

"There now, Parson, ye jist must wait, an' have that cup of tea, an' some of my fresh bread. We shan't tech Nellie's pies an' cake, cause ye kin hev her cookin' any time, bless her dear heart. How I wish she was here herself so I could look into her sweet face an' tell her meself how grateful I am."

Hardly had the parson seated himself at the table ere several piercing shrieks fell upon his ears. Rushing to the door he beheld John Medley hurrying towards the house with arms at right angles, and his face as pale as death.

"Child! Child! What is it?" shouted Mrs. Stickles.

"R-r-uth's k-k-illed! She f-f-ell from the la-la-der. Oh! Oh!"

Waiting to hear no more they hurried to the barn, and there they found the little form lying on the floor, still grasping in her hand the precious package.

"My poor lamb! My darlin' baby! are ye kilt, are ye kilt?" wailed Mrs. Stickles, kneeling down by her side. "Speak to me, my lamb, my little baby! Oh, speak to yer mammy!"

But no sign of recognition came from the prostrate child. Seeing this the mother sprang to her feet and wrung her hands in agony of despair.

"What will we do? Oh, what kin we do? My baby is kilt - my poor darlin'! Oh - oh - oh!"

Tenderly Parson John lifted the child in his arms, carried her into the house, and laid her on the settle near the stove. It was found that she was breathing, and soon a little water brought some color into her face. Presently she opened her eyes, and started up, but fell back again, with a cry of pain, fiercely clutching the package.

"What is it, dear?" asked the parson. "Where is the pain?"

"My leg! My leg!" moaned the child.

"Ah, I feared so," exclaimed Mr. Westmore, after a brief examination. "We must have the doctor at once. Is there anyone near who will go for him, Mrs. Stickles?"

"Not a man, sir, that's fit to go. They're all in the woods. Oh, what kin we do!"

"Don't worry, Mrs. Stickles," was the reassuring reply. "Midnight will go, and I will hold the reins. Come, Dan, the horse, quick."

As Midnight drew up to the door a few minutes later, Parson John came out of the house and affectionately patted the sleek neck of the noble animal.

"Remember, Midnight," he said, "you must do your best to-day. It's for the sake of the little lass, and she was getting hay for you. Don't forget that."

Chapter XIII

For the Sake of a Child

Night had shut down over the land as Midnight, with her long, swinging strides, clipped through the lighted streets of the prosperous little railway town of Bradin, and drew up at old Doctor Leeds' snug house. A fast express had just thundered shrieking by. A strong, cutting wind racing in from the Northeast was tearing through the sinuous telegraph wires with a buzzing sound, the weird prelude of a coming storm.

The worthy doctor was at home, having only lately returned from a long drive into the country. He and his wife, a kindly-faced little woman, were just sitting down to their quiet meal. Seldom could they have an evening together, for the doctor's field was a large one and his patients numerous.

"You have no engagement for to-night, I hope, Joseph," remarked his wife, as she poured the tea.

"No, dear," was the reply. "I expect to have one evening at home, and I'm very glad of it, too. I'm weary to-night, and am longing for my arm-chair, with my papers and pipe."

A sharp knock upon the door aroused them, and great

H. A. Cody

was their surprise to see the venerable Rector of Glendow enter.

"Parson John!" cried the doctor, rushing forward and grasping his old friend's hand. "It's been months since I've seen you. What lucky event brought you here to-night? Did you miss the train? If so, I'm glad. My chessmen are moulding for want of use."

But the parson shook his head and briefly told of the accident in the barn.

"And so the little lass is in trouble, hey? More worry for Mrs. Stickles."

"And you will be able to go to-night, Doctor?"

"Certainly. Sweepstakes hasn't been on the road for two days, and is keen for a good run."

"But, my dear," remonstrated Mrs. Leeds, "are you able to go? You have been driving all day, and must be very tired. Why not rest a little first?"

"And let the poor child suffer that much longer! Not a bit of it."

"I have heard doctors say," remarked the parson, as he and Dan sat down to their supper, "that they get so hardened to suffering that at last it does not affect them at all. I am glad it is not true with you."

"The older I get," replied the doctor thoughtfully, stirring his tea, "the more my heart aches at the pains and sufferings of others, especially in little children. As soon as I hear of someone in distress I can never rest until I reach his or her side. There always comes to me a voice urging me to make haste. Even now I seem to hear that child calling to me. She is a sweet, pretty lass, and how often have I patted her fair little head, and to think of those blue eyes filled with tears, that tiny face drawn with pain, and her whole body writhing in agony. However, you know all about this, Parson, so what's the use of my talking."

"But I am glad to hear you speak as you do, Doctor. Over thirty years have I been in Glendow, and I become more affected by suffering the older I get."

The doctor looked keenly into Mr. Westmore's face, as if trying to read his inmost thoughts.

"Do you ever become weary of your work?" he at length asked. "Do you not long for a more congenial field?"

"I have often been asked that question, Doctor," the parson slowly replied, "but not so much of late. I am getting old now, and young men are needed, so I am somewhat forgotten. However, I am glad that this is so. Years ago when a tempting offer came to me from some influential parish, though I always refused, it disturbed me for days, until the matter was finally settled. Now I do not have such distractions, and am quite happy. In the quiet parish of Glendow I find all that the heart can desire. The labour to me becomes no more monotonous than the work of parents with their children. They often are weary in their toil for their little ones, but not weary of it. The body gives out at times, but not the love in the heart. And so I always find something new and fresh in my work which gives such a relish to life. I have baptized most of the young

H. A. Cody

people in this parish, I have prepared them for Confirmation, given them their first Communion, and in numerous cases have joined their hands in holy wedlock. Some may long for a greater field and a wealthy congregation. But, remember, as the sun in the heavens may be seen as clearly in the tiny dewdrop as in the great ocean, so I can see the glory of the Father shining in these humble parishioners of mine, especially so in the children of tender years, as in the great intellects. As for travelling abroad to see the world and its wonders, I find I can do it more conveniently in my quiet study among my books. At a very small cost I can wander to all parts of the world, without the dangers and inconveniences of steamers and railroads. As to studying human nature, it is to be found in any parish. Carlyle well said that 'any road, this simple Entepfuhl road, will lead you to the end of the world,' and was it not the quaint and humble-minded Thoreau who expressed himself in somewhat the same way:

"'If with Fancy unfurled,
You leave your abode,
You may go round the world,
By the Marlboro road.'"

The doctor rose from the table and grasped Mr. Westmore's hand.

"Thank you for those words," he said. "I have thought of those very things so often, and you have expressed my ideas exactly. I must now be away. You will stay all night, for I wish to have a good chat with you upon my return."

"Thank you very much," the parson replied, "but we

must be off as soon as possible. My daughter is all alone and will be quite uneasy by my long absence. We shall go home by the way of Flett's Corner, and thus save three miles. But look, Doctor, don't send your bill to the Stickles. Send it to me. Now be sure."

"Tut, tut, man. Don't worry about the bills of others. Leave this matter to me. The Stickles won't have any cause for anxiety about the bill, and why should you? It's paid already."

What a noble picture these two men presented as they stood there! Both had grown old in a noble service for their fellow-men, and truly their grey heads were beautiful crowns of glory. One had charge of the cure of souls, the other of bodies, and yet there was no clashing. Each respected the work of the other, and both were inspired with the high motive which lifts any profession or occupation above the ordinary - the Christ-like motive of love.

Parson John remained for some time after the doctor had left, chatting with Mrs. Leeds, and when at length Midnight started on her homeward way it was quite late. They had not advanced far before the storm which had been threatening swept upon them. Although the night was dark, the roadbed was firm and Midnight surefooted. As they scudded forward the wind howled through the trees and dashed the snow against their faces. They fled by farm-houses and caught fleeting glimpses of the bright, cosy scenes within. Twice they met belated teams plodding wearily homeward. Without one touch of rein, or word of command, each time Midnight slowed down, swerved to the left and swung by. It was only when the dim, dark forms of the panting steeds loomed up for an instant on their right, and then disappeared into the blackness, were they aware of their presence. Occasionally the road wound for a mile or more through a wooded region, and in such places they found peace and shelter. Here the wind could not reach them, although they could hear its wild ravings in the tree-tops above. The snow came softly, silently down, and, although they could not see it falling, they could feel it flecking their faces and knew it was weaving its mystic robe over their bodies. In one place such as this a faint glimmer of light struggled through the darkness a short distance from the road.

"It's Stephen's cabin," the parson remarked. "It is a snug place on a night like this. I wonder what he is doing now. I wish we had time to call to give him a word of cheer."

About two hundred yards beyond the cabin they left the main highway and entered upon a lumber road. This latter was used in the winter time in order to avoid a large hill on the former and the huge drifts which piled from fence to fence. At first Midnight slowed down to a walk, but at length, becoming a little impatient to get home, she broke into a gentle trot. Then, in the twinkling of an eye, the sleigh gave a great lurch, and before a hand could be raised Dan found himself shooting over the parson and falling headlong into the soft yielding snow. Recovering himself as quickly as possible, and brushing the snow from his mouth, ears and eyes, he groped around to ascertain what had happened. Away in the distance he could hear a crashing sound as Midnight hurried along with the overturned sleigh. Then all was still. He called and shouted, but received no reply. A feeling of dread crept over him, and at once he started to walk back to the road. He had advanced but a few steps, however, when he stumbled and half fell over a form which he knew must be that of Parson John. He put out his hand and felt his coat. Then he called, but all in vain. Hastily fumbling in his pockets he drew forth several matches and tried to strike a light. His little hands trembled as he did so, and time and time again a draught blew out the tiny flame. In desperation he at length kneeled down upon the snow, sheltered the match with his coat, and ere long had the satisfaction of seeing the flame grow strong and steady. Carefully he held it up and the small light illumined the darkness for the space of a few feet around. Then it fell upon the prostrate form at his side. It touched for an instant the old man's face, oh, so still and white, lying there in the snow; and then an awful blackness. The light had gone out!

H. A. Cody

Chapter XIV

The Long Night

As Dan stood there in the darkness with snow to his knees, clutching between his fingers the extinguished match, the helplessness of his position dawned upon him. What had happened to the parson he could easily guess, for the place was full of old stumps, half protruding from beneath the snow. No doubt he had struck one of these in the fall. But of the result of the blow he could not tell, for placing his ear close down to the face he tried to detect some sign of life, but all in vain. Suppose the parson had been killed! He thought of Nellie, waiting anxiously at the Rectory. How could he tell her what had happened? Suddenly a new sense of responsibility came to him. Something must be done as quickly as possible, and he was the only one to do it. He thought of Stephen's cabin, which they had passed a short time before. He could obtain help there, and he must go at once. Taking off his own outer coat he laid it carefully over the prostrate man, and then struggled back to the road. Having reached this he imagined it would not take him long to cover the distance. But he soon found how difficult was the undertaking, and what a task it was to keep the road on such a night. The blackness was intense, and the snow, which all the time had been steadily falling, added to the difficulty. Every few steps he would plunge off into the deep snow, and flounder around again until he had regained the solid footing. The distance, which was not more than a mile, seemed never-ending. Still he plodded on, the thought of that silent form lying in the snow inspiring him with extra energy. At length, much exhausted, a welcome glimmer of light winged its way through the darkness. Dan's heart leaped within him. The place was near, and Stephen had not yet gone to bed. Panting heavily, and struggling unsteadily, he crept slowly forward, reached the door and pounded fiercely upon it with both doubled-up fists.

Slowly the door was opened, and great was Stephen's surprise to see the little snow-covered figure standing before him.

"Help! Come quick!" gasped Dan.

"What's wrong?" Stephen demanded, dragging the boy into the cabin. "Where's the parson?"

"Over there - in the snow - in the woods!"

"Sit down," said Stephen, noticing how weary and excited was the little lad. "Tell me now all about it."

Quickly and briefly Dan related about the drive through the storm, the accident on the "cut off," and Parson John's fall.

"Oh, God!" Stephen groaned when he had heard the story. "What will Nellie think? What will she say? It will break her heart! I must be off at once!"

Reaching for the lantern his hand trembled as he lighted it.

H. A. Cody

"Wait here," he commanded, "till I hitch Dexter to the pung; or no, you'd better come with me and give a hand. There is no time to lose."

Dan obeyed without a word and held the lantern while Stephen harnessed the horse.

"Where's Midnight?" Stephen asked, as he deftly drew the reins through the terrets.

"She ran away. I heard the sleigh crashing after her as she ran."

"She'll kill herself! But no, she's too wise for that. She'll go home and whinny at the door, and then what will Nellie think! We must hurry along as fast as possible. She will he frantic with fear."

"Guess we'd better bring the parson back to your place," Dan remarked as Dexter swung down the road.

"Bring him to my place!" exclaimed Stephen in surprise. "What can we do for him there?"

"Won't he need the doctor?"

"Yes, he may. But we can't go all the way to Bradin now."

"Guess you won't have to do that."

"Why, what do you mean?"

"He's at the Stickles'."

"At the Stickles'?"

"Yep. The little girl got hurt, so we went after the doctor."

"Oh, I see - I see now," Stephen mused. "That's a different matter. It's only three miles to the Stickles'. But the road will be bad to-night, for the wind's across country, and the drifts there pile fast and deep. But I shall go if necessary, even if I have to crawl on all fours. I won't have to do that, though, for Dexter will take me through if any horse can."

It did not take them long to cover the one mile of road between the cabin and the place where the accident had occurred. By the light of the lantern it was not difficult to find the spot. An uncanny feeling crept over them as they drew near, and saw the parson lying there in the snow just as Dan had left him. With the lantern in his hand Stephen leaped from the pung and looked intently into the face of the prostrate man. It did not take him long to ascertain that life still remained in his body, and a prayer of thankfulness went up from his heart as he thought of the dear old man and the anxious Nellie.

Quickly and as carefully as possible they lifted him into the pung, covered him with a warm robe, and then sped back to the cabin. As soon as they had laid him upon the bed, Stephen reached for a heavy coat hanging on the wall.

"I'm off now," he said. "You keep watch. I'll be back as soon as I can."

The injured man lay perfectly motionless, to all outward appearance dead. Dan stood looking at him for some time after Stephen had left, puzzled and bewildered. What could he do? What would Nellie

H. A. Cody

think of him now? He sank upon the stool by the bedside And buried his face in his hands - a forlorn little creature, trying to think. Presently he glanced towards the bed, and gazed long and intently upon the parson's face. Many were the thoughts which crowded into his mind as he sat there. A deep affection for the old man had sprung up in his heart. To him he was like some superior being with his great strength and wonderful knowledge. Then to think he should care for him, Dan Flitter, so small, who could neither read nor write, who was nothing but a sponger. The thought of Farrington's insult came to him, and what he had said about the parson. It had rankled continually in his breast, and now it arose in greater force than ever. Why were the people saying such things about this good man? He had listened to men talking in the store and along the road. They had said and hinted many things, and he had been silent. But, though silent, his mind and heart had been at work. Often while lying in his little bed at night he had brooded over the matter. He longed to do something to clear the parson, and show the people that they were wrong. But what could he do? They would not listen to him. They hinted that the parson had stolen the gold, and what could he say? It needed more than words. These were the thoughts which had been beating through his brain for days, giving him at times that listless manner, far-away look, and lack of interest in his studies, which worried Nellie so much. So sitting on guard by the injured man's side this night with large, dreamy eyes, thoughtful face - more thoughtful than ordinary for a child of his age - he recalled the various scenes since the night of the fire. Suddenly his face flushed, the dreamy expression faded from his eyes, as the dim light of dawn is dispersed by the fulness of day. They shone with a new radiance as he turned them upon the parson's face. He rose to his feet and walked quickly up and down the room. He was once again a creature of the wild. The glory of a lofty purpose fired his blood. He had experienced it before when, out in the woods, he had followed the tracks of the nimble deer, or listened to the whirr of the startled pigeon. But now it was a nobler chase, a loftier purpose, in which the honour of a faithful friend was at stake.

A sound from the bed startled him. Glancing quickly in that direction he noticed the lips of the wounded man moving. No sign of consciousness, however, did he give. He was in another world, the strange, mysterious world, where the mind roams at will and language flows from the fountain-head of the inner being.

"'The blood of our Lord Jesus Christ, which was shed for thee - drink this - .'" He was in church at the Communion service, administering the cup.

"Four thousand dollars." He was at the auction now, eager and intent.

"Poor lassie, poor little lamb." This time it was the injured Stickles child. And thus he rambled on from one thing to another, while Dan stood like a statue in the room staring upon him. Suddenly he opened his eyes, looked around in a dazed manner, and then fixed them upon the boy's face. He moved a little, and at once a cry of pain escaped his lips.

"Dan! Dan!" he exclaimed. "What is the matter? Where am I, and what is the meaning of this pain in my shoulder?"

The look in his face was most pathetic, and Dan longed

to do something to relieve his suffering.

"Does yer shoulder hurt much?" the lad asked.

"Yes, yes, the pain is intense. Tell me how it happened."

"We were chucked from the sleigh, an' I guess you struck a stump," was the reply.

"Is this Stephen's cabin?"

"Yep. He's gone fer the doctor, so I'm keepin' watch."

The parson remained very quiet, and did not speak for some time. He still felt confused, and his shoulder was giving him great pain. He realized, however, how much he owed to Dan. What if he had been alone when the accident occurred?

"Did you come back for Stephen?" he at length questioned.

"Yep."

"And you were not hurt? Are you sure?"

"Sure's I'm livin'."

"And you were not afraid to come alone to the cabin for help?"

"No, I didn't mind."

"You're a brave boy, Dan. You've done much for me to-night. Saved my life, in fact."

"Oh, I didn't do much. Not worth mentionin'," and the lad took his seat by the bedside.

How the time did creep by. Often Dan went to the door and looked out. He strained his ears in order to hear the sound of bells, but the wind moaning and tearing through the tree-tops alone fell upon his ears. At last, when his patience was almost exhausted, the door was flung open, and Doctor Leeds entered, covered with snow, and a most anxious look upon his face. It did not take long for the practised eye and hand to ascertain the trouble. The shoulder had been dislocated, and would have to be replaced.

Then the parson showed of what stuff he was made. Hardly a sound escaped his lips as the doctor, assisted by Stephen, performed the painful operation.

"There!" exclaimed the physician, as he bound up the wounded member, "we'll have you round again in a short time. Now, some would have squaked and yelled like a baby, but you're a man through and through." "Thank you, Doctor. You are very good. But how about the little lass? You didn't leave her for me? Tell me the truth," and the parson's eyes sought the doctor's face.

"Oh, don't you worry about her," was the good-natured reply. "Sweepstakes took me over the road like the wind, and I had the poor little leg all fixed up before Stephen arrived. She'll do very well now without my care. But come, we must get you home at once."

"Do you think I am able to go?"

"Able! certainly you're able. Home's the only place for

you, though the journey may cause you some pain."

"And you will come too, Doctor? You muat be very tired, and need a good rest."

"Yes, I'm going with you. I'm not going to leave you yet. You're worth fifty ordinary men, and we must not run any risk. Besides that, sir, I do want a glimpse of your dear Nellie, and a little chat with her. I haven't rested my eyes upon her for months, and do you think I'm going to miss such an opportunity? No, sir, not a bit of it."

Mr. Westmore was forced to smile in spite of his weakness as he looked into the doctor's strong, rugged face.

"God bless you," he replied. "This isn't the first time you have been a firm friend to me. I can never forget how you stood day and night by the side of my dear wife, doing all in your power to keep her with us a little longer."

"Tut, tut, man," and the doctor turned away to hide a mistiness in his eyes. "She was worthy of it, and her like can't be found every day. But come, Steve has been waiting at the door for some time, and we must be away."

Chapter XV.

Deepening Shadows

As Nellie stood at the study window the Sunday afternoon her father left for Craig's Corner a sense of depression and loneliness stole over her. How much longer could her father continue those hard drives, she wondered. He was getting old. His hair was so white and his steps feeble. What was to become of him when he could perform his beloved work no longer? She knew very well how they were pressed for money, and how much had gone to help Philip in his fight in British Columbia. How many things had they gone without! Even mere common necessities had been given up. Naturally her mind turned to the auction, and the money her father had paid down for the farm. Four thousand dollars! Where had it come from, and why would her father never tell her, or speak about it in her presence? How often had she lain awake at night thinking about it all! Then to hear people more than hinting about Billy Fletcher's gold, and what had become of it, was at times more than she could bear. Never for a moment did she doubt her father, but often she longed to ask him for an explanation of the mystery. Was the money his own, or was he handling it for someone else? If so, why should he not tell her - his only daughter - who was so dear to him?

H. A. Cody

She was aroused by the arrival of several children from the houses nearest the Rectory. Every Sunday afternoon Nellie found her real enjoyment with her little class. She had known them all since their birth, and they loved her. How longingly they looked forward to that brief Sunday gathering. There were no harsh, strict rules here, no perfunctory opening and closing, and no lifeless lessons droned forth in a half-rebellious spirit. It was all joy and love. How their voices did ring as Nellie played on the little harmonium some sweet hymn attuned to childish hearts and minds. Then, after the lessons were over, there came the treat of the day - a story read from one of those marvellous books kept on a shelf in a corner all by themselves. When at last the story had been finished and the class dispersed, Nellie locked the doors, and made her way to Vivien Nelson's. What a hearty welcome she received from them all! To Mr. and Mrs. Nelson, hard-working, God-fearing people, she was as their own daughter. She and Vivien, their only child, had been playmates together at school, and their friendship had never languished. There Nellie felt at home. She knew that no matter what disagreeable things were being said about her father throughout the parish, no word of reproach or blame was ever mentioned in the Nelson home. Others might think what they liked about Parson John, but the Nelsons had known him too long in times of sorrow and joy to believe any evil of their old Rector.

Here Nellie stayed until the following afternoon, and then made her way home to have the house comfortable before her father came back. As the evening drew near she anxiously watched for his return. She saw the dull grey sky and knew that a storm threatened. As the darkness deepened and the wind raved about the house, and the snow beat against the north windows, her anxiety increased. The supper table stood ready in its snowy whiteness; the kettle sang on the stove and the fire in the sitting-room grate threw out its cheerful glow. It was a scene of peace and genial comfort contrasted with the raging of the elements outside. But Nellie thought nothing of this, for her heart was too much disturbed. Had anything happened to her father and Dan? It was some relief to know that the lad was along, for two were better than one should an accident occur. Her eyes roamed often to the little clock ticking away on the mantel-piece. Six-seven-eight-nine. The hours dragged slowly by. She tried to read, but the words were meaningless. She picked up her needlework, but soon laid it down again, with no heart to continue. Once more she glanced at the clock. Ten minutes after nine. She thought it longer than that since it had struck the hour. She arose to attend the kitchen fire, when a loud knock upon the front door startled her. She turned back, and stood for an instant in the centre of the room. Her heart beat fast, and her face paled. Tramps were frequently seen in Glendow, working their way from one place to another. At times they were impudent and tried to force an entrance into houses. It was a likely night for them to seek shelter, and suppose one were standing out there now! What could she, a lone woman, do? Another rap, harder than the first, fell upon her ears. Something must be done, and at once. Crossing the room and pausing near the door she demanded who was there.

"Sam Dobbins," came the reply, and Nellie breathed more freely as she unlocked the door, opened it and admitted the visitor.

"'Tis a blasted night," the man remarked as he tried to

H. A. Cody

shake himself free from his mantle of snow and stamped upon the floor with his great heavy boots. "If I'd known 'twas so bad I'd never stirred one step."

"Is anything wrong?" questioned Nellie, fearful lest Sam was the bearer of ill news. "Have you seen my father?"

"Your father! Isn't he home?" and the man looked his surprise.

"No, he hasn't come yet, and I'm so uneasy."

"Well, I declare, and to think that I have come all the way to see him, and he's not here. When do you expect him?"

"I expected him home before dark, but now I don't know what to think. Is there anything I can do for you, Mr. Dobbins? Won't you take a seat?"

"No, there's nothin' you kin do, miss. I've got to see the parson, and only him. I hate the job, but I've got to do it. I'm the only constable in the place, and I've got to do my duty."

At these words a startled look came into Nellie's face. She took a step forward and looked keenly into the man's eyes.

"What do you mean?" she demanded. "I know you're a constable, but what do you want of my father? Oh, please tell me, quick!"

"Now don't get excited, Miss," Mr. Dobbins kindly replied, looking with admiration upon the excited young figure before him. "Remember, I've nothin' against your father. Haven't I shod every horse he had since he came to this place, long before you were born. He's been a good customer of mine, and I ain't got nothin' agin him. I'm only doin' my duty as a constable."

"But I don't understand, Mr. Dobbins. You come here to arrest my father and - "

"Only to serve the summons, Miss," interrupted the blacksmith. "I ain't goin' to arrest him. He'll be asked to appear at the trial, that's all."

"Trial! what trial?"

"Oh, it's in connection with a cow."

"A cow!"

"Yes. It seems that Si Farrington's hired man, Pete Davis, was takin' away the Stickles' only cow, when your father appeared on the scene, cut the rope, set the cow free, and sent Joe off in a hurry. Farrington's in a rage, and says he'll make the parson smart fer what he did. He's goin' to take legal action, and so I've been sent to serve the summons. That's all I know about it, Miss. I'm real sorry, but what else could I do?"

Nellie made no reply when the man ceased. Words would not come. Her bosom heaved, and she placed her hand to her forehead in an abstracted manner. Her eyes were fixed full upon the constable's face, though she did not see him. Her thoughts were away from that room, out through the storm and darkness to an old grey-headed man battling somewhere with the tempest,

H. A. Cody

for the sake of others. What had happened? What would he think when he reached home to find out what Farrington was doing?

The constable shifted uneasily from one foot to the other in an embarrassed manner before those pathetic eyes. He clutched his cap more firmly in his hands, and shuffled towards the door.

"Guess I'll go now, Miss," he stammered. "I'll step up the road to make a call and come back again. Maybe your father will be home then."

Nellie hardly heard the door open and close as the constable passed out into the night. She stood for awhile as if dazed, then sinking into a nearby chair she buried her face in her hands. The wind howled and roared outside, and the snow dashed and swirled against the window. A big grey cat rose from its position before the fire, came and rubbed its sleek fur against her dress, and gently purred for some attention. But Nellie did not heed it. How dark all seemed to her! One thing after another! Why were these clouds gathering so thick over her dear father's head? It did not seem possible that he could be kept in ignorance much longer. It was sure to be revealed through this last trouble.

A sound fell upon her ears which made her look quickly up. Was it the wind? She listened with fast-beating heart. Again it came - a pathetic whinny out in the yard. She sprang to her feet, and rushed to the back door. She knew that call, for how often had she heard it! Midnight was there, standing almost at the threshold. Her dim form could be seen as Nellie peered out. She hurried forth, heedless of the pelting storm, expecting to hear her father's voice. But no cheery greeting met her, neither could she find the sleigh. Feeling around with her hands she felt the trailing shafts, and the awful truth flashed upon her. An accident had happened! And what of her father? Forgetting the horse she turned back into the house, seized a cloak, threw it over her shoulders, and hurried out into the storm. How the wind did roar about her as she waded and half stumbled through the drifts, which were now filling the road. Anxiety lent speed to her feet. She dashed on her way, and at length almost breathless reached the Larkins' house. Upon the door she beat with her hands, and after what seemed a long time Mr. Larkins made his appearance.

"Nellie! Nellie!" he exclaimed in affright, as she staggered into the room. "What in the world is the matter? Tell me, quick!"

"F-father's - had - an - a-a-ccident. Midnight came home without the sleigh - dragging the shafts - oh, what can we do?"

"Do?" was the reply. "We shall do what we can! I shall harness the horses at once, get several of the neighbors, and go in search of him. Don't worry too much, Nellie. To be pitched out of the sleigh in the soft snow is not so bad. No doubt we shall meet him and Dan plodding wearily along."

This the worthy man said to calm Nellie's fears, though in his own heart there was real anxiety, and he was not long in placing the horses fast to the big sled. But before he left he stopped to turn Midnight into the barn floor, threw on her blanket, and left her quietly munching a liberal supply of hay.

Mrs. Larkins was not long in making her appearance, and did what she could to bring comfort to Nellie's anxious heart. She also went with her back to the Rectory to await her husband's return. How the time did drag by! At every wild gust of wind Nellie started and trembled. At length, however, the faint sound of bells was heard, and scarcely had the panting, snow-flecked horses stopped at the door ere Nellie, bare-headed, and with a shawl over her shoulders, appeared.

"Father, father!" she cried, as she rushed forward, and peered into the familiar face. "Are you safe?"

"Yes, dearie. I am home again," came the feeble response.

"Oh, thank God!" she replied, throwing her arms around his neck, and kissing him again and again. "What a night this has been - a horrible nightmare!"

"Come, lassie," demanded the doctor. "Away with you into the house. What are you doing out here in such a storm? We'll look after your dad."

Chapter XVI

For Sweet Love's Sake

All the next day the storm continued in its unabated fury. The roads were completely blocked from fence to fence, and all sources of communication in Glendow were cut off. Each house was a little world of its own, a lighthouse in the midst of an ocean of snow where the long drifts piled and curled like hungry foaming breakers.

"This is the first holiday I've had for some time," chuckled good Doctor Leeds as he leaned back comfortably in an easy-chair, and puffed away at his pipe. "No one can come for me to-day, that's certain."

Nellie, too, was glad, and as she watched the storm from the window a feeling of relief came into her heart.

"Dear storm," she said to herself. "How I love you to-day. You are a stern protector, keeping out all prying eyes and malignant tongues. Mr. Dobbins will not venture out while you are abroad, and so we will have peace a little longer."

Parson John passed a restless night, moaning much from the pain in his shoulder. Towards morning,

H. A. Cody

however, he passed into a comfortable sleep, and did not wake until near noon. Nellie and the doctor had a long chat together. He told her about the accident, and she related to him the incident of the constable's visit to the Rectory.

"The brute!" roared the doctor, when Nellie had finished. "Farrington's a scoundrel! Why can't he leave decent people alone! He's always meddling with someone. He's never happy unless he's persecuting people. Oh, I've known him for years. And so he wants to have your father arrested, does he, for saving the Stickles' cow?"

"Yes," Nellie replied, "and I'm dreading the effect it will have upon my father."

"I see, I see," mused the doctor, while his eyes closed in a dreamy sort of a way. "It will not be for his good, that's certain. But there's a way, lassie, there's a way; don't forget that."

"What do you mean, Doctor?"

"I was just thinking what a villain Farrington is, and in what an underhanded way he works. But he leaves a loophole every time. Let me tell you something."

Then the doctor leaned over, and what he said brought back the colour into Nellie's face, and made her heart beat fast, and sent her about her household duties with a new spirit.

During the next night the storm cleared, and the morning sun transformed the vast, white fields into a shining, sparkling glory. Nellie was early astir, finished her household duties, cared for her father, who was steadily improving, ere the doctor made his appearance.

"I'm going to leave you in charge awhile this morning," she remarked as the latter was eating his breakfast. "The day is bright and those large drifts are so tempting, that I long for a snowshoe tramp. I have been in the house so long that I must have a breath of fresh air."

"Good!" replied the doctor. "It's just what you need. You had better make the most of it, too, while I am here, for as soon as the roads are broken I must be away. There are many patients to be looked after."

"Thank you, Doctor, very much. I know father will not mind my absence for a short time," Nellie responded, as she hurried away to make ready for her tramp.

A pretty figure she presented as she stood a little later before the door and bade the doctor good-bye. Snowshoeing she loved, and she had often travelled for miles with Stephen in the clear bracing air. But to-day she was not on pleasure bent, and her heart beat fast as she moved on her way. No sign of life did she see as steadily she plodded forward over the yielding snow. An hour later when she stood before Farrington's house and laid aside her snowshoes, her face was flushed with a healthy glow caused by the vigorous exercise. Her courage almost failed as she knocked upon the door, and waited for it to be opened. It was Mrs. Farrington who came, and great was her astonishment when she found who was there.

"Why, it's Nellie Westmore, I do declare!" she

H. A. Cody

exclaimed. "Come right in, dear, and lay your wraps aside. I'm so glad to see ye. But how in the world did ye git here?"

"I snowshoed all the way," was the quiet reply, "and I have come to see Mr. Farrington. Is he in?"

"Why certainly. He's in the store. I'll call 'im at once," and Mrs. Farrington bustled off, wondering what in the world brought Nellie on such a morning.

As Farrington entered the house a few minutes later, Nellie rose to meet him. She knew that now was the crucial moment, and a prayer went up from her heart for guidance. She was surprised at her own calmness as she looked into the face of the man who was causing her so much worry.

"I'm very glad to see ye, Nellie," and Farrington stretched out a big fat hand. "Set down, please."

"No, thank you, Mr. Farrington," Nellie replied. "I prefer to stand. I do not wish to keep you long. I've come to see you this morning on behalf of my father."

"Umph!" ejaculated Farrington, as he threw himself into an easy-chair.

"You know," continued Nellie, "my father met with a bad accident night before last, and is now confined to his bed, and I have come to ask you not to let Mr. Dobbins trouble him while he is in his weak condition. I feel quite sure you will do this."

"Ye want me to spare 'im, do ye?" Farrington blurted

out. "Spare the man who has injured me above measure!"

"Indeed! And in what way?" Nellie applied.

"In what way? do ye ask. Why, didn't he outbid me in the Frenelle homestead? Doesn't he refuse to buy goods at my store; an' then, to cap it all, interfered with my hired man when he went after that cow? Hev I any right to spare 'im? Tell me that."

"You have the right of consideration for an old man. My father is aging fast, and any trouble worries him so much. He doesn't know about what you intend to do, and I hope I can prevail upon you to go no further."

Nellie's voice was low and pathetic, and she made some impression upon Farrington, for when she had finished he did not at once reply. He sat looking at her, thinking how pretty she was.

"Nellie," he at length remarked, "we've allus been very fond of ye. We've known ye ever sense ye was a baby, an' ye seem like one of our own. Ye hev a good eddication, an' bein' a lady ye are well fitted to adorn a good man's home. Now, our Dick is a most promisin' feller, who thinks a sight of ye, so if ye'd consent to look upon him favourably, it ud please us all mighty well. Besides - "

"Mr. Farrington!" interrupted Nellie, "what do you mean? What do I understand you to say? Do you - "

"Wait a minute, my dear," remonstrated Farrington. "It's jist as well fer ye to consider this reasonable proposition fust as last. Yer dad's gittin' old now, so he can't last much longer; an' ye'll hev a home."

"An' jist think, Nellie dear," spoke up Mrs. Farrington, "what an advantage it'll be to ye. Richard'll inherit the hull of our property some day. He will be a gentleman, an' the son of a gentleman, too - of a good old fambly. It'll be a very gratifyin' thing, too, fer ye to know that Richard's father was a Councillor of Glendow. So now, dear, give up that uncouth Frenelle boy, an' take on with our son Richard."

Nellie's cheeks were flushed a deep crimson now, and her eyes were flashing with an angry light. Her heart was filled with disgust at these cool, self-satisfied schemers. Had they been less confident of their own importance they would have realized that they were treading on dangerous ground. They could not comprehend that back of Nellie's quiet, reserved demeanour there was a moral courage which would rise to any height of self-sacrifice at the call of duty, or in defence of those she loved. They had known her from childhood, and to natures such as theirs her gentleness and retiring disposition were interpreted as weakness or lack of proper spirit. To be suddenly awakened from such an idea was startling in the extreme.

"Mr. Farrington," Nellie replied, holding herself in check with a mighty effort, "I am very much astonished at the words I have just heard. I came here to talk to you as a lady would talk to a gentleman. But great is my surprise to be insulted to my face. You have no right to speak to me as you have done this morning, or to take such liberties as regards Stephen Frenelle. He is a real gentleman's son, and has the true instincts of a gentleman. We were children together, and I do not wish you to speak of him or any friend of mine in a slighting manner. As to your remarks in reference to your son, they are so unworthy of a father and mother that they arouse in me the feelings of deepest pity for you. I blush to think that you should ever suggest such a thing, and am surprised that your better nature does not assert itself, and cause you to cover your heads in shame for having uttered such words."

Nellie spoke rapidly with her eyes fixed full upon Farrington's face. The latter shifted uneasily at this torrent of words, and occasionally glanced at his wife, who was sitting near with open-mouthed wonder.

"Dear me, dear me!" Mrs. Farrington replied. "I allus thought ye was sich a nice, modest little thing, an' to think that ye should go on like this. What would yer dear mother think if she was livin'?"

"You are a mother, Mrs. Farrington," Nellie responded, "and what would you think if anyone made such a proposition to Eudora as you have made to me?"

"Oh, that's a different question."

"And in what way?"

"Oh, Eudora will hev money, an' will not be left penniless, while you an' yer father are jist dependin' upon the parish."

"Yes, I know it only too well," Nellie bitterly answered. "We are little more than paupers, trusting to the voluntary offerings of the people for our support. But then, this has little to do with what I came here for. We have wandered from the subject. I came simply to speak on behalf of my father."

"Oh, that matter's settled now once and fer all," Farrington replied in a cool, matter-of-fact manner. "Ye've taken the bizness into yer own hands. We've made ye a good offer, an' ye've refused pint blank, so we'll consider this little affair atween us settled. Sam Dobbins is in the store waitin' fer me, so I shall tell 'im to go ahead an' serve the summons."

"Stop a minute," Nellie demanded, as Farrington rose to his feet, stretched himself, and started leisurely towards the door.

"There's something you evidently have not considered which might change matters a little. I came here this morning trusting to get your consent to leave my father alone without any unnecessary trouble. I appealed to your manhood, but in vain. Now, there is only one course open to me, which I will be obliged to take."

"Hey, what's this?" and Farrington's brow knitted in perplexity. "I don't understand you."

"No, certainly you don't, but you will presently. I would like to ask who it was you sent out after the Stickles' cow?"

"Why, Pete, of course; my hired man. He allus does that work fer me, an' has taken dozens of 'em at various times."

"Yes, so I have heard," and Nellie's voice was charged with a warning note. "But were you not afraid of the risk you were running, Mr. Farrington?"

"Risk? what risk? I never had any trouble. What do you mean?"

"But is Pete a constable?"

"A constable, be blowed! What are ye drivin' at?"

"Did he have a warrant from a magistrate to go to the Stickles' place, open the door, enter the barn, and try to take away that cow?"

"N-no, certainly not. But he never had one afore, an' everything was all right."

"Yes, it was all right as far as you were concerned, because no one interfered, and the people were always too poor to make a fuss. But do you know that you have laid yourself open to a grave offence? In the eyes of the law you tried to steal that cow from the Stickles."

"Girl! Girl! What do ye mean by talkin' this way?" and Farrington bounded from his chair in a rage. "Explain to me at once what ye mean by sich words!"

"There's nothing much to explain, Mr. Farrington. Without a warrant, or any legal authority, you sent your servant to break into a private barn, and lead away a cow belonging to Mr. Stickles. Because my father interfered you wish to have him arrested. I hope you see the point."

Farrington was certainly a study just then. His eyes glowered, and his face was inflamed with rage. He was in a trap and he knew it.

H. A. Cody

"Ye'll pay fer this!" he cried, stamping upon the floor, in anger. "Ye'll - Ye'll - !"

"Very well," Nellie calmly replied. "I've simply told you your position, so now if you wish to go ahead, do so. You will know what to expect. Perhaps I have been a better friend to you than you now imagine. Remember, we have friends, who know a thing or two, and besides, if you are not careful, something may go wrong on election day."

"Who told you this, girl?" Farrington demanded. "Who put ye up to this bizness?"

"That's my own affair. I have warned you, so go ahead if you care to. I shall say no more."

With that she turned and walked quietly out of the house, put on her snowshoes, and started on her homeward way. But the trying ordeal through which she had passed told upon her. She trembled violently, and a great weakness came over her. She felt that she would sink down upon the snow. How could she continue? She looked all around, but no sign of life could she behold; no one to aid her. What was she to do? She thought of her father. Was he waiting for her, perhaps wondering where she was? With a great effort she moved slowly forward, and presently found her strength returning. On and on she plodded. Never had the snowshoes seemed so heavy, or the way so long, and right glad was she to see at last the Rectory rise up large and homelike before her. She reached the door, doffed the snowshoes, entered the house, hurried to her own room, and throwing herself upon her bed, wept as if her heart would break. She was tired - oh, so tired. The tears brought a blessed relief to her surcharged feelings, and when she at length sought her father's side a sunny smile illumined her face, her step was firm, and little remained to show to a casual observer the fierce struggle through which she had recently passed.

H. A. Cody

Chapter XVII

Hitting Back

Farrington said very little after Nellie's departure. He even surprised his wife by his coolness, for instead of raging, swearing and stamping around the house he walked quietly out into the store. Here he busied himself with various matters, and talking at times to the few customers who straggled in. When no one was present he sat on a high stool by the window and gazed out over the snow. He was not thinking of money now, nor how much his eggs and butter would bring. His mind was dwelling upon that scene which had just taken place. He thought nothing of the brave defence Nellie had made on behalf of her father, but only of his own wounded feelings. At times his hands would clinch, and a half-audible curse escape his lips. He would get even, oh, yes! But how? He saw the danger of going any further in connection with the Stickles' cow affair. He must let that drop. There were other ways, he was sure of that; the difficulty was to know just what to do.

The door opened, and a tall, lanky man entered, with a pair of skates dangling over his left shoulder.

"Hello, Miles!" exclaimed Farrington, hurrying around to shake hands with him. "Haven't seen you fer an age.

What's the news at Craig's Corner? Set down, you look about tuckered out."

"Should say I was," Miles drawled forth. "Never got into such a mess in all my life. Skated down river Sunday evening and was caught in that blasted snow-storm, and so am footing it back."

"Dear me, that's hard luck," and Farrington sat down upon a soap-box. "Anyway, I'm mighty glad to see ye. Hope things are goin' well at the Corner. Much election talk, eh?"

"Considerable. The air's been full of it lately, but I guess Sunday's doings will give the folks a new subject for awhile. 'Twas certainly a stunner!"

"Why, what do ye mean, Miles? Nobody killed, I hope."

"What! Haven't you heard anything?"

"No, how could I with the storm blockin' the roads."

"Sure. I never thought of that. But I supposed the parson let it out."

"The parson!" and Farrington's eyes opened wide with amazement. "What in the devil has he to do with it? He was brought home night afore last with his shoulder out of jint"

"Whew! You don't say so! Well, I declare!"

"Tell me what ye mean, man," exclaimed Farrington, moving impatiently on his seat. "Let's have the yarn."

"Ha-ha! It was a corker! Just think of it; a funeral procession moving slowly across the river, with Tim Fraser and Parson John racing by like a whirlwind. I never saw anything like it, ha-ha!" and Miles leaning back laughed loud and long at the recollection.

Farrington was all attention now. A gleam of delight shone in his eyes, and a faint sigh of relief escaped his lips. He controlled his eagerness, however, for he wished to draw Miles out, and learn the whole story.

"Ye don't mean to tell me," he remarked, "that the parson was racin' on Sunday? Surely ye must be mistaken!"

"I'm a liar then," calmly replied the other, gazing thoughtfully down at his boots. "Yes, I'm a liar, and a fool! Why, didn't I see the whole thing with my own eyes? And didn't all the people of Craig's Corner see it, too? Ask them, they'll tell you the same."

"I don't doubt yer word, Miles, but it's so unusual. The parson never did anything like that before, did he?"

"Not to my knowledge. But he's mighty fond of a horse, and a fast one at that, so I guess when Tim Fraser clipped up he couldn't resist the temptation."

"Did he explain about it? Did he tell how it happened?"

"He didn't say much. I heard him tell some people that he never let the devil get ahead of him, and he was bound he wouldn't do it that time."

"Ho-ho! That's what he said? Nothing more?"

"No, not that I heard. I came away after that, so nothing new has reached me since, except what you tell me. Is he badly injured?"

"I don't know. Guess he'll come out all right; he generally does."

"He looked very well on Sunday. I'm really sorry he's met with this accident."

"Mebbe it had something to do with the race," suggested Farrington.

"In what way?"

"Perhaps it's a punishment fer what he did on Sunday."

"Surely, you don't say - !" and Miles' mouth opened in surprise.

"Oh, I don't say anything fer certain. I only know that sich things sometimes do happen. A man who will race on the Sacred Day of Rest must expect almost anything to happen. I've known of several sich cases. Something generally does happen."

"You don't say so! Well!"

"Now honestly," continued Farrington very delibe-rately, "do ye think sich a man is fit to be the minister of the Gospel in Glendow? Do ye think a man who stands in church on Sunday an' reads them solemn words about keepin' the Sabbath Day holy, an' then goes out on the ice an' engages in a horse-race - do ye think sich a man is fit to teach our people? What an example to set our children! When we tell 'em to remember the Day an' keep it holy, they will say, 'Oh, the parson raced his horse on Sunday!' Oh, yes, that's what they'll say. So you see what a condition the parish will be in."

"Well, I never thought of it that way," replied Miles, rising to his feet. "But I must be off. I see the road is being broken."

When the man had left the store Farrington stood for some time with his hands clasped behind his back. He was in deep thought, and occasionally his lips curled with a pleased smile. He then walked to the window, and watched the men breaking the roads. He saw his own hired man, Pete Davis, among the rest. Most of the able-bodied men of the neighbourhood were there with shovels and teams. It was an inspiring sight to see team after team in a long procession plowing their way forward among the high drifts. Where the snow was light the leading horses would plunge through, blowing, snorting, struggling, and at times almost hidden from view. In places shovels had to be used and then cuttings, narrow and deep, were made through the banks, just wide enough for one team to move at a time. For hours the work had been carried on, and at length the last drift had been conquered, and communication, from place to place once again opened up.

Farrington watching the horses surging through was not thinking of the fine appearance they presented. His mind was upon a far different matter. He stood there, saw the teams swing around and finally disappear up the road. It pleased him to see Miles riding upon one of the sleds. His ready tongue was as good as a newspaper, and he would spread the story of the Sunday race wherever he went.

Mrs. Farrington was surprised at her husband's jocular manner when he was called to dinner. He joked and laughed more than he had done in many a day. Not a word did he say about Nellie's visit; in fact he seemed to have forgotten all about it.

"Ye must have done a good bizness this mornin', Si," his wife remarked. "I haven't seen ye in sich fine spirits in a long time."

"Haven't sold as much as usual, my dear," was the reply. "Didn't expect to anyway, as the roads have jist been broken."

"But ye seem very happy. Has anything remarkable occurred?"

"Simply an idea, my dear, simply an idea."

"Well, well, who'd a thought it. I didn't know that an idea 'ud make one feel so good. Tell me about it, Si."

"No, not now. I haven't time. Besides, I want to see how it'll work, an' then I'll surprise ye."

Farrington rose from the table, and going to the store went at once to the small office. Here he spent some time writing, and at the end of a half hour gave a chuckle of satisfaction, laid aside the pen, folded up the paper and put it into his pocket. Next he went into the stable, and ordered Pete to harness the horse and have it at the door in fifteen minutes. At the end of that time he came from the house, wrapped in his large fur coat, cap and mittens. Soon he was speeding over the road, leaving Mrs. Farrington, Eudora and Dick watching him from the window, and wondering what it all meant,

Farrington was forth upon important business, and he knew exactly at what houses to stop. There were the Fletchers, he was sure of them; the Marshalls, their kinsmen; the Burtons, and several families who owed fair-sized bills at the store, and would be unable to pay for some time.

The sun was dipping big and red far westward when Farrington turned his horse's head homeward. He was well pleased with his afternoon's work. No one had refused to sign the petition he carried, and over twenty names had been scrawled upon the paper.

As he moved along his eyes rested upon a little cottage away to the right, nestling near a grove of large maple trees. Old Henry Burchill, the wood-chopper, lived there. Farrington's brows knitted as he thought of him. Would he sign the paper? He knew that Henry was once opposed to the parson for introducing certain things into the church. But then that was long ago, and he wondered how the old man felt now. Anyway there was that unpaid bill at the store. It would have some weight, and it was no harm to try.

Mrs. Burchill was at home, and was surprised to see the storekeeper enter the house. She was a quiet, reserved woman, who mingled little with her neighbours. The lines of care upon her face, the bent back and the toil-worn hands told their own tale of a long, hard battle for life's bare necessities. Her heart beat fast as she shook hands with her visitor, for she, too, thought of that bill at the store, which she and her husband had been bravely striving to pay.

"Is yer husband at home, Mrs. Burchill?" asked Farrington, seating himself on a splint-bottomed chair.

"No, sir. He's in the woods chopping for Stephen. I'm afraid he won't be home to-night."

"Dear me! that's too bad," and Farrington brought forth the paper from his pocket. "I wanted 'im to do a little favour fer me - simply to put his name to this pertition. But, if you'll do it, 'twill be jist the same," and he handed over the paper.

Mrs. Burchill put on her glasses, and slowly and carefully read the words written there. Farrington watched her closely and noted the colour mounting to her faded cheeks, and the look of reproach in her eyes as she at length turned them upon his face.

"And you expect me to put my name to this?" she demanded.

"An' why not?" smiled Farrington. "Have you read what the paper sez?"

"Yes, every word."

"An' don't ye think there's a reason why ye should sign it? Don't ye think the Bishop should know what kind of a parson we have?"

"Mr. Farrington," and Mrs. Burchill spoke very deliberately, "if the Angel Gabriel himself came with that paper for me to sign I should refuse. I'm an old woman now, and why should I commit such a sin in my declining years?"

"Sin! what sin would ye commit in simply signin' that paper?" Farrington demanded.

Mrs. Burchill did not reply at once, but placing her hand upon a Bible lying by her side she reverently opened it.

"Listen to these words," she said. "They are not mine, remember, but the Lord's. 'Touch not mine anointed,' He says, 'and do my prophets no harm.' Now Parson John is one of the Lord's anointed, set apart for a sacred work, and it's a dangerous thing to strive against Him."

"Tut, tut, woman! That's all rubbish! Them things happened in olden days. Besides, we have a just grievance. He is interferin' too much with the affairs of others. He takes too much upon himself. Then, what about that race on Sunday? Do ye think we should stand that?"

"Ah, sir, it's the same old story. Don't you remember how people said the very same thing about Moses and Aaron, long, long ago. They said that those two men were taking too much upon them, and a rebellion ensued. And what was the result? The Lord punished the people, the earth opened and swallowed them up. I often read that story to Henry in the evenings, and it makes us feel very serious. Oh, yes, it's a dangerous thing to interfere with the Lord's anointed. Something's bound to happen to the ones who do it."

Farrington could stand this no longer. He had met with such success during the afternoon that to hear this rebuke from Mrs. Burchill was most annoying.

"Woman!" he exclaimed, rising to his feet. "I don't want to hear all this. I didn't come here to be preached to about sich old-fashioned trash as the 'Lord's anointed!' I came here to git ye to sign that paper, an' not to be preached to! Will ye sign it or will ye not?"

"No, I shall not sign it!" was the quiet response.

"Very well, then, that's all I want to know. But remember, Mrs. Burchill, there's a little unpaid account on my books against your husband. Please tell 'im to call and settle it at once. If not - oh, well you know the result," and Farrington looked significantly around the room. "So, good-day. I must be off."

Mrs. Burchill stood at the window and watched Farrington drive away. Then a sigh escaped her lips. She went back to the chair where she had been sitting, and kneeling down buried her face in her hands. For some time she remained in prayer, but her earnest pleadings were not for herself or her husband, but for the old grey-headed man - the Venerable Rector of Glendow.

H. A. Cody

Chapter XVIII

Wash-Tub Philosophy

"I've been up to me neck in soap-suds ever sense daybreak, an' I ain't done yit."

So declared Mrs. Stickles as she wiped her hands upon her apron and offered a chair to her visitor, Betsy McKrigger.

"I'm rale glad to see ye, nevertheless," she continued, "fer it's been a month of Sundays sense I sot eyes on ye last. How've ye been? An' yer old man, is he well?"

"Only fairly," replied Mrs. McKrigger, laying aside her bonnet and shawl, and taking the proffered chair. "Abraham went to the mill this mornin' an' I came this fer with 'im. We were clean out of flour, an', although the roads are bad, there was no help fer it, so he had to go, poorly as he is. He'll stop fer me on his way back."

"An' what's wrong with 'im?" asked Mrs. Stickles, going back to her washing.

"The doctor thinks he's got delapitation of the heart. Abraham was never very strong there, and suffers most after eatin'. I'm gittin' very nervous about 'im."

"Oh, is that all?" and Mrs. Stickles paused in her work. "I wouldn't worry about that. Mebbe he eats too much. Men's hearts an' stummicks are purty closely kernected, an' what affects the one affects t'other. It's indigestion the man's got-that's what 'tis. It's a wonder to me they don't all hev it."

"Mebbe yer right, Mrs. Stickles. 'Abraham is certainly a big eater. But it wasn't eatin' which gave 'im the delapitation yesterday."

"What was it, then?"

"It was Si Farrington who gave it to 'im. That's who it was."

"Ugh!" ejaculated Mrs. Stickles. "Surely a cur like that wouldn't affect anyone, would it? I'm jist waitin' to run agin Farrington meself, an' then we'll see who'll hev palputation of the heart. It'll not be me, I reckon."

"It's very true what ye say," replied Mrs. McKrigger, bringing forth her knitting, "but when ye owe the man a bill at the store, an' heven't the money to pay, it makes a big difference."

"So he's been at you, has he? I s'pose he's been tryin' to git yer cow, horse or farm. He tried it here, but Parson John, bless his soul, soon stopped that."

"No, not like that. He only hinted what he'd do if Abraham didn't sign the pertition."

"Oh, I see. He's goin' to run fer councillor, an' wanted yer husband to sign his denomination paper, did he?"

"No, no, not that. It's about the parson."

"What! Parson John?"

"Yes, it's about 'im, poor man."

"Land sakes! What's up now?" and Mrs. Stickles paused in her work and stood with arms akimbo.

"Farrington thinks the parson's too old fer the work, an' that we should hev a young man with snap an' vim, like Mr. Sparks, of Leedsville. He believes the young people need to be stirred up; that they're gittin' tired of the old humdrum way, an' that the parish is goin' to the dogs. But that wasn't all. He thinks the parson isn't a fit man to be here after that disgraceful racin' scene on the river last Sunday. He sez it's an awful example to the young. So he's gittin' up the pertition to send to the Bishop."

Mrs. Stickles had left the wash-tub now and was standing before her visitor. Anger was expressed in her every movement.

"An' do ye tell me!" she demanded, "that yer husband signed that paper?"

"W-what else was there to do?" and Mrs. McKrigger dropped her knitting and shrank back from the irate form before her. "How could he help it?"

"Betsy McKrigger, I never thought ye'd come to this. Help it! Why didn't yer husband help Farrington out of the door with the toe of his boot?"

"But think of that unpaid bill, Mrs. Stickles."

"Unpaid bill, be fiddlesticks! Would ye turn aginst yer best earthly friend fer the sake of a bill?"

"What else could we do?"

"Do? Let yer cow or anything else go! What do sich things amount to when yer honour's at stake. Dear me, dear me! has it come to this?"

"Ye needn't make sich a fuss about the matter," and Mrs. McKrigger bristled up a bit. "It's a purty serious thing when yer whole livin's in the fryin'-pan."

"Livin', livin'! Where does yer livin' come from anyway, Mrs. McKrigger? Doesn't the Lord send it? I reckon He'll look after us. Didn't He tend to old 'Lijah when he done his duty. Didn't the ravens feed 'im? An' what about that widee of Jerrypath? Didn't her meal and ile last when she done what was right? Tell me that!"

"Oh, yes, that may be as ye say. I ain't botherin' about old 'Lijah an' that widow. If them people lived to-day they'd jine forces an' start the biggest flour an' ile company the world has ever seen. I wish 'Lijah 'ud come our way some day, fer me an' Abraham hev often scraped the bottom of the flour barrel an' poured out the last drop of ile, not knowin' where any more was comin' from."

"Tut, tut, woman!" remonstrated Mrs. Stickles. "It's wrong fer ye to talk that way. Hev ye ever really wanted? Didn't the flour and the ile come somehow? Whenever we're scrapin' the bottom of the barrel it seems that the Lord allus hears us, and doesn't let us want. I guess, if we stan' by the Lord, He'll stan' by us.

I'm mighty sorry yer man signed that pertition aginst that man of God. It don't seem right nohow."

"I'm not worryin' about that, Mrs. Stickles. Farrington has considerable right on his side. The parson is old. We do need a young man with snap an' vim. The parson's sermints are too dry an' deep. Abraham sleeps right through 'em, an' says it's impossible to keep awake."

"Well, I declare!" and Mrs. Stickles held up her hands in amazement. "To think that I should live to hear sich words in me own house. Ye say the parson's too old. Ain't ye ashamed of them words? Too old! D'ye want some new dapper little snob spoutin' from the pulpit who hasn't as much knowledge in his hull body as Parson John has in his little finger? I know there's many a thing the parson talks about that I can't understan', an' so there is in the Bible. I often talk the matter over with John. 'John,' sez I, 'Ye recollect when ye was makin' that wardrobe fer me out in the shed two springs ago?'

"'Well,' sez he.

"'An' ye remember how the children used to watch ye an' wonder what ye was makin'!'

"'Sartinly,' sez he.

"'An' how they used to pick up the shavin's ye planed off, an' brung them inter the house.'

"He kalkerlated he did.

"'Well then,' sez I, 'John, them children didn't

understan' what ye was makin', but they could pick up the shavin's an' make use of 'em. So when Parson John is preachin' an' I can't altogether foller him, I kin pick up somethin' here an' thar which I do understand, an' them are the shavin's which I kin use, an' do use. Oh! John,' sez I, 'hasn't the parson been droppin' shavin's fer over thirty years, an' not allus in the pulpit either, an' haven't we ben helped 'cause we picked 'em up an' made 'em our own?' John said I was right, an' he knows, dear soul."

"That may be all very well fer you an' John," replied Mrs. McKrigger, "but what about the young people, an' the older ones fer all that, who won't pick up the shavin's? Farrington sez we want a poplar young man who kin speak without any preparation, like Mr. Dale, the missionary who was here last summer. Now, there was a man up to whom the young men could look, a reglar soldier, who had been in the fight in Africy, had lived among lions, tagers and niggers. He was a hero, an' if we could git a rale live missionary like that, he'd make Glendow hum, an' the old church 'ud be packed to the doors every Sunday. It's them missionaries who has the hard time. Oh, they're wonderful people. Parson John's a good man, but he ain't in the same line with them nohow. He's too commonplace, an' don't stir the people up."

For a while Mrs. Stickles did not reply. She wiped her hands on her apron, and crossing the room took down a small pot, put in a little tea, filled it with water, and set it on the back of the stove to draw. Next she brought forth some large frosted doughnuts, and after she had poured a cup of tea for Mrs. McKrigger and one for herself she sat down upon an old splint-bottomed chair.

"Did I ever tell ye the conversation I had with Mr. Dale, that missionary from Africy?" she at length asked.

"No, I never heerd it," came the reply.

"Well, that's queer, an' it happened only last summer, too. Ye see, we all went to the missionary meetin' in the church, an' Mr. Dale told us about that furren land. Somehow I didn't take to the man, an' I liked 'im less as he went on. All the time he was speakin' I noted how eagerly Parson John listened. Often his buzum heaved-like, an' I thought I heerd 'im sigh. But when the speaker 'gun to compare Africy with Canada and Glendow, I got mad. 'Here the work is small,' sez he; 'thar it's mighty! Here ye hev yer hundreds; thar we hev our thousands. Here things is easy; thar hard.' As he talked on that way I looked at the parson an' saw a pained expression on his dear face. I jist longed to jump to me feet, an' pint out that old grey-headed man a sittin' thar, an' tell a few things I know. But I got me chance later."

"What! ye didn't say anything hard, I hope?" interrupted Mrs. McKrigger.

"Only the plain truth; jist what he needed. Ye see, me an' John was axed into the Rectory afterwards to meet the missionary an' hev a cup of tea. Mr. Dale did most of the talkin', an' told us a hull lot more about his experiences in Africy. But somehow he rubbed me the wrong way. He had little use fer Canada, an' said so, an' that was mor'n I could stan'.

"'Mr. Dale,' sez I, speakin' up, when his jaw stopped waggin' fer an instant. 'Would ye be willin' to leave yer present field of labour?'

"'No,' sez he, lookin' at me surprised-like.'

"'An' why not,' sez I.

"'Oh the work is so inspirin' out thar,' sez he. 'I'd about die in a - a - ' (I think he was goin' to say a country parish like this) but he said 'settled field whar the work is so quiet, ye know.'

"'An' ye wouldn't be willin' to give up Africy,' sez I, 'fer a poor parish like Glendow, if thar was no clergyman here?'

"'No,' sez he, in a hesitatin' way, fer he didn't seem to know what I was a drivin' at.

"'Exactly so, Mr. Dale,' sez I. 'It takes a heap of spunk, I reckon, to go to them furren fields, but I kalkerlate it often takes jist as much to stay to hum, feed pigs, hens, an' look after a hull batch of children. I've hearn men preach about sacryfice in big churches, but I generally find that, when a poor country parish gits vacant, they don't seem inclined to give up their rich churches an' step into a humbler place. Yet sometimes I've heerd of sich men goin' to furren fields. An' why is that, Mr. Dale?'

"'That they might do more work fer the Master,' sez he.

"'I think yer wrong thar,' sez I. 'Now, look here. To enter a country parish is to be almost unknown, an' people say, 'Oh, he's only a country parson,' an' they stick up their ugly noses, which they think are acristocat. But let a man go to a furren field, an', my

H. A. Cody

lands! they blubber over 'im an' make a great fuss. If he combs the head of a little nigger brat out thar in Africy - though no doubt he needs it - why the missionary magazines an' papers are full of it. If he pulls the tooth of an old Injun chief who has a dozen wives taggin' around after 'im, the people hold up thar hands in wonder, an' call 'im a hero. But let a man stay at hum in a parish like Glendow, an' no one hears of his doin's, cause they don't want to.'"

"My! ye didn't say all that?" exclaimed Mrs. McKrigger, "an' to a rale live missionary, too."

"Them's the exact words I said, an' them ain't all," rattled on Mrs. Stickles. "I had me tongue on 'im then, an' it did me good to see his face. He looked once towards the door as if he thought I'd jump at 'im. Oh, it was as good as a circus to see 'im shake," and she laughed at the recollection of it.

"'Remember,' sez I, 'I ain't got nuthin' agin furren missions, fer they do a heap of good. But I would like to see things levelled up a bit. If I git down on me knees an' scrub the floor, it's nuthin' thought of. But if a missionary does it, a great fuss is made. When Parson John is dug out of snow-banks every week, when his sleigh gits upsot an' throws 'im into the ditch, no one outside the parish ever hears of it. But let sich things happen to a furren missionary, an', my lands! it's wonderful.'

"I could see all the time that Mr. Dale was gittin' excited an' excititer.

"'Woman,' sez he in a lofty kind of way, which reminded me of a young rooster tryin' to crow, 'do ye realize what yer talkin' about? Do ye know yer treadin' on delicate ground?'

"'Yes,' sez I, 'when I tread on a man's toes, it's purty delicate ground.'

"'I don't mean that,' sez he. 'But do ye know that *I'm* a missionary, an' do ye know what it means to be away from hum seven years, away in a furren land?'

"'Yes,' sez I. 'It means a holiday of a hull year at the end, with yer salary goin' on, an' yer travellin' expenses paid. D'ye think, Mr. Dale, that the parson here ever gits sich a holiday? Y'bet yer life he doesn't. He's been here workin' like a slave fer over thirty years now, an' in all that time *he* never had a holiday.'

"At that the parson himself speaks up. 'I think yer wrong thar, Mrs. Stickles,' sez he. 'I had two hull weeks once, fer which I've allus been most thankful.'

"'An what are two weeks?' sez I. 'An' didn't ye pay yer own travellin' expenses?'

"'Yes,' sez he, 'I did.'

"'Thar now,' sez I to Mr. Dale. 'What d'ye think of that? Two weeks in over thirty years of hard work!' But that reminds me of somethin' else - an', sez I, 'Who pays yer salary, Mr. Dale? D'ye mind tellin' me that?'

"'The Mission Board' sez he.

"'An' do ye git it reglar?' sez I.

"'Every month,' sez he.

"'I thought so,' sez I. 'An' d'ye think the parson here gits his every month?'

"'I don't know,' sez he. 'But s'pose he does.'

"'Not by a long chalk,' sez I. 'He has to wait months an' months fer it, an' sometimes he doesn't git it at all, an' then has to take hay an' oats, or do without. I know that to be a fact. Old skinflint Reeker over thar owed two dollars one year to the church, an' he wondered how in the world he was to git out of payin' it. Durin' the summer a Sunday-school picnic was held on his place back in his grove, an' fer one of the games the parson cut down four little beeches about as big as canes. Thar was thousands of 'em growin' around, an' wasn't worth a postage-stamp. But old Reeker saw 'im cut 'em, an' the next day he went to the parson an' told 'im how vallable the beeches was - his fancy trees or somethin' like that - an' charged 'im fifty cents a piece, the amount he owed to the church. "Wasn't that so, Parson?" sez I, turnin' to 'im.'

"'Yes, yes,' sez he. 'But it ain't worth speakin' about now. I think we had better have our cup of tea, an' talk no more about the subject.'"

"Dear, good man," and Mrs. Stickles wiped her eyes with the corner of her apron. "He was kinder upsot at what I said. But not so, Nellie. Her sweet face jist beamed on me, an' when I went out into the kitchen to help her she put her arms about me old neck, an' gave me a good big thumpin' kiss. That's what she did."

Scarcely had Mrs. Stickles ended, ere bells were heard outside.

"Why, I declare, if Abraham ain't back already!" exclaimed Mrs. McKrigger, rising to her feet and donning her hat and wraps. "He's made a quick trip. I'm very grateful, indeed I am, fer the cup of tea an' the pleasant time I've had. Ye must come to see me as soon as ye kin."

Mrs. Stickles stood for some time at the window watching the McKriggers driving away. She was thinking deeply, and a plan was being evolved in her mind which made her forget her washing and the various household duties. At length she turned and entered the room where her husband and little Ruth were lying.

"John," she said, after she had related to him what Mrs. McKrigger had told her about Farrington and the petition, "d'ye think you an' Ruthie will mind if me an' Sammy go into the shore this afternoon with old Queen?"

"Why no, dear," was the reply. "But don't ye think the roads are too bad, an' besides, what are ye thinkin' of?"

"I don't mind the roads, John. They're purty well smashed down by now, an' Queen's very stidy. I've a plan, John, which comes right from me insides," and leaning over she whispered it into his ear.

"Land sakes, dear!" replied her husband. "D'ye think ye kin manage it? Will they listen to ye? Ye're only a woman, remember, an' what kin a woman do?"

"Yes, I'm only a woman, John, an' mebbe 'tain't a woman's place. But when men are too scart an' heven't as much spunk as a chicken jist outer the shell, what

H. A. Cody

else is thar to do? Is thar no one in the hull parish to stan' up fer the Lord's anointed? Tell me that. Didn't that beautiful Queen Ester stan' before her crank of a husband, Hazen Hearus, an' plead fer the lives of her people? An' didn't Jael do the Lord's will when she put old Sirseree outer the way, tell me that? Now, I ain't a queen like Ester, an' I hope I ain't a woman like Jael that 'ud drive a nail through a man's head. I'm jist plain old Marthy Stickles, but mebbe I kin do somethin' fer the Lord, even if I ain't purty or clever."

An hour later an old, lean horse fastened to a home-made pung was wending its way slowly along the road leading to the river. Holding the reins was Sammy, a queer little figure, wrapped from head to foot, bravely maintaining his precarious position on six inches of the end of the board seat. Towering above him, broad-shouldered and ponderous, sat Mrs. Stickles, the very embodiment of health and strength.

"Sammy," said she, as the sled lurched along the rough road, "I don't like this bizness. But when the Lord's work's to be did, somebody's got to set his face like flint, as the Bible sez, an' do it. Don't ye ever fergit that, Sammy. Don't ye ever disremember that yer ma told ye."

Chapter XIX

The Sting

The buzz of gossip once more filled the air of Glendow. This last affray between Parson John and Farrington and the part Nellie had taken gave greater scope to the numerous busy tongues. Up and down the shore road and throughout the back settlements the news travelled. It was discussed at the store, the blacksmith shop, the mill, and in the homes at night, wherever a few were gathered together. The Fletchers had never been idle since the night of old Billy's death. They stirred up others by various stories and conjectures, fashioned in their own suspicious minds. "Why," they asked, "did not the parson explain about that money he paid down for the Frenelle homestead? How was it that a poor country parson was able to buy such a farm? They were further incensed by an incident which happened several weeks after the auction. Tom Fletcher was determined that he would question the parson some day, in the presence of others. He prided himself upon his keenness of observation and shrewdness in detecting a guilty manner in those whom he suspected of wrong-doing. The first opportunity he seized when he met the parson at the blacksmith shop, waiting for his horse to be shod.

H. A. Cody

"Well, Parson, are ye goin' to sell the farm?" he asked in a sort of careless manner.

"What farm?" was the reply.

"Oh, the Frenelle place."

"No; it's not for sale."

"Well, is that so? Money's tight these times, an' I thought mebbe ye'd he glad to get rid of it."

"No. I'm not anxious to do so."

"But, isn't it a heap of money to be tied up in one place? Mebbe ye'd give us a hint how ye manage to do it. It's as much as us poor farmers kin do to live, let alone put four thousand in a place which we don't intend to use!"

Tom tipped a wink to several others in the shop, as much as to say, "Now, I've cornered him. Watch for the fun." Parson John saw the wink, and drew himself suddenly up. He realized that the man was drawing him out for some purpose, and it was as well to check him first as last.

"Tom, do you mind," he asked, "if I put one question to you?"

"Why, certainly not. Drive ahead."

"It's concerning that Widow Tompkins' place. Perhaps you will tell us how you got control of it? Such a thing doesn't happen every day."

Across Tom's face spread an angry flush, while a half-suppressed laugh was heard from the bystanders. All knew very well that Tom had cheated the widow out of her property, though no one ever had the courage to mention it to him before.

"What do you mean by that question?" demanded Fletcher.

"It's a simple one, though, is it not?" the parson quietly responded. "It naturally makes us curious."

"Then I'll not satisfy such d - curiosity. I tend my own affairs, an' I ax others to do the same."

"That's just the point, Tom," and the parson looked him square in the eyes. "You wish to be let alone with your business, and so do I. You don't wish to satisfy idle curiosity with your affairs, and neither do I. So we are quits."

This incident only caused the Fletchers to hate the parson more than ever. Their greatest ally was Farrington. He was a man of considerable means, and to have his support meant much. Never before was he known to be so liberal to the people who came to his store. Often he invited them into his house to sup with him, and then the grievances and election matters were thrashed out. Occasionally when a farmer came to make purchases, Farrington would see that a present was bestowed in the form of a piece of calico for the wife, or some candy for the children. This was done especially when Farrington was not sure of his man. He was playing his part, not only stirring up these men against the man of God, but also ingratiating himself into their good wishes against the day of the election.

When Farrington entered the field as a candidate for the County Council, he knew he would have a hard struggle against his opponent, Philip Gadsby, who was a man much respected, and had occupied the position of councillor with considerable credit for two terms. The storekeeper had been hard at work for some time with no visible success, for the Farrington family with their high-flown ideas were much disliked by the quiet, humble-minded folk of Glendow. The idea, therefore, of him being Ifteir representative was at first abhorrent to most of the people. But this new ruse of Farrington's was proving most successful. The Fletchers drew with them all the loud-talking and undesirable element of Glendow. This Farrington well knew, and by espousing their cause he was greatly strengthening his own. The election day was only a few weeks off, so Farrington and his party had no time to lose.

During all this buzz of gossip, Parson John, the man most vitally concerned, was perfectly oblivious of the disturbance. Of a most unsuspecting nature, and with rot a particle of guile in his honest heart, he could not imagine anyone harming him by word or deed. Happy in his work, happy in the midst of his flock, and with Ms pleasant little home guarded by his bright house-keeper, he had no thought of trouble. To his eyes the sky was clear. His humble daily tasks brought him comfort through the day, and sweet, undisturbed rest by night.

But with Nellie it was different. She heard what her father did not. Fragments of gossip drifted to her ears, which paled her cheek and set her heart beating fast. Occasionally Dan bore her news he had picked up at the store, or from the boys of the neighbourhood, who were not slow in talking of the things they had heard from their elders. Nellie longed to tell her father, that he might he able to answer some of the charges which were made. Several times had she determined to do so. But when she had looked upon his calm face, noted his white hair, and gazed into his clear, unsuspecting eyes, her resolution always took wings and disappeared. Then she would surprise her father by twining her arms about his neck and giving him a loving kiss.

Two weeks had now passed since the accident, and Parson John was rapidly improving. Two Sundays had he missed from church, something which had happened but once before in his long ministry in the parish. Winter was passing, and signs of spring were beginning to be seen and felt. The snow was steadily disappearing from the hills, and the fresh, balmy air drifted gently in from the south with its exhilarating influence.

It was Saturday night, and Parson John was looking forward to the morrow, when he could take his accustomed place at the parish church. He and Nellie were sitting quietly in the little room, when Mr. Larkins entered with the mail. The postman had met with an accident on the icy road, and was several hours behind time. Usually Dan went to the office, but on this occasion Mr. Larkins was down to the store, and had brought along the mail for both families.

"Letters for us!" Nellie exclaimed as Mr. Larkins entered. "Oh, how good of you to bring them!"

"Stay, stay," insisted the parson, as the worthy neighbour was about to retire and leave them to the enjoyment of their letters. "You have not had a whiff with me for a long time, and here is a new church-warden waiting to be broken in."

"But, I shall interrupt you," Mr. Larkins replied.

"No, no, not in the least."

"Well, then, I agree to remain for one smoke, if you will promise that you will read your letters, and not mind me. I see a new magazine on the table which looks very tempting."

Ensconced in a large easy-chair, he was soon deeply immersed in the fascinating pages, at the same time endeavouring to enjoy the long "church-warden," which was not altogether to his taste. Silence reigned in the room, broken only by the cutting of envelopes and the occasional rattle of the letters.

Mr. Larkins was startled by a sudden cry of astonishment, and looking quickly up he saw the parson sitting erect in his chair, clutching a sheet of paper in both hands, and staring at it in a dazed manner. Nellie at once sprang to his side to ascertain the cause of the commotion.

"Look! Look!" he cried, thrusting the paper into her hand. "It's from the Bishop! Read it, quick, and tell me what it means! Am I losing my senses, or is this only a dream, or a joke?"

Although Nellie's face was pale as she sprang to her father's side, it went white as death as she quickly scanned the missive, drinking in almost intuitively every word and its meaning. Then, flinging it aside with an impatient gesture, she placed her arms about her father's neck, and tried to soothe him.

"Father, father, dear, never mind," she pleaded. But her voice faltered, and she simply clung to him like a tender vine to some sturdy oak.

"Girl! girl!" demanded the parson, "what does it mean? Do you know anything? Tell me, quick!"

"Father, father," urged the maiden, "calm yourself. Don't get so excited."

"But, do you know anything about this? Tell me at once!"

"Yes -"

"Yes, what? Don't stop. Go on," and the old man leaned forward so as not to miss a single word.

"Oh, father, give me time," sobbed Nellie. "I will explain all. What will Mr. Larking think?"

"True, true. What will he think?" and the parson turned towards his visitor.

"You will pardon me, sir, for acting so strangely. But I am much upset. There, please, read this. A letter from my Bishop, full of the most remarkable utterances a man ever wrote. My people turned against me! My people charging me with being a common thief! No, no! It cannot be true! Read it - read it for yourself," and with a trembling hand he passed over the letter.

"My dear Westmore," so began the epistle. "What is the trouble between you and your parishioners in Glendow? I have recently received a petition signed by twenty of your people asking for your removal, on the following grounds:

"*First*. That you are too old to do the work; that many parts of the parish are being neglected, and that a young man should take your place, who will be able to hold the flock together.

"*Second*. That you alone attended the deathbed of an old man, William Fletcher by name, who was possessed of a considerable sum of money, all in gold. The money, it is well known, was always kept in the house in a strong, iron box. The night you attended him the house was burned to the ground, but no trace of the money has since been found. Even at the time you were suspected by some, as it was well known you were much involved in some mining transactions out in British Columbia and badly in need of money to carry on the work. But not until shortly after the fire, when at a public auction you purchased a large homestead and paid down the amount, four thousand dollars, in cash, did the whole parish suspect that something was radically wrong.

"*Third*. That on your way to attend a funeral at Craig's Corner on a recent Sunday, you engaged in a horse-race with one, Tim Fraser, a most notorious character.

"Such in brief is the purport of the petition which now lies before me, and I am asked not only to remove you, but to make a thorough investigation concerning the whole affair. I am much grieved at this matter, and cannot understand it at all. You have ever been looked upon as a faithful priest in the Church of God, and I believe you will be able to explain everything to the satisfaction of all. At first I thought it well that you should write to me. On second consideration, however,

I think it better to make a visit to Glendow, and see if the matter cannot be quietly settled. I do not wish this trouble to get abroad or into the newspapers. I wish to have the people of the parish come before me, one by one, that I may hear what they have to say, and thus be in a better position to form a sound judgment. I have written the petitioners to this effect, and have told them that I shall be in the vestry of the church next Thursday, morning and afternoon, to hear what they have to say. I have also written to your wardens - whose names, by the way, do not appear on the petition - stating the case, that they may give due notice throughout the parish."

Silently Mr. Larkins returned the letter, not knowing what to say.

"What does it all mean?" questioned the parson, looking keenly into his neighbour's face. "Am I only dreaming, or is it a joke?"

"Neither, father, dear," Nellie replied, taking a seat near his side, and tenderly clasping his hand, which was trembling with excitement. "It is all real, ah, too real! The people have been saying these things."

"What, girl! Do you mean to tell me that these things have been talked about ever since the night of the fire?" demanded the parson.

"Yes, father, some have been saying them."

"And you knew about these stories, Nellie?"

"Y - yes, some of them."

"And you never said a word to me! Never gave me a hint of warning, but let me remain in ignorance the whole of this time!"

"We thought it was for the best, father. Don't get angry with me. I suppose I should have told you, but I thought the gossip would soon cease."

"You thought so, did you! Girl, I didn't think you would deceive me - your father, in his old age! Have all my friends turned against me? Yes, yes, and even she, of my flesh and blood - the darling of my heart for whom I would die! God help me!"

"Father, father, dear! don't talk that way," pleaded Nellie."You will break my heart. You don't know what I have suffered. Day and night the trouble has been with me. I loved you so much that I wished to spare you the worry. I thought it was for the best, but now I see I should have told you. You have friends, true and tried, who do not believe a word of these charges."

The parson who had been gazing straight before him, rested his eyes upon his daughter weeping by his side. His face softened, and the old look returned.

"Forgive me, darling," he said, placing his arm tenderly about her. "I have wronged you and all my dear friends. But, oh, the blow is so sudden! I hardly know what to think. What can I do?"

For over an hour they sat there and discussed the matter. As Mr. Larkins at length rose to go, he looked into Parson John's face so drawn and white, and almost cursed the wretches who had brought such trouble upon that hoary head.

Chapter XX

The Overseer

The service at the parish church Sunday morning was largely attended. Word had spread rapidly that the Bishop would arrive during the week, and it was confidently expected that the parson would touch on the question from the pulpit.

"Guess we'll git something to-day," one man remarked to another, near the church door.

"Y'bet," was the brief response.

"D'ye think the parson will say anything about old Billy?"

"Mebbe he will, an' mebbe he won't."

"But I think he will. The parson likes to hit from the pulpit when no one kin hit back."

"Is that what brought you to church to-day? You seldom darken the door."

"Sure! What else should I come fer? I'm not like you, Bill Flanders, wearin' out me shoes paddin' to church every Sunday. I kin be jist as good a Christian an' stay

H. A. Cody

at home. I kin read me Bible an' say me prayers there."

"I'm not denying that, Bill, but the question is, Do ye? I reckon ye never open yer Bible or say yer prayers either fer that matter. If you were in the habit of doin' so you never would hev signed that petition to the Bishop."

"Well, I'm not alone in that. There's Farrington, a church member an' a communicant, who headed the list, an' if he - "

"Hold, right there, Bill. Farrington never signed that paper."

"Yes, he did."

"But, I say, he didn't. He promised to do so, but jist after he sent it away he made a fuss an' said that he had fergotten to do it."

"Ye don't say so!" and Bill's eyes opened wide with surprise. "But are ye sure?"

"Sartin. I had it from Tom Fletcher himself, who feels rather sore about it. It is well known that Farrington wanted the parson removed on the plea of old age, but didn't want that clause in about Billy's death. The Fletchers insisted, however, an' in it went."

"The devil! Well, it's queer, I do declare."

Just then the bell rang out its last call, and they entered the church with others.

Parson John looked greyer than usual as he conducted

the service and stood at the lectern to read the Lessons. But his voice was as sweet and musical as ever, though now a note of pathos could be detected. His step was slow and feeble as he mounted the pulpit, and a yearning look came into his face as he glanced over the rows of heads before him.

"Remember my bonds," was the text he took this morning, and without a note to guide him, he looked into the numerous faces, and delivered his brief message. A breathless silence pervaded the sanctuary as he proceeded to draw a picture of St. Paul, the great champion of the faith, in his old age enduring affliction, and appealing to his flock to remember his bonds. The arm of the parson still in the sling, and the knowledge the people had of the reports circulated about him, added much to the intense impressiveness of the scene. For about fifteen minutes he spoke in a clear, steady voice. Then his right hand clutched the top of the pulpit, while his voice sank and faltered. "Brethren," he said, straightening himself up with an effort, "St. Paul had his bonds, which were hard for him to bear; the bond of suffering, the bond of loneliness, and the bond of old age. You, too, have bonds, and will have them. But how sweet to know that your friends and loved ones will remember your bonds, will understand your sufferings, peculiarities, and will sympathize with you, and be considerate. I, too, have bonds: the bond of unfitness for my great work, and the bond of old age. These two shackle and impede me in the Master's cause. But I ask you to think not so much of these as of another which binds me soul and body - it is the bond of love. I look into your faces this morning, and think of the many years I have laboured among you in evil report and good report. I have learned to love you, and now that love is my

H. A. Cody

greatest bond, for it enwraps my very heart. When parents see their darling child turn against them, their love to him is the hardest bond to bear, because they cannot sever it. They remember him as a babe in arms, as a little, clinging, prattling child. They think of what they have done and suffered for his sake and how the cord of love has been silently woven through the years. My love to you is my greatest bond, and, though some may grow cold, some may scoff, and some repudiate, never let the lips of any say that your rector, your old grey-headed pastor, now in his fourth and last watch, ever ceased in his love to his little flock."

There was a diversity of opinion among the listeners to these pathetic words, which was quite noticeable as the congregation filed out of the church. The eyes of some were red, showing the intensity of their emotion, while others shone with a scornful light.

"The parson fairly upset me to-day!" blurted out one burly fellow. "I heven't been so moved sense the day I laid me old mother to rest in the graveyard over yonder."

"Upset, did ye say?" replied another, turning suddenly upon him. "What was there to upset ye in that?"

"Why, the way the parson spoke and looked."

"Umph! He was only acting his part. He was trying to work upon our feelings, that was all. Ah, he is a cute one, that. Did ye hear what he said about the bond of love? Ha, ha! That's a good joke."

There was one, however, who felt the words more deeply than all the others. This was Nellie, who sat straight upright in her pew, and watched her father's every movement. She did not shed a tear, but her hands were firmly clasped in her lap and her face was as pale as death. As soon as the service was over she hurried into the vestry, helped her father off with his robes, and then supported his feeble steps back to the Rectory. She made no reference to the sermon, but endeavoured to divert her father's mind into a different channel. She set about preparing their light midday repast, talked and chatted at the table, and exhibited none of the heaviness which pressed upon her heart. Only after she had coaxed her father to lie down, and knew that he had passed into a gentle sleep, did she give way to her pent-up feelings. How her heart did ache as she sat there alone in the room, and thought of her father standing in the pulpit uttering those pathetic words.

Thursday, the day of the investigation, dawned bright and clear. Not a breath of wind stirred the air. It was one of those balmy spring days when it is good to be out-of-doors drinking in freshness and strength.

The Bishop had arrived the night before, and had taken up his abode at the Rectory. About ten o'clock the following morning, he wended his way to the church, there to await the people of Glendow. Some time elapsed before any arrived, and not until the afternoon did most of them come. Tom Fletcher was among the first, and at once he made his way into the vestry, and confronted the Bishop.

The latter was a small-sized man, clean shaven, and with his head adorned with a mass of white, wavy hair. His face and massive forehead bore the stamp of deep intellectuality. He was noted as a writer of no mean

H. A. Cody

order, having produced several works dealing with church questions, full of valuable historic research. His every movement bespoke a man of great activity and devotion in his high office. His eyes were keen and searching, while his voice was sharp and piercing. "Sharp as a razor," said several of his careless clergy. Merciless and scathing in reference to all guile, sham and hypocrisy, he was also a man of intense feeling, sympathetic, warm-hearted, and a friend well worth having.

He was poring over certain church registers as Tom Fletcher entered, and, glancing quickly up, noted at once the man standing before him. He rose to his feet, reached out his hand to Fletcher and motioned him to a chair.

"Fletcher is your name, you say - Tom Fletcher," and the Bishop ran his eyes over several lists of names before him.

"Yes, sir, that's my name."

"You signed the petition, I see."

"Yes."

"Well, then, you must know about these charges which are made against your rector. Now, as regards the first. It states here that he is neglecting certain parts of the parish. Is that true?"

"I understand so."

"Where?"

"Oh, I hear he hasn't been to Hazel Greek an' Lands-down Corner fer over two years."

"Any other place?"

"No, I guess them's the only two, but it seems to me to be a purty serious matter fer sich places to be neglected so long."

"Ah, I see," and the Bishop looked keenly into Tom's face.

"You're not a vestryman, Mr. Fletcher?" he remarked.

"No, never was one."

"Did you ever attend an Easter Monday meeting?"

"No, never had time."

"Do you take a church paper?"

"Should say not. Much as I kin do is to pay fer the newspaper."

"But, of course, you read the Synod Journal, which is freely distributed. It contains each year a report from this parish."

"Yes, I read it sometimes, but there isn't much to interest me in that."

"But surely, Mr. Fletcher, you must have read there that Hazel Creek and Landsdown Corner were cut off from Glendow over two years ago, and added to the adjoining parish, and are now served by the rector of

Tinsborough. They are more accessible to him, and the change has been a good one."

"What! Ye don't tell me!" and Tom's eyes opened wide with surprise. "I never knew that before. The parson never said a word about it."

"Did you ever ask him? Or did you inquire why he never went to those places?"

"No. I thought - "

"I don't want to know what you thought," and the Bishop turned sharply upon him. "Explanations are not needed now. You have proven conclusively that you know nothing about the church affairs in this parish, and care less. According to these registers I find that you never come to Communion and never contribute one cent to the support of the church. But we will let that pass, and consider the next charge made here."

"What, about Uncle Billy?"

"Yes. You know the charge made, and as you signed the petition you must have some substantial proof to bring forth."

Tom twisted uneasily on the chair and twirled his hat in his hands. He was mad at the way the Bishop had cornered him, and at what he had said. But he was also afraid of this man who knew so much and seemed to read his inmost thoughts. He began to dread the questions which he knew would come, and longed to be out of the vestry. He was not feeling so sure of himself and wished he had stayed away.

"The second charge made here," continued the Bishop, "is of a most serious nature. It is to the effect that your rector stole the gold from William Fletcher the night the house was burned, and used some of it to buy a farm. Is that what it means?"

"I - I - don't know," Tom stammered, now on his guard, and not wishing to commit himself.

"But you should know," the Bishop insisted. "You signed the paper, and I ask you what it means, then?"

"The gold is gone, sir, an' the parson was the only one there with Uncle Billy. Besides, where did he git all of that money?"

"But that's no proof. I want facts, and I expect you to give me some."

"That's all I know," was the surly response.

"And upon the strength of that suspicion you signed this paper?"

"Yes."

"And you would swear that you know nothing definite?"

"Y - yes - that's all I know."

The Bishop remained silent for a short time, musing deeply.

"Do you know," he at length remarked, "that you have put yourself in a very awkward position?"

"How's that?"

"You have virtually said that Mr. Westmore stole that gold. If you cannot prove your statements you have laid yourself open to prosecution for defamation of character. Your rector, if he wished, could bring in a charge against you of a most serious nature."

"I never thought of that."

"No, I know you didn't. You may go now, but remember the position in which you have placed yourself."

Tom waited to hear no more. He fairly sprang to the door, his face dark and frightened. He spoke to no one, neither did he notice the sturdy form of Mrs. Stickles standing there waiting to be admitted into the vestry.

The Bishop looked up as the door opened and Mrs. Stickles entered. She always proved the dominating factor wherever she went, and what her size could not accomplish was well supplied by her marvellous tongue. The Bishop winced as she seized his hand in a vise-like grip.

"It's real glad I am to set me eyes on ye," she exclaimed. "I heven't seen ye in a dog's age, an' I'm mighty pleased ye look so well. How did ye leave the missus, bless her dear heart? My, I'm all het up, the church is so hot," and she bounced down upon the chair Fletcher had recently vacated.

The Bishop's eyes twinkled, and his care-worn face brightened perceptibly. His exalted position made him a lonely man. There was so much deference paid to him. People as a rule were so reserved in his presence, and showed a longing to be away. "Many people desire a high office," he had once said, "but very few realize the responsibility and loneliness it entails. So much is expected of a Bishop, and his slightest words and acts are criticized. I often envy humble workmen, smoking and chatting together. They have many things in common. They may say what they like, and much heed is not given to their remarks."

It was therefore most refreshing to have this big-hearted woman seated before him acting and talking so naturally, without the least restraint, the same as if she were in her own house.

"You have come, I suppose," said the Bishop, "in connection with this petition," and he pointed to the paper lying on the table.

"Oh, that's the thing, is it?" asked Mrs. Stickles, as she leaned forward to get a better view. "Be very keerful of it, Mr. Bishop. Don't scratch it or bring it too close to the fire."

"Why, what do you mean?" asked the Bishop.

"What do I mean? Don't ye know that's the work of the devil, an' there's enough brimstone in that paper to burn us up in a jiffy. It's soaked through an' through, so I advise ye to handle it keerful."

"So you think these charges in this petition are not true? What can you say to the contrary, then?"

"What kin I say to be contrary? I kin say a good deal, an', indeed, I hev said a good deal. When I heered

H. A. Cody

about that pertition my buzum jist swelled like the tail of an old cat when a hull bunch of yelpin' curs git after her. But I didn't sit down an' weep an' wring me hands. No, sir, not a bit of it. Me an' Sammy went to them in authority, an' sez I to them church-wardens, sez I, 'will ye let that old parson, the Lord's anointed, be imposed upon by them villains?'"

"'What kin we do?' sez they.

"'Do!' sez I.' Do what the Lord intended ye to do, fight. Didn't the Holy Apostle say, 'Quit ye like men, be strong?' 'Git up a pertition,' sez I, 'an' git every decent, honest man in Glendow to sign it, an' send it to the Bishop. Tell 'im?' sez I,' that the parson isn't neglectin' his parish an' that yez hev full confidence in 'im.'

"'We don't like to do it,' sez they.

"'Why not?' sez I.

"'We don't like to stir up strife,' sez they. "'Tisn't good to hev a disturbance in the church. We're men of peace.'

"'Peace,' sez I, 'an' let the devil win? That's not the trouble. Yer afeered, that's what's the matter. Yer too weak-kneed, an' hain't got as much backbone as an angle worm.' That's what I said to 'em, right out straight, too. Now kin ye tell me, Mr. Bishop, why the Lord made some people men instead of makin' 'em chickens fer all the spunk they've got?"

"But, Mrs. Stickles," replied the Bishop, who had been staring in amazement at the torrent of words, "what has this to do with the question before us?"

"I'm comin' to that, sir, only I wanted to tell ye my persition. When I found that them in authority wouldn't make the start, I concluded that the Lord meant me to do the work. So me an' Sammy an' our old horse Queen travelled up an' down the parish fer three solid days, with this result," and, drawing a paper from a capacious pocket, she laid it on the table. "Thar 'tis, read it fer yerself, an' jedge."

The Bishop's eyes grew a little misty as he read the words written there, and noted the long list of names testifying to the worthiness of the rector of Glendow.

"Mrs. Stickles," he at length remarked, and his voice was somewhat husky, "the Lord will reward you for what you have done. While others have been simply talking, you have been acting. Like that woman of old, you have done what you could, and this deed of love, believe me, will be remembered in the parish of Glendow for generations to come. You may go now; you have done your part."

Chapter XXI

Decision

With his chair drawn tip close to the window, Parson John watched the people as they moved along the road to and from the church. He recognized them all, and knew them by their horses when some distance away. As clothes betray a person when his face is not observable, so do horses and sleighs on a country road. They seem to be vital parts of the owners, and to separate them would be fatal. No one could imagine Mrs. Stickles seated in a finely-upholstered sleigh and driving a high-mettled horse. She and Sammy, the home-made pung and the old lean mare plodding onward, were inseparably connected with the parish of Glendow. The parson's face brightened as he saw this quaint conveyance shaking along the road. In Mrs. Stickles he knew he would have one champion at least, though all the others should turn against him. Team after team he watched, but none turned aside into the Rectory gate to say a word to the old grey-headed man, sitting before the window.

The hours dragged slowly by, and still he sat there. Nellie went quietly about her household duties, but a great weight kept pressing upon her heart. Her father was so quiet, took no interest in his books, and did no writing. Often she would stop and watch him as he sat there. He seemed to be greyer than usual; his head was more bent, and his face wore a sad, pained expression. "If he would only utter some word of complaint," thought Nellie, "it would not be so hard. But to see that dumb, appealing look is almost more than I can bear."

Though very quiet, Parson John was fighting a hard, stern battle. His eyes were often turned towards the road, but his thoughts were mostly upon other things. Over his desk hung two pictures, and occasionally his gaze rested upon these. One was that of a sweet-faced woman, who looked down upon him with gentle, loving eyes-such eyes as Nellie inherited.

"Ruth, Ruth," he murmured, "my darling wife. Thirty-five years since I brought you here as a fair young bride. Thirty-five years! We knew not then what lay before us. We knew not then how one must walk for years by himself and at last tread the wine-press alone."

His eyes drifted to the other picture hanging there - the Master kneeling alone in Gethsemane. Long he looked upon that prostrate figure with the upturned face. He thought of His agony in the Garden, the betrayal, desertion and suffering. "I have trodden the winepress alone," he softly whispered as into his face came a new light of peace and strength. Opening a well-worn volume lying on the desk he read again that Garden scene, when the Master knelt and fought His terrible battle. Forgotten for a brief space were his own trials as he pored over that sacred page. How often had he read that story, and meditated upon every word, but never before did he realize the full significance of the scene. "Wonderful, wonderful," he murmured again, as he reverently closed the Book. "Thank God - oh, thank

God for that life of suffering and sorrow! He knows our human needs. He trod the winepress alone, and must I, His unworthy servant, expect to escape? So, my Father, do with me what is best. 'Not my will, but Thine be done.'"

At this moment Nellie entered the room. She noticed the changed expression upon her father's face, and, crossing to where he was, stood by his side.

"Do you feel better, father?" she asked.

"Yes, dear. My heart was very heavy a short time ago, but it is lighter now. I seem to see my way more clearly. The darkness has passed, and a new peace has come to me. Will you sing something for me, dearie?"

"Certainly, father. What shall it be?"

"Your mother's favorite hymn. The one she sang just before she left us."

Taking her seat at the little harmonium, Nellie gently touched the keys, and in a clear, sweet voice sang the old favourite hymn:

> "The sands of Time are sinking,
> The dawn of Heaven breaks,
> The summer morn I've sighed for.
> The fair, sweet morn awakes.
> Dark, dark has been the midnight,
> But dayspring is at hand,
> And glory, glory dwelleth
> In Emmanuel's land."

Softly she sang the whole hymn through, her father

leaning back in his chair with closed eyes, drinking in every word and sound.

"I're wrestled on towards Heaven,
'Gainst storm and wind and tide;
Lord, grant thy weary traveller
To lean on Thee as guide."

"That's what I must do now, Nellie. 'Lean on Him as guide.' Oh, it gives me such comfort. And He will guide right; we must never doubt that."

When the Bishop had finished his investigation in the vestry, he sighed as he closed his small grip and left the church. Slowly he walked up the road lost in deep thought. There were numerous things which disturbed his mind. He had listened to what the people had to say, but everything was so vague. Yet there was some mystery, he believed, connected with the whole matter. That missing gold, the Rector's need of money and then the purchase of the farm were still shrouded in darkness. Thinking thus he reached the Larkins' house where he had been invited to tea.

"It will help Nellie to have the Bishop here," Mrs. Larkins had said to her husband, "for she has enough care at the present time."

Keenly she watched the Bishop's face as he came into the house, hoping to obtain some clue to his thoughts. To her the trouble at the Rectory was as her own, and she longed to know the outcome of the investigation. At first she dreaded the thought of having the Bishop to tea. Had she not often heard of his sharp, abrupt manner? Anxiously she scanned the tea-table, with its spotless linen, with everything so neatly arranged, and

H. A. Cody

wondered what she had omitted. Her fears were soon dispelled, however, for the Bishop made himself perfectly at home. It was a pleasure to him to sit at the table with these two true, honest souls, of whom he had heard much from Parson John. They were so natural, and made no effort to be what they were not.

"You must be tired, my Lord," said Mrs. Larkins, "after this trying day."

"Not so much tired as puzzled," was the reply.

"And did you get no light on the matter?"

"Not a bit. Look at all those notes I took - not worth the paper on which they are written. Everything is hearsay - nothing definite. And yet there is some mystery attached to the whole affair. I am sorely puzzled about that missing gold and where the Rector obtained the money to buy that farm."

"And didn't he tell you, my Lord?" asked Mrs. Larkins, pausing in the act of pouring the tea.

"No, he will not tell me. He is as silent as the grave. When I pressed him to speak and thus clear himself, he begged me with tears in his eyes not to urge him. 'It's honest money,' he said, 'which purchased the farm, but I can tell you no more now.'"

"You have heard, my Lord, that he is involved in some mining transaction out in British Columbia. It is now in litigation and the parson is contributing all be possibly can."

"Yes, I learned of that to-day, and it only tends to

complicate matters. I cannot believe that your Rector had anything to do with that gold. But oh, if he would only explain. Are you sure that that box is not still among the ashes and ruins of the old house?"

"I am certain it is not there," Mr. Larkins replied. "We have searched the place thoroughly, and even sifted the ashes, but all in vain. Not a trace could we find of the box or the gold."

The evening was somewhat advanced as the Bishop bade the Larkins good-night and made his way over to the Rectory. He found Parson John seated in a deep chair, gazing silently before him. Nellie was sitting near reading, or trying to read. She greeted the Bishop with a bright smile, drew up a chair for him to the pleasant fire, and took his hat and coat.

"Have I kept you up, Nellie?" he asked. "Your father must be tired."

"No, no, my Lord," she replied. "It is not late yet. But you must be tired."

"A little, my dear. The day has been somewhat trying."

From the time he had entered Parson John had kept his eyes fixed full upon the Bishop's face with a mute, questioning look which spoke louder than words. "What have you found out?" He seemed to be saying. "What stories have they been telling about me? Who have been my foes and friends?"

"The vestry was converted into quite a court-room to-day," said the Bishop, reading the questioning look in the parson's face. "There were certainly several lively scenes, especially when Mrs. Stickles made her appearance."

"You have reached a conclusion then, I suppose?" and Mr. Westmore leaned eagerly forward.

"No, not yet. I cannot give my decision now. I want to think it carefully over, and shall notify you by letter."

"I thank you, my Lord, for the trouble you have taken in the matter," and the parson resumed his former position. "But I have been thinking deeply since hearing these reports concerning me, and my mind is made up as to the course I shall pursue."

"Indeed, and in what way?" queried the Bishop.

"To-morrow morning I shall hand to you my resignation of this parish."

The effect of these words was startling, and Nellie's face went very white as she glanced quickly at her father.

"Do you mean it?" inquired the Bishop.

"Yes, my Lord. I have not come to this decision without much thought, prayer, and struggle. I have been too blind. I forgot how old I am, though God knows my heart is as young as ever. It's only natural that the people of Glendow should desire a change; a man who will infuse new life into the work, and draw in the wandering and indifferent ones. May God forgive me that I did not think of it before!"

His head drooped low as he uttered these words, and

the pathos of his voice denoted the intensity of his feelings. It was impossible not to be much moved at the figure of this venerable man, this veteran warrior of his church, without one word of complaint, willing to relinquish all, to give up the command to another, that the Master's work might be strengthened. The Bishop was visibly affected, although he endeavoured to conceal his emotion.

"Westmore," he replied, "I always believed you to be a noble man of God, though I never knew it as I do to-night. But where will you go if you leave Glendow? How will you live?"

"I am not worrying about that. He who has guided me all of these years; He, who has given me strength for the battle, will not forsake me now in my fourth and last watch when I am old and grey-headed. My brother and his wife at Morristown have for years been urging us to pay them a long visit. We will go to them, and stay there for a time. Perhaps the Master will open to me some door in His vineyard that I may do a little more work ere He take me hence. I have no means of my own, but the parish owes me six months' salary, and no doubt the people will gladly pay it now to be rid of me."

"Why not sell that farm you purchased?" suggested the Bishop. "It should bring a fair price, and the money would keep you for some time. I cannot place you on the Superannuated list at present, but there may be a vacancy soon and the money from the sale of the farm will keep you until then."

"I can't sell the place, my Lord, it is impossible."

"But you bought it; it is yours."

"It's not mine to sell! It's not mine to sell!"

The look upon the old man's face and the pathos of his words restrained the Bishop from saying more on the subject.

"And so you think you must go?" he remarked after a painful silence.

"Yes, I see nothing else to do."

"But remember all have not turned against you. See this list," and the Bishop handed over the petition Mrs. Stickles had given him.

Eagerly the parson read the words, and scanned the names scrawled below.

"And did Mrs. Stickles do this?" he asked.

"Yes. She went up and down the parish for three days."

"God bless the woman!" murmured Mr. Westmore. "What a comfort this is to me; to know that all have not deserted me. I did not expect it. But it will not change my mind. My eyes have been suddenly opened to my own inability to do the work. Another will do much better. I've explained everything to you, my Lord, that I can explain, and about that horse-race, too. It is better for me to go."

"Father," said Nellie, "let us go to Uncle Reuben's for a month or so. You need a rest, and a vacation will do you good. Perhaps then you will see things differently."

"Capital idea!" exclaimed the Bishop. "It's just the thing! Go to your brother's and stay there for a month or two."

"But what about the parish? It will be left vacant the whole of that time. If I resign a new Rector can take charge at once."

"Oh, I will arrange for that," responded the Bishop. "There is a young man fresh from college who will be ordained shortly. I will send him here during your absence. We will thus give the people a change, and then, no doubt, they will be glad enough to have you back again."

Parson John sat for some time in deep meditation, while Nellie watched him with an anxious face. The clock in the room ticked loudly, and the fire crackled in the hearth.

"Very well," he assented at length with a deep sigh. "If you think it best, my Lord, that this should be done I shall not oppose your wish. But I am firmly convinced that it will be just the same as if I resigned. When once the new man comes and begins the work, the people will not want their old Rector back again. But, nevertheless, it will be all for the best. 'My times are in His hands,' and I feel sure that ever 'underneath are the Everlasting Arms.'"

H. A. Cody

Chapter XXII

In the Deep of the Heart

It did not take long for the news of Parson John's intended departure to spread throughout Glendow.

Tongues were once more loosened and numerous conjectures made.

"Guess the Bishop found things pretty crooked," remarked one, "an' thinks it high time for the parson to get out."

"I've thought the same myself," replied another. "The parson's been dabblin' too much in furren affairs. As I was tellin' my missus last night, we never know what will happen next. When them as is leaders goes astray, what kin be expected of the sheep? I've given a bag of pertaters each year to support the church, but dang me if I do it any more!"

But while some saw only the dark side and believed the parson to be guilty, there were others who stood nobly by him in his time of trial. Various were the calls made, some people driving for miles to say good-bye, and to express their regrets at his departure.

Among the number was Mrs. Stickles. She was the

first to arrive, and, bustling out of the old broken-down wagon, she seized the parson's hand in a mighty grip as he met her at the gate.

"God bless ye, sir!" she ejaculated. "I'm more'n delighted to see ye. I was on me knees scrubbin' the kitchen floor when Patsy Garlick dropped in an' told me the news. It so overcome me that I flopped right down an' bawled like a calf."

"Dear me! dear me!" replied the Rector. "What's wrong? did you receive bad news? I hope nothing's the matter with Tony."

"Oh, no. I don't mean 'im, sir, though I ain't heered from 'im fer months now. He's so shet up thar in the woods that it's hard to hear. But I feel he's all right, fer if he wasn't I'd soon know about it. No, it's not fer 'im I bawled, but fer you an' the darlin' lass. To think that ye are to leave us so soon!"

"Oh, I see," and the parson placed his hand to his forehead. "Thank you very much for your kindness, Mrs. Stickles, and for what you did concerning that petition. So you have come all the way to bid us good-bye. You must go into the house at once, and have a bite with us. I shall send Dan to give the horse some hay."

"Thank ye, sir. I didn't come expectin' to be taken in an' fed, but seein' as it'll be some time afore I hev sich a privilege agin, I don't mind if I do."

Spring had now come in real earnest. The days were balmy, the sun poured its bright rays upon hill and valley, and the snow disappeared as if by magic.

Thousands of streams and rivulets rushed racing down to the river, sparkling and babbling, glad of their release from winter's stern grip. The early birds had returned, filling the air with their sweet music, and the trees, awakened from their long slumber, were putting forth their green buds. Everything spoke of freshness and peace.

But within the Rectory there was an unusual silence. A gloom pervaded the house, which even Nellie's sunny presence could not dispel. Dan had disappeared, and no trace of him could be found. He had departed in the night so silently that even Nellie's ever-watchful ear did not hear his footsteps upon the floor. They knew no reason why the lad should do such a thing, and anxiously they discussed the matter over the breakfast-table. Inquiries were made throughout the parish, which only served to set tongues wagging more than ever.

"I knew when the parson took him in," said one knowing person, "that something 'ud happen. Ye can never tell about sich waifs. They generally amount to nuthin' or worse."

Nellie missed Dan very much. She had come to love the lad with all his quaint ways and dreamy far-away look. He had always been so ready to do anything for her, and often she found him watching her with wondering eyes. In her heart she could not believe that the boy had run away because he was tired of living at the Rectory. She felt sure there must be some other reason, and often she puzzled her brain trying to solve the problem.

As the days passed preparations were made for their

departure. There was much to do, for numerous things they must take with them. The parson took but little interest in what was going on. He seemed to be living in another world. So long had he lived at the Rectory that the building had become almost a part of himself. How many sacred associations were attached to each room! Here his children had been born; here he had watched them grow, and from that front door three times had loving hands borne forth three bodies, - two, oh, so young and tender - to their last earthly resting-place in the little churchyard. In youth it is not so hard to sever the bonds which unite us to a loved spot. They have not had time fully to mature, and new associations are easily made and the first soon forgotten. But in old age it is different. New connections are not easily formed, and the mind lives so much in the past, with those whom we have "loved long since and lost awhile."

It was hard for Nellie to watch her father as the days sped by. From room to room he wandered, standing for some time before a familiar object, now a picture and again a piece of furniture. Old chords of memory were awakened. They were simple, common household effects of little intrinsic value. But to him they were fragrant with precious associations, like old roses pressed between the pages of a book, recalling dear and far-off, half-forgotten days.

Nellie, too, felt keenly the thought of leaving the Rectory. It had been her only home. Here had she been born, and here, too, had she known so much happiness. Somehow she felt it would never again be the same; that the parting of the ways had at last arrived. Her mind turned often towards Stephen. She had seen him but little of late. Formerly he had been so much at the

Rectory. Seldom a day had passed that she did not see him. But now it was so different. Sometimes for a whole week, and already it had been a fortnight since he had been there. She knew how busy he was bringing his logs down to the river. He had told her that stream driving would soon begin, when every hour would be precious to catch the water while it served. She knew this, and yet the separation was harder than she had expected. There was an ache in her heart which she could not describe. Often she chided herself at what she called her foolishness. But every evening while sitting in the room she would start at any footstep on the platform, and a deep flush would suffuse her face. She had come to realize during the time of waiting what Stephen really meant to her.

Thus while Nellie worked and thought in the Rectory, Stephen with his men was urging his drive of logs down the rough and crooked Pennack stream. How he did work! There was no time to be lost, for the water might suddenly fall off and leave the logs stranded far from the river. All day long he wrestled with the monsters of the forest. At night there was the brief rest, then up and on again in the morning. But ever as he handled the peevy there stood before him the vision of the sweet-faced woman at the Rectory. She it was who had moved him to action, and inspired him. through days of discouragement. His deep love for her was transforming him into a man. He longed to go to her, to comfort her in her time of trouble. But he must not leave his work now. Too much depended upon that drive coming out, and she would understand. So day by day he kept to his task, and not until the last log had shot safely into the boom in the creek below did he throw down his peevy. It was late in the evening as he sprang ashore and started up the road. His heart was happy. He had accomplished the undertaking he had set out to perform.

And while Stephen trudged homeward Nellie sat in the little sitting-room, her fingers busy with her needle. All things had been completed for their departure, which was to take place on the morrow. Parson John had retired early to rest, and Nellie was doing a little sewing which was needed. The fire burned in the grate as usual, for the evening was chill, and the light from the lamp flooded her face and hair with a soft, gentle radiance. Perfect type of womanhood was she, graceful in form, fair in feature, the outward visible signs of a pure and inward spiritual nobleness.

So did she seem to the man standing outside and looking upon her through the window with fond, loving eyes. His knock upon the door startled the quiet worker. She rose to her feet, moved forward, and then hesitated. Who could it be at such an hour? for it was almost eleven o'clock. Banishing her fear she threw open the door, and great was her surprise to behold the one of whom she had just been thinking standing there. For a brief space of time neither spoke, but stood looking into each other's eyes. Then, "Stephen," said Nellie, and her voice trembled, "I didn't expect to see you to-night. Is anything wrong?"

"No, not with me," Stephen replied as he entered. "But with you, Nellie, there is trouble, and I want to tell you how I feel for you. I wanted to come before; but you understand."

"Yes, I know, Stephen," and Nellie took a chair near the fire.

As Stephen looked down upon her as she sat there, how he longed to put his strong arm about her and comfort her. He had planned to say many things which he had thought out for days before. But nothing now would come to his lips. He stood as if stricken dumb.

"Nellie."

"Stephen."

Silence reigned in the room. Their hearts beat fast. Each realized what that silence meant, and yet neither spoke. With a great effort Stephen crushed back the longing to tell her all that was in his heart, and to claim her for his own. Would she refuse? He did not believe so. But he was not worthy of her love - no, not yet. He must prove himself a man first. He must redeem the homestead, and then he would speak. Sharp and fierce was the struggle raging in his breast. He had thought it would be a simple matter to come and talk to her on this night. He would bid her a conventional good-bye, and go back to his work, cheered and strengthened. But he little realized how his heart would be stirred by her presence as she sat there bowed in trouble.

"Nellie," he said at length, taking a seat near by. "I'm very sorry you're going away. What will the place be like without you?"

"Yes, I'm sorry to go, Stephen," was the low reply. "'Tis hard to go away from home, especially under - under a cloud."

"But, surely, Nellie, you don't think the people believe those stories?"

"No, not all. But some do, and it's so hard on father. He has had so much trouble lately with that mining property in British Columbia, and now this has come."

Stephen sat thinking for a while before he spoke. When at last he did he looked searchingly into Nellie's face.

"There is something which puzzles me very much, and partly for that reason I have come to see you to-night."

"Anything more in connection with father, Stephen?"

"Yes. Nora has been worse of late, and the doctor said that the only hope of curing her was to send her to New York to a specialist. Mother was very much depressed, for we have no means, and under the circumstances it is so hard to hire money. I had about made up my mind to get some money advanced on the logs. I would do anything for Nora's sake. The next day your father came to see her, and mother was telling him what the doctor said, and how much he thought it would cost. Two days later your father sent mother a cheque for the full amount, with a letter begging her to keep the matter as quiet as possible. I cannot understand it at all. I know your father is in great need of money, and yet he can spare that large sum. Do you know anything about it?"

Nellie listened to these words with fast beating heart. She knew her father had been over to bid Mrs. Frenelle and Nora good-bye, but he had said nothing to her about giving the money. The mystery was certainly deepening. Where had that money come from? A sudden thought stabbed her mind. She banished it instantly, however, while her face crimsoned to think that she should believe anything so unworthy of her father.

"Nellie," Stephen questioned, after he had waited some time for her to speak, "do you know anything about it?"

"No, Stephen; nothing. It is all a great puzzle. But it is honest money! Never doubt that! Father keeps silence for some purpose, I am sure. He will tell us some day. We must wait and be patient!"

She was standing erect now, her eyes glowing with the light of determination, and her small, shapely hands were clenched. She had thought of what people would say if they heard this. It would be like oil to fire. No, they must never know it.

"Stephen," she cried, "promise me before God that you will not tell anyone outside of your family about that money!"

"I promise, Nellie. Did you think I would tell? I know mother and Nora will not. Did you doubt me?"

"No, Stephen, I did not doubt you. But, oh, I do not know what to think these days! My mind is in such a whirl all the time, and my heart is so heavy over the puzzling things which have happened. I just long to lie down and rest, rest, forever."

"You're tired, Nellie," replied Stephen, as he straightened himself up in an effort to control his own feelings. "You must rest now, and you will be stronger to-morrow. Good-bye, Nellie, God bless you," and before she could say a word he had caught her hand in his, kissed it fervently, flung open the door, and disappeared into the night.

H. A. Cody

Chapter XXIII

Where Is Dan?

During the whole of this time of excitement Dan had been doing his own share of thinking. He heard the rumours of the parish, listened to the stories told at the store or blacksmith shop, tucked them away in his retentive mind, and brooded over them by day and night. The purpose which had taken possession of him as he sat by the parson's side during his lonely watch in Stephen's camp grew stronger as the days passed by. He told no one, not even Nellie, what was in his mind. It was a sacred thing to him, and he dreamed over it, as a mother over her unborn child. Not until the dream had become a reality, a living deed, must the world know of it.

Formerly he had been indifferent as to his studies. His listless manner was a great cause of worry to Nellie. But after the accident a change took place. His eagerness to know how to write surprised her. Often she found him painfully scrawling huge letters upon any old piece of paper he happened to find. Time and time again he asked her how to spell certain words, and when she had printed them for him he copied them over and over again with the greatest care. Every day he watched the mail-carrier as he rattled by in his rude buckboard. To him this man was a wonderful being.

Knowing nothing of the postal system, Dan imagined that Si Tower conducted the whole business himself. "How much he must know," he thought, "and what long journeys he must take." It was therefore with considerable trepidation he one day stood by the roadside watching the postman rattling along.

"Hello, kid! Watcher want?" was Si's salutation as he pulled in his old nag, and glared down upon the boy.

"You give this to Tony, please," and Dan held up a little folded slip of paper.

Tower looked at the paper, and turned over the wad of tobacco in his cheek before replying. Then a quaint twinkle shone in his eyes.

"I can't take that," he said. "'Tain't lawful. No stamp. Say, kid, guess the only way fer ye to deliver that is to take it yerself. Git up, Bess," and with a hearty laugh the postman swung on his way, and all that day told the story wherever he stopped.

"Ye should have seen his face an' eyes," he chuckled. "It was as good as a circus. Thar was no stamp on the letter, an' when I told 'im to go himself an' deliver it, he jist stared at me. Ha, ha, it was too funny fer anything."

But Dan, as he stood in the road watching Tower drive away, did not see anything funny. His faith in the postman had received a rude shock. His hero was made of common clay after all. He sighed as he walked back to the house, clutching in his hands the little crumpled piece of paper. As the days passed and the new trouble arose at the Rectory, Dan became very restless. He knew of everything that was going on, and when the

H. A. Cody

Bishop arrived he gazed upon him with awe mingled with fear and anger. Often he would draw forth the letter, from a deep, capacious pocket, and look long and carefully upon it.

At length the moment arrived when his mind was fully made up. He bade Nellie and her father good-night, and crept upstairs to his own little room. For some time he sat upon the bed lost in thought. He heard Nellie come up the stairs and enter her own room. Drawing up the blind and turning down the light, he looked out of the window. How dark it was, and dismal. He would wait awhile until it became lighter. Throwing himself upon the bed without undressing, he drew a quilt over him and ere long was fast asleep. When he opened his eyes a dim light was struggling in through the window, and contending slowly with the blackness of night. Dan was sleepy, and the bed so comfortable, that he longed to stay where he was. But this feeling was soon overcome, and springing to his feet he stood listening and alert, as a creature of the wild startled from its lair. Not a sound disturbed the house. Everything was wrapped in silence. Quietly he moved out of his room, and crept softly down the stairs, fearful lest at every creak Nellie should be aroused. Reaching the kitchen he put on his shoes, which he had left by the stove. Next he went into the pantry, found some cold meat, bread, cheese and biscuits. A paper bag lying near was soon filled and securely tied with a stout string. Dan sighed as he donned his cap, drew on his mittens, closed the back door, and stood by the little outside porch. In his heart he felt it was wrong to go away without telling Nellie and her father where he was going. But on the other hand he was quite sure they would not be willing for him to go so far away, and besides he did not wish to tell them anything until the deed had been accomplished.

The early morning air was cool, clear and crisp. The sun had not yet risen, but far away in the eastern sky the glory of another new-born day was clearly visible. Dan's heart responded to the freshness and the beauty which lay around him. As the daylight increased the feeble chirp of half-awakened birds fell upon his ears. The old longing for the wild filled his soul. He thought of his father, the little cabin in the valley, and the woodland haunts he knew and loved so dearly. His eyes sparkled with animation, and the blood tingled and surged through his body. He felt like shouting at the mere joy of being alive.

"Guess I must be like the bears," he thought. "They stay in their dens all winter and come out in the spring. I'm just like one now."

He knew the direction, for had he not listened time and time again to the conversations in the store? The talk had often turned upon Rodgers & Peterson's big lumbering operations in Big Creek Valley. Yes, he was sure he could find the place. Up the river to Rocky Point, from thence along a big cove, then over a hill and down into a valley. He had dreamed of the way; how long it would take him, and what he would say when he got there. All day long he plodded steadily onward, and when night shut down he stopped by a large stack of hay which had been brought from the lowlands when the river was frozen. He was tired, and the soft hay inviting. Into this he crawled, and ere long was fast asleep. Early the next morning he was up and on again. His supply of food was now getting low. At noon he ruefully viewed the little that was left. "Enough only for supper," he murmured. "Maybe I'll get there to-morrow."

During the day he learned from several people he met that he was on the right road. They had looked with interest upon the little figure, and asked him numerous questions. But Dan gave only indefinite answers. He wished to go to Big Creek Valley to Rodgers & Peterson's lumber camp. When the second night arrived he was very weary and footsore. He had eaten his last scrap of food before sundown, and as he trudged on he wondered what he would do in the morning. He disliked the idea of asking at any of the farm-houses for food. His father had always scoffed at tramps and beggars. "They are spongers," he had often said, "and people cannot afford to have such useless people around."

That word "sponger" as it came to Dan caused him to straighten himself up and step forward more quickly. He was not a sponger now. His face flushed at Farrington's insult. He would show the whole world that he could pay for his keep, and if he could not do it in one way, he would in another.

That night no friendly haystack stood by the road-side, but over there in the field he saw a barn near a farm-house. He could find shelter in that. Waiting until it was dark, he crept cautiously through a small sheep door, and entered. He heard in another part of the building the cattle munching the last of their evening meal. It was good to know that they were near, and that he was not altogether alone. As he threw himself upon a small bunch of straw which he found as he felt around with his hands, a great feeling of loneliness came over him. He longed for the Rectory and a glimpse of Nellie's face. Was she thinking of him, he wondered, or had she forgotten him, and believed him to be an ungrateful scamp? He clenched his hands, and the blood surged to his face as he thought of it. No, he would show her he was not a scamp, but a real man. Oh, she should know what he could do!

Thinking thus he found himself no longer in the barn, but back again at the Rectory. He could see the fire burning brightly on the hearth, and a number of people standing around. They were all looking upon him, and he saw the doctor there, too. But Nellie's face riveted his attention. She was gazing upon him with such a deep look of love. And yet it did not seem altogether like Nellie, and, when she spoke, it was a different voice. Suddenly a strange sound fell upon his ears. The room at the Rectory faded, and in ita stead there was the rough barn floor, and the bunch of straw on which he was lying. For an instant he gazed around him in a bewildered manner. He could not realize just where he was. A childish laugh caused him to turn his head, and there looking in at him from a small door to the left was a little maiden, with curly, auburn hair and cheeks twin sisters to the rosiest apples that ever grew.

"Oo azy ittle boy!" she cried, clapping her hands. "Oo must det up. Turn, daddy, tee azy, azy ittle boy."

Presently there apppeared at her side, a large man, holding a pail in his left hand.

"What is it, dearie?" he asked. "What's all the fun and chattering about?"

"Tee, tee, azy boy," and she pointed with a fat little finger to the corner of the barn floor.

By this time Dan had leaped to his feet, and stood confronting the man. He felt that he was a trespasser, and perhaps he would be punished. But as he looked into the big man's eyes he read with the instinct of a wild animal that he had nothing to fear, for only pity shone in those clear, grey depths.

"Did you sleep there all night?" the man asked, pointing to the straw.

"Yes, sir," was the reply. "I hope you're not cross."

"I'm cross, boy, to think that you didn't come to the house and ask for a bed."

"I didn't like to, sir. I didn't like to bother anybody. But I knew whoever owned the barn wouldn't mind if I slept here. It's a comfortable place, and I was tired."

"Did you have any supper last night?" the man asked, looking keenly into Dan's face.

"Yes, sir; a piece of bread."

"What, nothing more?"

"No. But I had a grand drink from that spring back yonder, and with the good sleep I've had, I think I can manage to-day."

"Look here, boy, you'll not leave this place until you have your breakfast. So come. Marion, you found this little stranger, and you must take him to the house."

But Dan drew back, as the little maiden toddled up to take him by the hand.

"I can't go," he stammered. "I've got no money, and I won't be a sponger."

"A what?" asked the man.

"A sponger. I hate a sponger, and so did my father. I'll split wood for my breakfast if you'll let me, sir, for I am hungry."

"That's a bargain," said the man, much pleased at the spirit of the boy. "So hurry off now. I haven't much time to lose."

Proudly the little maiden conducted her charge to the house, and told in broken language about her marvellous find. Dan felt much at home with Marion's mother, and during breakfast he told her where he was going.

"What! to Rodgers & Peterson's camp!" exclaimed: the big man at the head of the table. "That's where I'm going myself, and that's why I'm up so early this morning. I'm glad to hear of that, for I'll have company."

"But I must split the wood," Dan insisted. "I shall try to earn my breakfast, but what about the ride?"

"Oh, I'll give you work along the way," laughed the man. "You'll have plenty to do, so don't worry."

While the horses were being harnessed Dan vigorously swung the axe in the wood-house. Perched upon the door-step Marion watched him with admiring eyes. He knew that she was looking at him, and his bosom swelled with pride. He was not a sponger, but a man working for his breakfast. At times he stole a glance at the little figure sitting there. "How pretty she is," he thought. "I wish I had a sister like her. He longed to stay there, to be near the little maiden, and to work for the big, kind man. He sighed as he laid down the axe, and gazed at the wood he had chopped.

"It ain't much," he remarked, as he stood ready to climb into the waggon. "Wish I had more time."

"It will do," responded the big man. "I am satisfied if you are."

Dan had no time to answer, for at that instant a little voice sounded forth. Looking quickly around he beheld Marion hurrying towards him holding in her hand a small rose.

"Me div dis to oo, ittle boy," she cried. "It's off my own woes bus. Oo must teep it."

Hardly knowing what he did Dan took the little flower, and stood staring at Marion.

"Come, lassie," cried her father, catching her in his arms and giving her a loving hug and a kiss. Take good care of mother. We must be off."

"Oo div me tiss, too," and she lifted up her lips to Dan's.

The latter's face flushed scarlet, and he trembled. Never in his life had he kissed a little girl like that. What should he do? He longed for the ground to open or something dreadful to happen. He would have welcomed anything just then.

"Tiss me, ittle boy," urged Marion. She had him by the coat now with both hands, drawing him down to her. There was nothing for him to do. He must go through the ordeal. Suddenly he bent his head and shut his eyes. His face came close to hers; he felt her lips touch his cheek, and heard her childish laugh of delight.

"Dood ittle boy!" she exclaimed. "Now dood-by. Don't lose my pitty fower."

Too much confused to say a word Dan scrambled into the waggon, and soon the horses were speeding off down the lane to the road. For some time he sat bolt upright on the seat, silent and thoughtful, clutching in his hand that tiny rose. The big man at his side asked no questions, but seemed intent solely upon managing his horses. But not a motion of the little lad at his side escaped his notice. He loved children, and had the rare gift of understanding them. A faint smile played about his mouth as from the corner of his eye he saw Dan take a piece of paper from his pocket, shyly place the rose between the folds and then return it to its former place. He could not hear the boy's heart thumping hard beneath his jacket, but he understood, and what more was needed?

All day long they jogged over the road, stopping only at noon to feed the horses and eat a lunch Marion's mother had tucked away in the corner of the waggon. Dan found it easy to talk to the big man sitting by his side. He told him about his father's death, Parson John, and the accident, to which his companion listened with much interest. But concerning the object of his visit to the lumber camp, Dan was silent. Several times he was at the point of explaining everything, but always he hesitated and determined to wait.

"I did not tell Nellie," he said to himself, "and why should I tell a stranger first?"

The sun was sinking far westward as they wound their way along a woodland road. Down to the left the water of Big Creek Brook raced and swirled. Occasionally they caught glimpses of the rushing torrent as the road dipped closer to the bank.

"We should meet the drive ere long," the big man remarked, as he flicked the horses with his whip. "I'm afraid the logs have jammed in Giant Gorge, or else they would have been here by this time. It's a bad, rocky place, and seldom a drive gets through without trouble."

Presently he pulled up his horses before a little log shack standing to the right.

"I shall leave the horses here for the night, boy," he said. "There's a path down yonder to the left. If you're in a hurry you can take that. It will lead to the stream, and you can follow it up until you meet the men. If they ask any questions tell them you came with Big Sam, and everything will be all right. Take care and don't fall into the water."

Dan was only too anxious to be on foot. He was cramped from sitting so long in the waggon. Moreover, he was restless to get to the end of his journey, and accomplish his business. Thanking the big man, he leaped from the waggon and was soon speeding down the path, and in a few minutes reached the edge of the brook, roaring and foaming between its steep banks. Looking up-stream he could see no sign of the drive, but the well-beaten path was there, and along this he hurried. Ere long he reached a bend in the stream and as he rounded this, and lifted up his eyes, a wild, terrible scene was presented to view. Away to the right he beheld Giant Gorge, a narrow gash in the rocks, through which the waters were seething and boiling in wildest commotion. On the hither side a flood of logs was sweeping and tearing down, like a mighty breastwork suddenly loosened. Dan started back in terror at the sight, and was about to spring up the bank to a place of safety, when his eyes rested upon the form of a man out in the midst of that rush of destruction, vainly trying to free himself from the watery chasm which had suddenly yawned beneath his feet. Dan's heart beat wildly at the sight. But only for an instant did he hesitate. Then forward he leaped like a greyhound. Forgotten was the rushing torrent, and his own danger. He thought only of that frantically clinging man. He reached the edge of the stream, leaped upon the nearest logs, and, with the agility of a wildcat, threaded his way through that terrible labyrinth of grinding, crashing, heaving monsters.

Chapter XXIV

The Rush of Doom

To bring a drive of logs down Big Creek Brook required skill, patience and courage. It was a nasty, crooked stream, filled with sunken rocks, bad bends and stretches of shallow water. Rodgers & Peterson had their logs in the stream early, and everything pointed to a successful season's work. For awhile all went well, but then mishap after mishap held them back. The logs jammed in several places, and days were lost in getting them cleared. Then they grounded upon bars and shoals, which caused a great delay. But the most serious of all was the hold-up in Giant Gorge. This was the most dreaded spot in the whole stream, and seldom had a drive been brought through without some disaster. Much blasting had been done, and a number of obstacles blown away. But for all that there were rocks which defied the skill of man to remove. Two flinty walls reared their frowning sides for several rods along the brook. Between these an immense boulder lifted its head, around which the waters incessantly swirled. But when the stream was swollen high enough the logs would clear this obstacle at a bound, like chargers leaping a fence, and plunge into the whirling eddies below.

When the "R & P" drive, the name by which it was

commonly known, reached Giant Gorge, it was confidently believed that there was enough water to carry it safely through. But such reckoning was wrong. As the logs came sweeping down and were sucked into the Gorge they began to crowd, and, instead of rushing through loose and free, they jammed against the rocky walls, while a huge monster became wedged on the sunken boulder, and, acting as a key log, held in check the whole drive. Then began a wild scene, which once beheld can never be forgotten. Stopped in their mad career, the logs presented the spectacle of unrestrained passion. The mighty, heaving, twisting mass groaned, pressed and writhed for freedom, but with the awful grip of death the sturdy key log held firm. Steadily the jam increased in size, and whiter threw the foam, as one by one those giant logs swept crashing down, to be wedged amidst their companions as if driven by the sledge of Thor.

The drivers stood upon the bank and watched the logs piling higher and higher. Well did they know what the delay might mean to Rodgers & Peterson. Much depended upon that drive coming out, and for it to be held up during summer meant almost ruin to the firm. They were a hardy body of men who stood there late that afternoon discussing the matter. They were great workmen these, well versed in woodland lore. All winter long had they taken their part in that big lumber operation, and, now that the work was almost completed, it was certainly aggravating to be thus checked.

As the men talked, and several lighted their pipes, one strapping fellow stood on the bank, his eyes fixed upon that immovable key log. During the whole winter Tony Stickles had been the butt as well as the curiosity of the men. His long, lank figure was the source of much ridicule, while his remarks, which were always slow and few, were generally greeted with merriment. From the first night in camp he had been a marked man. Ere he threw himself into the rude bunk he had knelt down on the floor in the presence of them all, and said his evening prayer. A boot had been thrown at his head, and a laugh had gone about the room. Tony had risen from his knees, and with a flushed face sought his couch, surprised at the action on the part of these men. But one middle-aged man of great stature and strength had watched it all. He sat quietly smoking for several minutes after the laughter had subsided.

"Boys," he said at length, taking his pipe from his mouth, "I'm real sorry at what ye've done to-night. I've six little ones of me own, an' I hope to God when they grow up they'll not be afeered to kneel down an' do as yon lad has done to-night. I'm not a good man meself, more's the pity. But that boy's had a good mother's teachin'. I honour her an' 'im. An' let me tell ye this, men, if I ketch ye doin' agin what ye did to-night, ye'll have to reckon with me. So jist try it on, an' I won't give a second warnin'."

Jake Purdy calmly resumed his smoking, and the men looked at one another in silence. They knew very well from certain past unpleasant experiences what it meant to cross this quiet, plain-spoken man. He said little, and never entered into a quarrel without some reason. But when he did there was cause for the stoutest heart to quake.

Tony listened to it all concealed away in his bunk. His heart thumped beneath his rough shirt, and he wished to thank Jake for taking his part. But strive as he might he never had the opportunity. The big woodsman never seemed to notice him. Days passed into weeks, and still Tony did not utter the gratitude which was lying in his heart. To him Jake was more than ordinary - a hero. He watched him as he chopped, and drank in greedily the few words he let fall from time to time in the camp.

"Boys, that drive must go through."

It was the boss who spoke, as he jerked his thumb towards the Gorge. "Yes, it's got to go through to-night, or it's all up. The water's falling off fast, and if we wait till to-morrow, we'll wait till next fall. I've always said there should be a dam at the head of the Gorge, and I say it now more emphatically than ever. But as it is not there, it's up to us to get this d - n thing through as best we can. I've never been stuck yet in bringing out a drive, and I hope this won't be the first time."

"But what's your plan?" asked one. "Hadn't ye better pick one of us to go down into that hell-hole, an' cut that key log?"

"No, that isn't my plan," and the boss scratched the back of his head. "I'm not going to be responsible for the carcase of any man. If I say to one 'Go,' and he goes and gets pinched, I'll worry about it to my dying day. I'd rather go myself first. But if we draw for it, then it's off my shoulders, and I stand the same chance as the rest of ye. I believe that whatever is to be will be, and the right man to go down there will be chosen. Do you agree to that, boys?"

"Ay, ay," came the response. "Go ahead, Tim. We'll stand by the agreement."

H. A. Cody

Some brown paper was accordingly found, and cut with a big jack-knife into twenty pieces, according to the number of the men. On one of these a large X was marked with a blue lead-pencil, which one of the men had in his pocket. A tin lunch can was next produced, and into this the pieces of paper were all thrown and the cover shut down tight. When the can had been thoroughly shaken, the men came up one by one, shut their eyes, put in their hands and drew forth a slip. A tense silence reigned during this performance, and the hearts of these sturdy men beat fast as each glanced at his paper to see what it contained. Jake Purdy was one of the last to approach, and, thrusting in a huge, hairy hand, jerked forth his piece, and as he looked upon it his face turned pale, though he said not a word as he held up the slip for all to see the fatal X scrawled upon it. At that instant Tony Stickles started forward, and confronted Jake. His eyes were wide with excitement, and his long, lank figure was drawn up to its full height.

"You mustn't go!" he cried. "No, no! You've got six little ones at home, an' a wife who wants ye. I'll go in yer place."

Big Jake looked at Tony in surprise, and into his strong, determined face came an expression of tenderness which the men had never seen before.

"No, lad," he replied, "it can't be. The lot's fallen to me, an' I'm the one to do it. I thank ye kindly all the same."

Tony waited to hear no more. His eyes glanced upon an axe lying near. Springing towards this he seized it, and before a restraining hand could be laid upon him he bounded towards the Gorge, sprang down the bank and leaped upon the logs.

Big Jake rushed after him, calling and imploring him to come back. But his cries were unheeded. Tony was now between the rocky walls, working his way over those tossed and twisted monsters, deaf to all entreaties from the shore.

"Come back, Jake!" roared the men from behind. "It's no use for you to go now. He's taken the matter into his own hands, an' one's enough."

Reluctantly he obeyed, and stood with the rest watching with breathless interest to see what would happen.

Tony had now reached the front of the jam, and was carefully picking his way to the gripping key log. Balancing himself as well as he could he chose a spot where the strain was the greatest. Then the axe cleaved the air, the keen blade bit the wood, and the whirling chips played about his head. Deeper and deeper the steel ate into the side of the giant spruce. Suddenly a report like a cannon split the air, the axe was hurled like a rocket out into midstream to sink with a splash into the foaming eddies. Tony turned, leaped like lightning back upon the main body of logs, and started for the shore. But he was too late. With a roar of pent-up wrath the mighty drive moved forward. Down through the Gorge it surged, gaining in speed every instant from the terrible pressure behind. And down with it went Tony, enwrapped with foam and spray. Nobly he kept his feet. He leaped from one log to another. He dodged monster after monster, which rose on end and threatened to strike him down. It was a wild race with death. Should he miss his footing or lose his head only for an instant he would have been ground to pieces in that rush of doom. The watching men stood as if transfixed to the spot. They saw him speeding onward and drawing nearer to the shore at the sharp bend in the stream. It looked as if he would gain the bank, and a cheer of encouragement rang out over the waters. But the words had scarcely died upon their lips ere they beheld the logs part asunder right beneath Tony's feet, and with a wild cry he plunged into the rushing current below. Frantically he clutched at the nearest logs, and endeavoured to pull himself up from that watery grave. At times he managed to draw himself part way out, but the swirling waters sucked him down. It needed only a little help, but the logs were wet and slippery, and there was nothing on which to obtain a firm grip. His body was becoming numb from the icy waters, and at each terrible struggle he felt himself growing weaker. He knew he could last but little longer in such a position. Was he to drown there? His thoughts flashed to his little home in Glendow. Were they thinking of him? he wondered. What would his mother say when they carried her the news? Oh, if he could only feel her strong hand in his now, how soon he would be lifted from that awful place. Suddenly there came into his mind her parting words when he had left home.

"Tony," she had said, "ye may be often in danger out thar in the woods. But remember what the good Lord said, 'Call upon me in the day of trouble an' I will deliver ye.'"

And there in the midst of that swirling death he lifted up his voice. "Oh, Lord!" he cried, "help me! save me!"

And even as he prayed, and made one more mighty struggle, a small hand reached out and grasped his. It was all that was needed. He felt the watery grip loosen, and numbed to the bone he sprawled his full length across a big log at Dan's feet. And not a moment too soon had that helping hand been stretched forth, for glancing back he saw the logs had closed again, grinding and tearing as before. They had struck a wild eddy and all was confusion. He staggered to his feet at the shock and barely escaped a huge log which suddenly shot up from below. But Dan was not so fortunate, for a glancing blow sent him reeling back, a helpless, pathetic little figure. Tony was all alert now. Leaping forward he caught the unconscious boy in his arms, and started for the shore. Then began a fierce, determined fight, a hand-to-hand encounter with cold, relentless death. Step by step Tony staggered forward, baffled here, retreating a few paces there, but steadily gaining. At first he did not mind Dan's weight, but after a few minutes the burden began to tell. He was weak anyway from the terrible strain and experience through which he had recently passed. Could he hold out until he reached the shore? His face was drawn and tense; his eyes stared wildly upon those rolling, moving, writhing things beneath his feet. They seemed like thousands of serpents trying to capture him as he leaped from one to the other. His brain reeled; he was falling, but at that moment he felt strong arms about him. His burden was snatched away. He heard voices, friendly, encouraging and cheering, and then, oblivion.

When Tony opened his eyes he found himself lying upon the shore with several men standing near, watching him with keen interest. There was no merriment or ridicule in their faces now, but only anxiety and sympathy. The hearts of these rough men

H. A. Cody

had been touched by what they had recently witnessed. Most of them were with the drive, but a few had been told off to look after the two lads.

"Where's that boy?" asked Tony as the terrible scene flashed back into his mind.

"Over there," replied one, jerking his thumb to the left.

"Is he all right?" was Tony's next query.

"Can't say. He's not come to yet."

At this Tony struggled to his feet, and walked slowly over to where Dan was lying, unconscious still, and breathing hard.

"Who is he? Where did he come from?" were the questions which these men asked one another as they rubbed Dan's body, and bathed his forehead.

Something white sticking from a little pocket in Dan's coat caught Tony's eye. Reaching down he drew it forth, and as he did so the little crushed rose dropped to the ground. One of the men picked it up and holding it in his big, rough hand looked curiously upon it. But Tony did not notice the flower, for his eyes were fixed upon the paper on which he saw his own name. Slowly and with difficulty he spelled out the queer letters scrawled there.

"deR toNy," so the missive began. "cUm hoM qiK they say paRson John sTol ol bilees goLD i tHINK yoU nO weR IT ISS

"yeR friEND TruLEE

"*Dan.*"

Tony held the letter in his hand for some minutes and stared at those quaint words. He had heard from his mother of the death of old Billy and the burning of his house. But of the trouble later he knew nothing, for letters from home had been few. Now a new light dawned upon his mind. Something must be wrong, and this lad had come all the way for him! But who was Dan? He had never seen nor heard of him before.

"As he stood there Big Sam drew near. He started with surprise as he saw the boy lying on the ground, his little pale face resting upon a rough coat.

"What! what's this?" he exclaimed. "Why, this is the boy who came with me to-day! Has he fallen into the stream? I warned him to be careful."

"Poor boy! poor boy!" he remarked when the story of the brave deed had been related. "Do you think he's badly hurt?"

"Can't say," replied one. "But do ye know who he is?"

"Yes," and Big Sam in a few words told all that he knew.

"We must get him away from this as soon as possible," said the former speaker. "He needs the doctor. Where had we better take him?"

"Look here, boys," said Sam after a moment's thought. "As soon as those horses have munched their oats they shall head for home. I'll take the boy with me, and my wife will care for him. The doctor lives near."

Tony stood by listening to it all with his eyes fixed intently upon Dan's face, while his hand still clutched the letter. He was weak, and ready to drop. But a burning desire throbbed within his breast. He partly realized the situation at Glendow. There was trouble, deep, serious trouble, and he was needed.

Chapter XXV

Beneath the Ashes

Far away in the West the sun was sinking low as Stephen Frenelle stood on the shore looking out over his newly rafted logs. Not a ripple disturbed the surface of the noble river, or the waters of the little creek lying between its semi-wooded banks. It was a balmy spring evening when the whole world seemed at peace. On a night such as this new longings and aspirations swell the heart, and the blood tingles joyfully through the body. Stephen had remained after the rest of the men had gone home. He wished to examine the logs to see that the work was well done. As he now stood on the shore his thoughts were not upon the glassy river or Nature's loveliness. His mind was disturbed. All through the winter he had been looking forward to the time when the logs would be floating there secured by their wooden bonds. He had planned to have Nellie come to see the completion of his work. He knew how she would rejoice at what he had accomplished, and in his mind he had heard her words of congratulation. But now all was changed. The work was done, but Nellie was not there to behold his victory. How lonely seemed the parish since her departure. He had thrown himself with great energy into his task, and the days had sped by. But, try as he might, he could not free himself from the weight which

H. A. Cody

pressed upon his heart. Everything in the parish moved on as before. The new clergyman came, and service had been held in the church as usual. Many spoke favourably of the new man. He was young, full of spirit, and a clear, forcible speaker. But to Stephen it was not the same as formerly. He missed the white-haired, venerable man in his accustomed place. The moment he entered the church his eyes sought the seat where Nellie always sat. It was empty. That form so dear to him was not there. He saw her Prayer Book and Hymn Book in the little rack, and a lump came into his throat, as he knew they would not be used.

He thought of these things, standing there on the shore. His tall, manly figure was drawn to its full height. He gazed straight before. It was a far-off vision he beheld, and suddenly there came into his heart a peace such as he had not known since she left. She seemed to be very near, standing right by his side. He saw her face, beheld her eyes looking into his, and heard her voice bidding him to be of good cheer, and to look up.

A sound near by startled him. He glanced quickly around, half expecting to see Nellie standing there. Instead, however, he beheld the tall, lank form of Tony Stickles approaching. His face was gaunt, his step weak and slow. But Stephen did not notice these, so surprised was he to see him.

"Tony!" he exclaimed, reaching out his hand, "where did you drop from? I thought you were on the big drive."

"So I was, Steve," Tony replied, taking a seat upon a large boulder.

"Didn't get fired, eh?"

To this Tony made no response. He looked thoughtfully before him for a while.

"Say, Steve," he at length remarked. "How's Parson John?"

"He's gone, Tony. Driven from Glendow."

"What!" and Tony sprang to his feet in excitement. "When did he leave?"

"Last week."

"Then I'm too late! I was afraid of it! But I came fast - I ran sometimes; but it was no use. Is he in the lockup?"

"In the lockup! What do you mean?" and Stephen stared at him in amazement.

From the depth of a capacious pocket Tony brought forth Dan's soiled letter, and held it up.

"Read that," he said. "It's all I know."

Quickly Stephen scanned the quaint words, drinking in almost intuitively the meaning of it all.

"Did Dan give you this?" he demanded.

"Yes."

"And where is the boy now?"

Tony's eyes dropped at the question, and he did not answer.

"Is anything wrong?" Stephen insisted.

"Yes, I'm afraid so. But set down close, Steve. I've somethin' great to tell ye."

And sitting there in the dusk of even Tony poured into his companion's ears the story of that terrible scene in Giant Gorge, and of Dan's brave deed.

Stephen listened spell-bound to the tale. The meaning of Dan's departure was all clear now. While people had been blaming the lad as an ungrateful runaway he had fared forth in loving service on behalf of his guardians. A mistiness blurred Stephen's eyes as Tony paused.

"Where is Dan now?" he asked.

"At Big Sam's house. We brought 'im down on the waggon, an' I helped carry 'im in."

"Who is Big Sam?"

"Oh, he's the teamster. The booms are near his place whar the raftin' will be done. Sam hauls the stuff fer the gang."

"And you don't know how badly Dan is hurt?"

"No, I came away at once. I wanted to help the old parson. An' say, Steve, did they find the gold?"

"Find it? No. And I don't think they will now. It's a great mystery."

"An' they say the parson took it?"

"Yes, some do."

"An' didn't they find the iron box?"

"No."

"Did they look beneath the ashes?"

"They searched every nook and corner, and even sifted the ashes, but could find nothing."

"An' didn't Billy say nuthin'?"

"No, he was too weak. He tried to speak after the parson had carried him out, but no one could understand him."

Tony did not speak for a while, but remained lost in thought.

"Steve," he at length remarked. "I'd like to go to that old place. Will ye go with me?"

"What! to-night?"

"Yes, right away."

"It will be dark there now, Tony. Why not wait until morning?"

"No, no. I must go to-night. We kin git a lantern, an' I want a shovel, too. Will ye come?

"Yes, if you want me," was Stephen's reluctant reply.

"But you might as well save yourself the trouble. The place has been so thoroughly searched by daylight that I don't see we can do much at night. Anyway, I shall go with you."

Together they moved on their way up the road, Stephen carrying his peevy upon his shoulder. As they came to the store he stopped.

"Wait here, Tony," he said, "till I run in and get the mail. I shall be only a minute."

Entering the building he found Farrington sitting behind the counter writing. He looked up as Stephen entered, and laid down his pen. He was affable to all now, for election day was but a week off, and he needed every vote.

"Raftin' all done, Steve?" he asked as he handed out the mail.

"Yes, all finished," was the reply.

"Ye'll be to the p'litical meetin' to-night, Steve, won't ye?"

"Oh, I had forgotten all about it."

"But ye must come. I want ye to hear what I hev to say. Gadsby'll be thar, an' I've got a dose fer 'im which he won't soon fergit. I'll show 'im a thing or two, an' the people'll learn that they need a real, live practical man for councillor. Ye must certainly come."

"I'm not sure that I can come," Stephen replied. "I have an engagement to-night. I may be there, however, if I can get through in time. But I must be off now; Tony's waiting for me."

At these last words Farrington started, and an expression of concern swept over his face. He leaned anxiously forward and looked intently at Stephen.

"Did ye say that Tony Stickles is out thar?"

"Yes. He has just arrived."

"Why, w - what's he back so soon fer?"

"Special business, so he tells me. But I must be off."

Stephen noted Farrington's remarkable interest in Tony's return, and wondered what it meant. He had no mind to tell him about Dan, for he preferred to have as few words as possible with this man who was such a thorn in the flesh. He left Farrington standing in the door and proceeded with Tony up the road. As they moved along he noticed how his companion lagged behind. Usually he was such a rapid walker, and this slowness was a surprise to Stephen.

"Are you not well, Tony?" he asked.

"I'm all right," was the reply. "I've had a long walk to-day."

"Since when?"

"Daybreak."

"And did you rest?"

"No."

"Look here," and Stephen faced sharply about "Have you had anything to eat to-day?"

Tony's face flushed, and he gave a slight, evasive laugh. But Stephen was not to be put off.

"No, that won't do. I want to know. Have you been walking all day without any food?"

"Oh, I didn't mind, Steve. I was in a hurry to get home. Besides I - "

"Yes, I know," interrupted Stephen. "You didn't have your pay, and were too proud to beg. Oh, you're a great one. But you shall have supper with me at once before you go digging among those ashes."

For a while Tony was stubborn, but in the end Stephen led him off in triumph. Supper was ready, and Mrs. Frenelle gave the visitor a hearty welcome, and in his own quaint way he told of his work in the woods, and his experience on the drive.

"I feel like a new man," he said, rising from the table. "I was about tuckered out. Now I'm ready fer that bizness up yon. Guess we'll turn up somethin' tonight, or my name ain't Tony Stickles."

It was quite dark by the time they reached the ruins of the old house. The lantern threw its fitful light over the charred sticks and blackened stones.

"My! this is a scary place!" Tony exclaimed as he glanced around. "Poor old Billy was good to me, an' many a square meal I've had here. Now let's begin operations."

The wreck of the old-fashioned chimney stood out gaunt and desolate, while the large fire-place was filled with sticks and stones. These Tony began to clear away, tossing them far from the foundation. Placing the lantern in a secure position, Stephen assisted him in his task. Why he did so he could not tell, but there was something so sure and masterful about Tony's words and actions that he felt compelled to do something.

"Now fer the shovel, Steve. We'll soon see what's here," and Tony began to dig up ashes and earth in a lively manner. "I think this is the place. Yes, right down under the big hearth-stone, a little to the right. He told me about it time an' time agin. Poor Billy! Poor Billy! Ye never thought it 'ud come to this."

Stephen was all attention now. He watched Tony, digging and talking, uncertain whether the lad was really in his right mind. Had the fearful experience in Giant Gorge turned his brain? he wondered. He had read of such things. There was something uncanny about the way Tony talked to himself, and, brave though he was, a strange feeling crept through Stephen's body, making him long to be away from the spot. And still the digging went on, down through the yielding soil.

"Should be here purty close," Tony remarked. "Under the hearth-stone, well to the right. I ought to be near - Hello! what's this?"

The exclamation was caused by the point of the shovel striking something hard. Again and again the thrust was made, and each time a hollow sound was produced.

"It's it! It's it!" shouted Tony, now much excited. "I knowed it was here," and he dug away frantically, until presently an iron box about a foot long and six inches wide was exposed to view. Throwing aside the shovel, he seized the treasure with both hands, tore it from its hiding-place and held it aloft.

"Look, Steve!" he cried, trembling with excitement, "I knowed thar was somethin' here!"

Stephen was now as much aroused as Tony. "What's in it, do you think?" he asked.

"Gold! that's what's in it! Ye'll soon see," and Tony pulled back a little iron pin and threw up the cover. As he did so he gave a cry of surprise, for the light falling upon the interior showed nothing there but a few pieces of paper. Tony rubbed his eyes in amazement, and then looked at Stephen.

"Whar's that gold?" he fiercely demanded. "What has become of it?"

Stephen scarcely heard him, for a terrible idea had flashed into his mind. Someone had taken it, and was it - ? He hardly dare let the name beat for an instant through his brain. It was cruel. No, no, it could not be! That white-haired man of God would not stoop to such a thing! But where was the gold?

The moon rose clear and full above the distant horizon. It seemed to ask silently the same question. A dog from a farm-house up the road split the air with its hoarse bark of wonder. Stephen placed his hand to his forehead in an abstracted manner. Then he glanced at the box, and the papers lying therein arrested his attention. He reached down and took them in his hand. They were tied with an old piece of tarred twine, and were much blackened and soiled. Drawing forth the first and holding it close to the lantern, Stephen read the brief words recorded there. It took him but a minute to do this, and then followed an exclamation which gave Tony a distinct start.

"What is it, Steve?" he asked. "What hev ye found?"

"Read this, and judge for yourself," Stephen replied, thrusting the paper into his companion's hands.

As Tony spelled out the words his eyes bulged with astonishment.

"Oh, Steve!" he gasped, "I'm so glad it isn't the parson. But do ye think this is all right?"

"It. looks like it. See the date, November 10th of last year. And notice, too, these words 'for safe keeping' and 'until called for.' Why, it's as plain as day. Then, here's the amount, 'five thousand dollars, all in gold, to be left in the iron box marked with a cross in white paint.'"

"Say, Tony," Stephen asked, "did Billy have such a box, another one like this?"

"Why, yes, I do remember one very well. It was smaller than this; 'twas stouter an' had a lock an' key. He kept some papers an' loose change in it. It allus sot on the old mantel-piece over the fire-place."

"Tony!" said Stephen, looking hard at the paper, "if that box of gold is there yet, and that man has been silent and let another take the blame, it's the smallest, vilest piece of work of which I ever heard."

"Sure 'tis, an' I say let's go an' ax 'im 'bout it."

"But he's at the meeting now."

"Well, all the better. It's right that the people should hear. But say, Steve, what's that other paper?"

"Oh, I forgot it. Maybe it will explain things further."

"Why, it's Billy's will!" cried Stephen, running his eyes over the closely written sheets, "and he's left the whole of his property, gold, farm and all, to you."

"To me! To me!" exclaimed Tony. "Ye must be mistaken."

"Read it for yourself, then," and Stephen passed over the will. "It's all there in black and white."

As Tony read, his face flushed, and his hands clutched the paper in the intensity of his feelings. His eyes flashed as he turned them hard upon Stephen.

"I understand now!" he cried. "That villain has tried to cheat me outer all this. He thought the will an' every-thin' else was burned. But he was mistaken. Oh, yes, he didn't know what was beneath the ashes. Come, Steve, let's go an' ax 'im a few questions. Mebbe he'll explain things. Anyway we'll give 'im a chance. Come, let's hurry!"

Chapter XXVI

A Rope of Sand

Silas Farrington was much disturbed by Tony Stickles' arrival in Glendow. He had always laughed at the lad, considering him a stupid, ungainly creature. Occasionally he had overtaken Tony on the road trudging wearily along, but it had never occurred to him to offer him a seat in his waggon or sleigh.

"It spiles sich people," he had often said, "to take too much notice of 'em. They have a sartin place in life, an' should be made to keep it." But standing in the store that evening after Stephen's departure, the despised Tony occupied an important place in his mind. He would have laughed to scorn anyone who had suggested such a thing. But down deep in his heart, small and narrow though it was, dwelt considerable unrest. "What had the lad come back for?" he asked himself over and over again. "What was the special business which brought him so unexpectedly? Did he know anything?" Harrington's face twitched as he thought of these things. He strode up and down in the store. Once he paused before the safe standing in the corner, and looked long and thoughtfully upon it. A muttered curse escaped his lips. This was succeeded by a scornful laugh. "What a fool I am!" he exclaimed, "to worry about sich things! What is thar to find out? Let 'em do their best and be damned! We'll see who holds the stoutest and longest rope. That Steve Frenelle's a cur, an' I hate 'im. He's jist the one to stir up trouble. I've suspected 'im all along. He knows too much fer one of his age. Wait 'till I'm councillor, an' then I'll show 'im a thing or two." Waggons rattling along the road startled him. He glanced at his watch. "My! I didn't know 'twas so late; almost time for the meetin'. I must git ready."

The big public hall of Glendow was packed to the door. People came from all over the parish to this political meeting, for lively scenes were expected. The two candidates opposed to each other were to be there to discuss various problems of local interest. On the front seat sat Mrs. Farrington, Eudora and Dick.

Philip Gadsby was the first speaker. He was a man tall and somewhat thin, with a kind, thoughtful face. His voice was soft, well modulated, and his words carefully chosen. There was nothing of the orator about him, in fact his speech was somewhat of a hesitating nature. But he was possessed of a convincing manner, and all who were there knew they were listening to a man who was more than his words, and that what he said he would endeavour to accomplish to the best of his ability. He spoke about the needs of the parish, better roads, improvement of the schools, and the efforts which should be made to form an agricultural society in Glendow, which was essentially a farming community.

"Our watchword," he said in conclusion, "should be progress. Look at our roads. Money is spent upon them every season, but not in an intelligent way. We find men at times appointed roadmasters who seldom drive over the highway. Mud and sods are heaped up in the centre in a confused fashion, late in the fall. Let us do less, do it well, and use more gravel. Look at our schools. The buildings are old, ill equipped, and sometimes fifty to sixty children are crowded into one room fitted only to accommodate twenty, and one teacher to manage all. And we do need an agricultural society. We are farmers. We need to read, study, meet together and hear addresses from experts. New methods are employed elsewhere, while we are behind the times. Yes, we must advance. I have the welfare of the parish at heart, and whether elected or not I shall still take my part in the forward movement."

Often during the speech Gadsby was greeted with cheers and clapping, for those present realized the effectiveness of what he said, and he sat down amid great applause.

It was then that Farrington rose to his feet and mounted the platform. He had listened to Gadsby's speech with amused tolerance, and occasionally whispered something to his wife sitting by his side. He was a man possessed of an abundance of words, and he turned his attention at once upon the first speaker. Gadsby had made no personal allusion to his opponent. He simply stated his case and ceased. But not so Farrington. From the first word he uttered he began to pour forth contempt and ridicule. He laughed at Gadsby's ideas of progress.

"I think we're purty well advanced," he shouted. "The schools an' roads are good enough fer me. Progress means more money, an' more money means bigger taxes. The children of Glendow are well supplied, an' as fer the roads they're good enough. As fer an agricultural society - well," and here he cast a significant look at Gadsby, "them who talk sich things had better look at their own farms. Before I go out shoutin' about progress I had better be sure that my own bizness is on a good footin'. I generally find that sich people spend too much time gaddin' about instid of attendin' to their own home affairs."

And thus Farrington talked for over an hour. He wandered off into all kinds of subjects, made jokes at which the boys laughed, and told funny stories. He imagined he was putting his hearers in good humour, and he took their cheers and stamping as signs of approval. But he little knew what the serious-minded were thinking about. They were slow of speech, but they were keen observers, and they were mentally comparing the two candidates before them. Farrington knew nothing of this. He was in a rollicking, fine humour. He felt pleased with the people for their apparent approval, but more pleased with himself for the speech he was making. "I'm real glad to see so many of yez here," he said in conclusion. "I think nearly all the voters are present, at any rate every family is represented. Now if any of yez would like to ax a question I shall be glad fer 'im to do so. I take it that the meetin' is open fer free discussion."

"Guess I've made a hit," Farrington whispered to his wife as he resumed his seat by her side. "The people know a good thing when they find it."

"Ye done well, Si," was the reply. "I'm sartinly proud of ye. Thar's no doubt now about yer election."

The clapping and stamping had not ceased ere a man was noticed pushing his way through the crowd to the front of the hall. As he mounted the platform the noise suddenly stopped, for all were much surprised to see Stephen Frenelle standing there. Never before had he been known to do such a thing, especially at a political meeting. What could he have to say? All wondered. And Stephen, too, was surprised. He was not accustomed to public speaking, and shrank from the thought of facing so many people. But he was very calm now, and in his eyes flashed a light which bespoke danger. In his right hand he clutched several papers, which all noted. He looked steadily over the heads of the people before speaking, and an almost breathless silence ensued.

"You wonder why I am here," he began at length. "I am not used to the platform, and only a matter of great importance would ever make me mount it. The last speaker has given permission for all to ask questions. He has said that nearly all the voters are here, and that every family is represented. I will tell you of one voter who is not here, one who on an occasion like this was generally present. I need hardly mention his name, for you all know. I now ask why isn't Parson John with us to-night?" He paused as if for an answer, and looked into the faces before him. "You all know," he continued, "as well as I do. Because he was actually driven from the parish. He left it almost a heart-broken man."

At these words, Farrington sprang to his feet.

"What has all this nonsense to do with the election?" he cried. "He's out of order, an' I appeal to the chairman to stop 'im."

"Hear! hear!" yelled several. "Go ahead, Steve!"

shouted others.

"Yes, I intend to go ahead," replied the latter. "You will find out, Mr. Farrington, before I am through the meaning of my words, and perhaps I will not be the only one out of order. It's more likely to be disorder.

"I was asking the question when I was interrupted, 'Why was Parson John driven from the parish?' Because of vile stories which were circulated about him. And what were those stories? You know as well as I do. I need not mention them all; of one only shall I speak. When old Billy Fletcher's house was burned to the ground, and the gold which he was supposed to have could not be found, what did some say? That Parson John took it. Yes, that's what they said, and you all know it. I've heard it ever since then. His friends knew it was a lie, but what could they say? What proof could they bring forward? I now ask you what became of that gold? It is a secret no longer. The witness is here," and Stephen held the papers aloft. The silence which now pervaded the hall was most intense. Every ear was strained to its utmost, and every eye was fixed full upon that up-lifted hand.

"Here is my witness," repeated Stephen, "and I ask the man, the last speaker, whose name is signed to this paper, to stand up and give us an explanation."

During the latter part of this speech, Farrington had turned as white as death. He sat bolt upright, with his hands clutching convulsively the edge of the seat. He felt that something terrible was pending, and a horrible, craven fear overwhelmed him! He knew that paper held up there only too well. It was simply a sheet of cheap writing-paper, and yet it was his ruin. It was damning him as a scoundrel and a sneak in the presence of these people!

"Cannot the last speaker explain how his name happens to be here and what he knows about that gold?"

These words fell like the knell of doom upon Farrington's ears. What was he to do? But something must be done.

"What d'ye mean?" he gasped. "What d'ye want me to explain?"

"About this writing."

"What writin', an' whar did ye git any writin' of mine? It's some mean trick!" he shouted, jumping to his feet. "This villain has come here fer the purpose of injurin' me! I tell ye it's false! it's false!"

"But what about this?" Stephen insisted, calmly holding up one of the papers. "And there are others."

"What is it? What is it? Read it, Steve," came the cry from the audience.

"I say it's false!" shouted Farrington, springing again to his feet, his face blanched with terror. "It's a mean trick! Put the villain out! Will ye let an honest man be put upon in this way?"

"Read the paper, Steve," urged several. "Let's know what's the matter. We don't understand this fuss."

Farrington made a pathetic figure as he stood there

uncertain what to do. He knew he was in a trap, but he had not the moral courage to stand up and face the worst like a man. Had he done so there were many who would have pitied him. But he blustered and raved and threatened what he would do.

"If that man will be still for a few minutes," said Stephen, "I shall tell you what these papers contain."

"Sit down, Farrington!" came a general yell. "We'll hear you later."

"Now," began Stephen. "I shall read this one first. It is not long.

"'To-day October 30, 18 - I placed the sum of $5,000 in gold in Silas Farrington's safe for him to keep until called for. The money is locked in a stout, iron box marked with a cross with white paint. I do not like banks - they are not to be depended upon, and are always failing. This seems to be the best place to put my money. I am to give Mr. Farrington one dollar a month for the use of the safe. 'WILLIAM FLETCHER.'"

As Stephen finished the reading, a movement took place among the people and angry, threatening words were interchanged.

"It's a lie!" yelled Farrington. "It's made up to ruin me! Will ye believe sich a story?"

"Just wait a minute," continued Stephen, holding forth another small piece of paper. Here is further evidence which might be of some service. Listen to this.

"'Glendow, Friday, Oct. 30th, 18 - Received from William Fletcher, the sum of $5,000 in gold, in an iron box, to be kept for him in trust in my safe until called for, he promising to pay me one dollar a month for the use of my safe. 'SILAS FARRINGTON.'"

An intense silence now reigned in the hall. All were waiting to see what would happen next. It was the calm before the storm. The people were more than surprised, they were dumfounded at this sudden turn of events. The purpose of the meeting was forgotten. Then one wild cry went up. There was confusion everywhere, all talking and shouting at once. At this the chairman rose to his feet, and held up his hand for peace. Gradually the commotion subsided, and all waited to hear what he had to say.

"We are much astonished at what has happened," he began. "It is a very serious matter. These papers are of a most damaging nature to one of the candidates here to-night. He has emphatically denied the statements made therein. But we demand further proof. Let him now come forward and speak. Perhaps he can explain matters fully."

"Hear! Hear!" came from every part of the building.

Half dazed and trembling, Farrington staggered forward, and grasped the back of a chair for support.

"It's a lie, I tell ye!" he shouted. "But I want to ax one question. Whar did them papers come from? Ye all know very well that everything was burned which old Billy had in the house. Not a scrap of anything was left, and how did them papers escape? That's proof enough to show what a mean trick has been played upon me. I am the one to ax fer an explanation."

"That shall be granted at once," Stephen replied, and in a few words he told of Tony Stickles' arrival, their search beneath the large hearth-stone, and the discovery of the iron box containing the valuable papers.

"Tony is here," said Stephen in conclusion, "and if you do not believe me, ask him."

But there was no need for Tony's witness. The evidence was already strong enough, and the people were aroused.

"Mr. Farrington," said the chairman, motioning the audience to be quiet. "If you have that gold in your safe, it will save considerable trouble if you produce it at once. If it is there and you have kept silence and allowed that man of God to suffer, you deserve the severest punishment. Is it the wish of the people here that the safe should be opened?"

"Ay, ay!" came like a roar of thunder.

"Ye can't do it!" yelled Farrington, rising to his feet. "It's my private property, an' I defy anyone to touch my safe."

"Oh, we'll not touch it," the chairman coolly remarked. "We'll not lay hands on it. All we ask you to do is to throw open the door and show us what's inside."

"It ain't lawful, I say," shouted the desperate man.

"Maybe it isn't lawful. But we'll attend to that, I

reckon. Sometimes people take the law into their own hands, and I guess that's what we'll do to-night. In my opinion there's not a judge or a jury in the whole land but would support our action. Come now, you'd better do as we desire at once."

Farrington, excited though he was, found it necessary to do some rapid thinking. He knew he could not delay that angry assembly much longer. One hope only remained, and upon this he acted.

"Very well," he replied, "I might as well go at once. Come when you like, you kin examine everything in the safe. I'm not afeer'd fer ye to look."

He took a step or two forward with the intention of leaving.

"Wait a minute," said the chairman. "Don't be in too big a hurry. We'll go along with you. It's always good to have company on such occasions."

"I don't want anyone," snapped Farrington, turning angrily upon him.

"No, I know you don't. But we're not considering your feelings just now."

"Then, I'll not go! Do what you like with me!" and Farrington sank back upon the seat, a pitiable bundle of wretched humanity.

Chapter XXVII

In the Toils

During the whole of this excitement, Mrs. Farrington had remained motionless, striving to comprehend the meaning of it all. At first a great rage filled her heart at the thought of Stephen Frenelle talking in such a way to her husband. But when the papers had been read her anger was changed to fear, which was much increased by Farrington's excited condition. She realized that he was placed in an unenviable position, but thought not so much of the meanness of his deed as of what the neighbours would say. How could she ever hold up her head again? she wondered. How the women would talk! And then to think that Si was in danger of losing the election, all on account of this Stephen Frenelle. What business had he to interfere? It was no concern of his. She watched everything which took place, and listened eagerly to each word. She heard the chairman ordering her husband to wait until several went with him to search his safe. Then when she had seen him sink upon the seat at her side, she gave one cry and fell prostrate upon the floor.

At once several people sprang forward, and strong arms bore her through the crowd into the open air.

Farrington hardly noticed what was taking place. He

sat huddled upon the seat where he had dropped, helpless and full of despair.

"Come, Mr. Farrington" - it was the chairman's voice - "we must get through with this business, and we are determined to get through with it to-night. Will you go quietly and open that safe, or must we carry you there?"

No answer coming from the wretched man, the chairman continued: "Very well, then, men, there's only one thing left - and what's your wish?"

"Drag him there," was the shout, and a yell of derision arose whilst a number of sturdy forms rushed forward. The people were wildly excited now. They realized the nature of the trick which had been imposed upon an innocent man. Had the money been merely stolen, or had Farrington committed forgery, they would have let the law take its course. But in this case the vile meanness of the deed, the criminal silence of months, stirred their hearts, inflamed their passions, and carried them beyond the bounds of reason.

"Let me alone!" yelled Farrington, as a dozen hands were laid upon him.

"Will you come, then?"

"Y-y - es," was the quaking reply.

"Well, hurry up about it," and as the wretched man started for the door, he was rushed forward by the crowd which surged about him. Hatless and almost breathless, with wild staring eyes, Farrington staggered along the road. The store was reached.

"Unlock the door," was the command, "and make haste about it."

This was soon done and the crowd pressed into the building.

"Now open the safe!" the chairman demanded, "and show us what's there."

But just here Farrington, terrified though he was, hesitated. Like the man who, about to die on the gallows, cherishes hope of deliverance almost to the last, so did he. Perhaps his friends would interfere to save him from the ignominy. But alas! his former boon companions, Tom Fletcher and his gang, were nowhere to be seen. They had quietly slunk away, fearful for their own safety from the infuriated people. Now that safe door stood only between Farrington and eternal disgrace. It was no wonder that he paused. How could he do it? The perspiration stood in great beads upon his forehead, and his knees would hardly support his body.

"I can't!" he gasped, looking imploringly around.

A yell was the only response to his appeal.

"Boys," cried the chairman, when the confusion had subsided, "there's a coil of new rope over there in the corner, and a stout tree stands outside. Suppose we give him his choice. He can either open the safe or go up to the first limb."

"Hear, hear!" was the reply, and a rush was made for the rope, a long piece cut off and a loop formed. The chairman had no idea of carrying out the latter design, and he knew very well that such an extreme measure would not be needed. It was simply a ruse to get the safe open. And in this he was right. When Farrington heard their terrible words, and saw the noose made ready, with a groan he sank upon his knees before the safe. With trembling hands he turned the steel disk, but somehow the combination would not work. Again and again he tried, the people becoming more and more impatient. They believed he was only mocking them, while in reality he was so confused that he hardly knew what he was doing. But at length the right turn was made and the heavy door swung open upon its iron hinges.

"Bring out the stuff," demanded the chairman.

One by one the articles were brought forward, and last of all from a back corner Farrington slowly dragged forth an iron box with a white cross mark upon it.

A shout of triumph rose from those who first beheld it, and then yells of derision.

"Order!" commanded the chairman.

"Is that Billy Fletcher's box?"

"Y-y-es."

"And you knew it was there all the time, and let Parson John get the blame for stealing it?"

"Y-y - es. B-b - ut fer God's sake have mercy! I - I - didn't mean to do it! I was o-only j-j - okin'! I intended to ex-p-plain everything."

There was an ominous movement among the

bystanders, and those in the rear did some excited talking, while several left the building. Presently the sound of heavy blows was heard in the store-room adjoining the shop. Then a rush of feet ensued, and Farrington was suddenly caught and hurried forward. The light of a small lamp shed its feeble beams over the place, making it look more ghostly than ever. The intentions of his captors flashed into Farrington's mind. Standing there was a large cask of tar used for boats and the roofs of houses. The head had been smashed in, and the odour was pouring forth.

"Fer God's sake not that!" shrieked the wretched man. "Oh, help, help! Murder!"

But his cries were all in vain. Rough hands were laid upon him, his clothes were hurriedly ripped off, and he was lifted bodily, and lowered feet first into the black, slimy depth. He resisted, but it was useless. He was forced down upon his knees, and the tar covered him to his very ears. Silence reigned now in the room. They were determined men who were handling this nasty job, and with set mouths and intense grimness they watched the victim flounder about and then give up in despair.

When he had been soused and soaked to their satisfaction he was helped out, and with the tar dripping from his body he was led back into the main store. There a large feather-bed was seen spread out upon the floor. It had been ripped open, and into this Farrington was plunged. He yelled and cursed, but to no avail. He was rolled over and over among the yielding feathers, and when at length he was allowed to stand upon his feet he presented the picture of a strange, incongruous bird with the head and feet of a man. No hand touched him now, and he stood there not knowing what to expect.

"Go," cried the chairman pointing to the back door leading into his house, "and the sooner you pull up stakes and leave the parish the better for yourself and family."

As soon as Stephen knew that his services were no longer needed, he stood back and let matters take their course. He followed the crowd to the store to see what would happen. Not until he had seen the box with his own eyes could he be completely satisfied with his evening's work. But when at length the safe was opened and the box exposed to view, he gave a deep sigh of relief. He had waited to see what the men would do with Farrington. He knew that the punishment inflicted was just. Stephen did not believe in the mob spirit, but he realized that the most effective remedy at times was that administered when the people aroused in righteous indignation tarred and feathered the culprit, bestowed the cat-o'-nine-tails or ducked him in the nearest pond. Though not in accordance with the British Constitution it is certainly the most effective way of dealing with some mean, contemptible cases. And Farrington's was one of them. With clever legal counsel he might be able to prove that he was acting within his right in holding the money "until called for," according to the wording of the paper he had signed, while the real motive that prompted him to keep silence might not be considered at all.

Having thus seen Farrington receive his just deserts, Stephen hurried home. A light was burning in the sitting-room which his mother had left for him ere she retired for the night. He threw himself into an armchair

H. A. Cody

and reviewed the exciting scenes of the evening. A weight had been suddenly lifted from his mind, and his heart was filled with thankfulness. He thought of the joy which would shine in Nellie's face when she earned how her father had been cleared of that terrible charge. He longed to see her, to look into her eyes, to clasp her hands and tell her what had so unexpectedly happened. Was she thinking of him? he wondered, and what was she doing? He realized more than ever what she meant to him. Life was unbearable without her sweet, loving presence.

At length, taking the lamp in his hand he sought his own room, but not to sleep. He threw himself upon the bed, clothes and all. But try as he might his eyes would not close. Ever before him rose that white-haired old man, with the weary face, bearing so patiently the burden of injustice. Why should he carry the load any longer? Why should he not know the truth as soon as possible? And how would he know unless someone went at once? Acting upon the thought he sprang from the bed, lighted the lamp and stole softly downstairs. He was about to leave the house, when he paused, and turning back went to a little writing-desk and drew forth a sheet of paper. Taking a pencil from his pocket he wrote a brief message to his mother, and laid it upon the dining-room table, where she would be sure to find it in the morning.

Having accomplished this he left the house and made his way to the barn. His favourite horse was startled from his sleep, and laid back his ears in resentment as the saddle was placed upon his back, and he was led out of the stable. The moon was flooding the whole land with its silver beams as Stephen sprang into the saddle and headed Dexter for the main road. Then the ring of steel-shod hoofs echoed upon the still air as horse and rider sped through the night, on to a little village far away beyond the hills.

H. A. Cody

Chapter XXVIII

Waiting and Serving

"I feel completely side-tracked now. Life moves forward, but here I am a useless burden."

It was Parson John who spoke, as he leaned back in an easy-chair and gazed dreamily out of the window.

Nellie laid down the book she had been reading aloud and looked anxiously at her father. This was the third day they had been at Morristown, and it was the first time her father had uttered any word of complaint. The change had been restful, and he had enjoyed it thoroughly. There had been so many things to see and to talk about with his brother that he hardly missed the separation from Glendow. A sense of glad freedom had been his. There was no responsibility of parish work, and no long, tiresome drives ahead. He need not worry about sermons for the following Sunday, nor feel concerned for any who might be sick. It was a luxury to sit there quietly in the large, airy room with the fresh breath of spring pervading the place, and to watch the trees putting forth their tender leaves and the fields donning their robe of green, yellow and white. Occasionally Nellie read to him from some favourite author, although much of her time was taken up helping her aunt with various household duties. The change which she beheld in her father caused her much joy. "It is just what he needs," she thought. "A good rest will restore him more than anything else." So now on this bright afternoon to hear him complain of being side-tracked, of no use in the world, worried her.

"You must remember, father dear," she replied, "it is well to be side-tracked sometimes. Engines are often laid by for repairs, and I have heard you say that we need rest that mind and body might be strengthened."

"True, very true, Nellie. But I seem to be useless. There are so many things to be done, and but little time in which to do them. When one has been engaged in a work for over thirty years it is not easy to lay it suddenly aside. It becomes part of one's life. Some may think that rest is sitting still and doing nothing. But to me such a thought is terrible. 'Rest,' as a great poet has well said, 'is not quitting life's busy career. Rest is the fitting of self to one's sphere!'"

"Yes, father, but did not blind old Milton say that 'They also serve who only stand and wait.'"

"But how am I serving, Nellie? What is there for me to do here? I sit all day long and think, while others serve me."

"Father," Nellie replied after a brief silence, "I believe a stroll would do you good. You have been staying in the house too much. I have discovered some very pleasant walks out from the village, and, if it will not weary you, suppose we start off now."

Her father looked up quickly at the suggestion.

"Capital!" he exclaimed. "It's just what I need. I am becoming too moody, and the fresh air will revive me."

He was almost like a child now in his eagerness to be off. With his stout cane in one hand, and leaning upon his daughter's arm, he moved slowly along the dry road, through the village and out into the country where the houses were few.

"Oh, this is life, grand, true life!" and he stood for a few minutes looking far away across the broad fields. The air laden with the freshness of spring drifted about them; the birds flitting overhead were pouring forth their joyous music, while on every side early flowers were lifting their tiny heads. All nature seemed to combine to give a glad welcome to these two wayfarers.

At length, coming to a cross road, Nellie paused.

"Look, father," and she pointed to a large tree near by. "What a cool, shady spot! Suppose we rest there for a while, and I will read some from the little book I have brought with me."

Willingly Mr. Westmore conceded to her wish, and soon they were snugly seated on the grassy sward. With his back against the tree, Parson John breathed a sigh of relief as he wiped the perspiration from his forehead with a large, white handkerchief.

So absorbed did they both become in the book that neither noticed the black clouds which had been gathering away to the south, and were now rolling up fearful and threatening beneath the sun. A distant peal of thunder, followed by a bright flash of lightning, startled them.

"A storm is coming!" exclaimed Nellie, springing to her feet. "We must hurry home at once! The road to the right is shorter. I know it quite well; we had better take that."

They had not proceeded far, however, before the peals of thunder became more intense, and soon large drops of rain came spattering down.

"We're in for a heavy storm," panted Mr. Westmore. "It's about to burst upon us. We must seek shelter!"

"There's a house right ahead," Nellie replied. "Perhaps we can get in there."

They plodded on in silence now, and turned in at a little gate none too soon. Scarcely had they entered the small porch in front of the house ere the storm broke. Hail, mingled with rain, came thundering down upon the roof, and, dashing against the glass, threatened to smash in every pane. The thunder crashed and shook the house, while the lightning streaked the air with blinding flashes.

"This is terrible!" exclaimed Nellie, clinging to her father's arm, her face very white. "We must get into the house!"

They knocked upon the door, but received no response. Again they rapped louder than before, and at length a key was slowly turned and a woman, neatly dressed and fair to look upon, peered timidly forth. A relieved look came into her face as she saw the two standing there.

H. A. Cody

"Come in," she said, giving a little nervous laugh. "This fearful storm has quite overcome me."

She led the way into a cosy sitting-room, and offered her visitors chairs.

"You will pardon our intrusion, I am sure," explained Mr. Westmore. "We came simply for shelter. We are much obliged to you."

"Not at all, sir," replied the woman. "I am so glad you came. I am alone with the children, and they are all much frightened."

"And your husband is away?"

"Yes. He's been gone all winter. He was working in the woods for Rodgers & Peterson, and is now on the drive."

"Dear me! it must be hard for you to have him away so much."

"It is, sir. But he will stay home after this. He has earned enough this winter to make the last payment on our farm. We have been struggling for years, saving every cent and working hard to get the place free from debt, and now it will be our very own if - if - ," and the woman hesitated.

"How glad your husband will be to be home," said Nellie, with her eyes fixed upon several bright little faces in the doorway. "He must long to see you all."

"Ay, indeed he does, but especially Doris. She is our invalid girl, you see, and is very dear to us. She can't romp and play like the others, and I suppose for that reason she appeals to us the more."

"Has she been ill long?" questioned Mr. Westmore, becoming now much interested.

"For five years. It's hip disease, and she will never walk without a crutch, if she does then. Perhaps you would like to see her."

They were conducted into a small bedroom, and the sight which met their eyes moved them both. Lying on the bed was a girl of about fifteen years of age, with a sweet, fair face, large, expressive eyes, and a high forehead crowned by a wealth of jet-black hair, parted in the middle and combed back with considerable care. The room was as neat and clean as loving hands could make it. A bright smile illumined the girl's face, which Nellie thought the most beautiful she had ever looked upon.

"It's so good of you to come to see me," she said. "Very few come, and I do get lonely at times."

"You will be glad when your father comes home, will you not?" Nellie remarked, taking the girl's thin, white hand.

"Oh, it will be delightful! He has been away so long. Let me see," and she counted on her fingers. "He has not been home since Christmas."

"But he writes to you, though?"

"Yes, such lovely letters, all about his work. But the last one was so sad. I have cried over it many times. I

H. A. Cody

have it right here. Would you like to read it? It's so interesting."

"Suppose you tell us about it, dear," said Mr. Westmore, taking a chair by the side of the bed. "That will be better."

The girl's face flushed a little, and she hesitated.

"I'm afraid I can't tell it half as well as father does in his letter. You know, the men were bringing the logs down Big Creek Brook, and they all got stuck in a nasty place called Giant Gorge. One big log in some way, I don't understand, stopped the rest, and it had to be cut out. It was a dangerous thing to do, and the men drew lots to see who would go down into that awful place. And just think, papa drew the paper with the mark upon it, which meant that he was to do it! I shudder and cry every time I think about it. Well, as dear papa was about to go, a young man, Tony Stickles, sprang forward and said he would go, because papa had six children and a wife who needed him. Wasn't that lovely of him? I should like to see him. And just think, before papa could stop him he sprang upon the logs, cut away the one which held the rest, and all rushed down right on top of him. Papa said he was sure Tony would be killed, but he jumped from one log to another, and when all thought he would get to the shore, the logs opened and he fell into the water. Then something wonderful happened, so papa said. As Tony was clinging there a boy suddenly came along, jumped upon the logs, ran over them, and pulled Tony out just in time. But a log hit the poor little boy, and Tony had to carry him ashore. Don't you think that's a lovely story, and weren't they both very brave, real heroes like you read about in books? Oh, I lie here hour by hour and think it all over!"

The girl's face was quite flushed now, for she had spoken hurriedly, and her eyes shone brighter than ever. She was living the scene she related.

"What a nice story you have told us," Nellie replied when Doris had finished. "I am glad to hear what a brave deed Tony did, for we both know him."

"What! you know him?" cried the girl.

"Yes, very well. Ever since he was a baby."

"How nice it must be to know a real hero!" sighed the girl. "Please tell me about him."

And there in the little room Nellie told about Tony, his mother, brothers and sisters, to which Doris listened most eagerly.

"We must go now," said Mr. Westmore rising to his feet and looking out of the window. "The storm has cleared and the sun is shining brightly."

"But you will both come again, won't you?" Doris inquired as she held out her hand.

"Yes, if you want us to do so," Nellie replied. "But we don't wish to tire you."

"You won't tire me. I long for someone to talk to, and you know so much."

Parson John had now left the room, and Nellie was holding the girl's hand. She glanced at the door to make sure that her father could not hear, then she bent over the bed.

"Did your father tell you the name of that boy who saved Tony's life?"

"No. He said he didn't know."

"Did he say what he was doing there?"

"No, only he had a funny little letter for Tony. It was in his pocket, and when they opened it a small rose fell out."

"And he didn't say what the letter was about?"

"No."

"Thank you, dear, I must go now," and as Nellie stooped down and gave the girl a kiss, Doris suddenly clasped her arms about her neck.

"I love you! I love you!" she murmured. "You are so beautiful and good! Come soon, will you?"

"Yes, dear, to-morrow, perhaps," and as Nellie left the room her eyes were moist with the tears she found impossible to restrain.

As she walked along the wet road by her father's side her mind was busy thinking over what she had just heard. Who was that boy? He must be a stranger to that place, and what was the letter about? Could it be Dan? How often had she and her father talked about the boy. They believed that he would come back some day. Suddenly there flashed into her mind the persistent efforts Dan had made to write a letter, and how he had time and time again asked her the way to spell certain words. She had thought little about it then, but now she remembered that one of the words was "Tony." Her father looked up in surprise as Nellie paused, and clutched his arm more firmly.

"What's the matter, dear?" he asked. "Are you tired? Perhaps we are walking too fast."

"No, father," and Nellie gave a little laugh. "I was Only thinking, and my thoughts run away with me sometimes. But I am glad we are almost home, for the walking is heavy and our shoes are covered with mud. See that beautiful rainbow, father!"

They both stood still for a few minutes, and looked upon the grand arch spanning the heavens and resting upon earth.

"The bow of promise, Nellie," said Mr. Westmore. "It appears to-day, the same as of old, to remind us all that 'His mercies still endure, ever faithful, ever sure.'"

"Perhaps it's a sign to us, father, that our storm has past, and the sun will break forth again." "It may be true, child. God grant it so," and Mr. Westmore sighed as he turned in at the gate leading to his brother's house.

Chapter XXIX

Rifted Clouds

Again the next day they both visited the invalid girl. Nellie read to her, while Parson John sat and listened. They were becoming firm friends now, and Doris chatted unreservedly.

"I shall tell papa all about you," she said. "I have a letter almost finished, and shall mail it to-night. How I wish you could see him."

All through the day Dan had been much in Nellie's mind. The idea which had come to her the evening before was growing stronger. She believed it was Dan and no other who had rescued Tony. It was just like him, and she thought of the afternoon he had saved her and her cousin on the river. Should she tell her father? That was the question which she debated with herself hour after hour, and when they returned from their visit to Doris, she had not yet decided.

That evening she strolled out of the house, and down the road leading to a little brook. The air was balmy and fresh, and this was her favourite walk. Trees lined the way, stern old oaks, beeches and maples - the grove on her uncle's farm, the place where people came for miles to hold picnics.

As Nellie walked along her thoughts turned often to Glendow. She wondered what Stephen was doing, and if his logs were rafted. She missed him greatly. They had been so much together, had grown up as children, but not until this separation had she fully realized what he meant to her. She thought of the night he had come to tell about Nora and to say good-bye. Her face flushed, and a sweet peace came into her heart as she dwelt upon Stephen's manner that night - his confusion - his stammering words - and the burning kiss upon her hand. She stood on the little bridge now, in the quiet dusk of even, leaning against the railing and looking pensively down into the shallow water below. Suddenly she raised her hand and pressed it again and again to her lips - the same hand which Stephen had kissed.

A step upon the bridge startled her, and her heart beat fast. Had anyone seen what she did? She thought she was alone, but somebody was coming. She turned away her flushed face, and gazed down into the water, leaning her arms upon the railing. The steps drew nearer. They were opposite her, and soon they would pass. Some neighbour, no doubt, going home. If he had seen her action he would tell others, and soon every person around would know. Presently the steps paused. The silence frightened her. It was dusk; no house in sight, and she was alone. Quickly she faced about, and there standing before her was Stephen. A cry of surprise escaped her, and the next instant she felt his strong arms about her and his lips fervently pressing her own.

"Stephen!" she cried, struggling to free Herself. "How dare you! When did you come?"

H. A. Cody

"Just from home, and was resting under that big tree," Stephen replied still holding her tenderly. "I dared much after I saw what you did a few minutes ago. Oh, Nellie, Nellie. I have been waiting long for this moment! Surely, surely you are mine at last!"

The flush had left Nellie's face now, leaving it very white, though in the deepening twilight this was not noticeable. Her heart was beating tumultuously, and a new feeling of peace and rest was stealing over her. How powerful seemed the man standing there. So long had she been called upon to be strong, always helping, ever taking such a responsible place in life, caring for her father, strengthening him in his work - and upon her he depended. But now to feel that she could give herself up to another, one who had passed through a stern fight in the strength of his sturdy young manhood, and had come forth as victor. Yet mingling with this new-found joy came the thought of the dark shadow hanging over her father's life. How could she be happy when he was in trouble? For his sake she had kept the brave spirit and presented only the bright sunny face, and cheery words of hope. The tension for weeks, nay months, had been a severe strain - and now this sudden joy! It unnerved her. Words would not come to Stephen's passionate pleading, but in their stead tears stole down her cheeks, while her form trembled with convulsive sobs.

Stephen started in surprise.

"Nellie! Nellie!" he cried. "What have I done! Forgive me! I did not mean to hurt you! I thought you would understand. If you only knew how I love you - if you only - "

"I know it, Stephen - I know it. I am very foolish. Please forgive me. I cannot explain these tears - they come unbidden."

"Then you're not unhappy, Nellie? You are not cross with me?"

"Cross, dear Stephen, no. I am so happy, very happy. But why should I he happy when my father is in trouble? How dare I! Is it right?"

"Then you love me, Nellie! Oh, speak the word - let me hear it from your own lips!"

"Yes, Stephen, I do love you, don't you know it? I am yours, your very own."

"Thank God! thank God!" he cried, drawing her closer to him, and kissing her again and again. She did not resist now, but allowed him to hold her there while he breathed into her ear his sweet words of love. They were no studied, well-rounded phrases, but such as leaped from a true, noble heart, and the woman listening knew their worth.

"Why didn't you write to me, Stephen?" Nellie whispered, "and tell me you were coming? I have been worried lately, and it would have been something to look forward to."

"I didn't know I was coming until this morning," came the reply.

"Didn't know?"

"No - I left in the night."

H. A. Cody

"This is more mysterious than ever."

"Yes, I left very early this morning, and should have been here by the middle of the afternoon, but Dexter threw a shoe about five miles back. I had to leave him at a farm, and walk the remainder of the way. I was resting by the bridge when you came along. I was quite put out to think I had to tramp that distance and be so late. But now I know it was for the best. Doesn't everything turn out right, Nellie?"

"Y-y - es, some things do," was the reluctant reply. "This has, anyway, and I try to believe that all things concerning my poor father will come out right, too. I think we had better go to him now and tell him of our happiness. It may brighten him up a bit."

Side by side they walked slowly along the road, and Stephen told the whole story of Tony's return, the hidden box, the political meeting, the discovery of the gold in the safe, and Farrington's ignominious punishment.

They had reached the house by the time he had finished, and stood for a moment on the doorstep before entering. In Nellie's heart was such a joy that words would not come to her lips. She felt she must be asleep, and would awake to find it only an unsubstantial dream. But Stephen's arm around her, and his strong presence near, assured her that it was a blessed reality.

They found Mr. Westmore sitting alone in his little room, reading by the shaded lamp. He glanced quickly up and was surprised to see Stephen standing by Nellie's side. He saw the look of rapture upon their faces, and read at once the meaning of it all, and into his own weary face came a light which Nellie had not seen in many a day. She tried to speak, but words failed, and moving quickly forward she threw her arms about her father's neck, and kissed him fervently.

"Oh, father, I am so happy!" she whispered. "Do you know? Can you understand?"

"Yes, darling," he replied. "I do understand. Come near, Stephen, my son," and as the young man approached, he joined their hands, and bade them to kneel before him. Then stretching out his hand over the bowed heads, and in a voice trembling with emotion, he gave them his benediction. "May the Lord bless you and keep you," he said. "May the Lord make His face to shine upon you, and be gracious unto you, and keep you true to Him and to each other unto your lives' end."

Sitting by Mr. Westmore's side that evening, Stephen told the story he had recently related to Nellie. Parson John sat straight upright in his chair, and his eyes never once left Stephen's face.

"And do you tell me!" he cried, when the latter ceased, "that Dan is injured - lying unconscious?"

"He was when Tony left."

"Poor dear boy! and he did it all for me!" murmured the parson. "What a sacrifice to make of his bright young life I I must go to him, Nellie, at once! In the morning! Poor Dan! Poor Dan!"

Thus the three sat for some time talking of the accident

H. A. Cody

and planning for the journey. Not once did Mr. Westmore speak about the recovery of the gold, but that night in the quietness of his own room he poured out his soul, in a great, fervent prayer of thankfulness to the Father above, and also he sought His aid on behalf of a little wounded lad lying on a bed of pain in a farm-house miles away.

Chapter XXX

Beneath the Surface

Across the mouth of Big Creek stream a long double boom cradled the large"R & P" drive. The last log had shot safely down the crooked brook and rested calmly by the side of its companions. There were thousands of them there, scarred and battered by rock and flood; worthy veterans were they, this hardy army of the forest, reposing now after their fierce, mad charge.

The work of the drivers was done, and the last peevy had been tossed with a resounding thud among its companions. A score of men were they who for months had been confined to the lonely life of the woods, and who for days had often been face to face with death. Naturally their eyes turned towards the river some distance away. There on its bank nestled the little town, and there, too, stood the Flood Gate Tavern, the most notorious place in the whole countryside. How often during the winter evenings had they talked of the many wild scenes which had been enacted there, and of the wages of months squandered in a night. Though they talked about the place and cursed it, yet, like moths singed by the candle's flame, they had returned spring after spring to the Hood Gate Tavern to spend the wages needed at home. Their money, too, was awaiting them there in the Company's

H. A. Cody

office. But now they hesitated. Never before had such a thing been known. Formerly there was a rush to the town when the last log had come in.

It was evening as the men stood there, and the sun was hanging low far in the west. The yearning for the tavern was strong - it called, it appealed to them. But another power was holding these rugged drivers in check. Their hearts had been much stirred these last few days, although not one acknowledged it. A little helpless, suffering child was unconsciously restraining the brute nature within them. He was holding them in leash, binding them by strange, invisible cords. In silence they ate their supper in the rafting house near by.

"Boys," said Jake Purdy as the men sat outside smoking. "I'm goin' down town to see if there's any mail. Any of ye comin'?"

It was all that was needed, and at once every man responded. Down the road they marched, their great boots making a heavy thud as they moved along. Into the post office they tramped, and stood around while the few letters were doled out. For Jake, there was one, written by a child's trembling hand. Eagerly he opened it, and, as he read, his face underwent a remarkable change. The rugged lines softened, and when he turned to the men waiting for him, there was no gruffness in his voice.

"'Spose we git our money, lads, an' hike back," he remarked.

"Ay, ay," was the response, but in several hearts there was a keen longing to remain.

Right in front of the Company's office stood the Flood Gate Tavern. The proprietor had been expecting the drivers and was well stocked up. He saw them coming into town and watched them enter the office for their money.

"They'll be here soon, Joe," he said to his assistant, "an' mind ye don't let an opportunity slip. Them bottles must go tonight. I know there'll be lively times about here. Them d - n temperance workers are dead set agin us, an' it looks as if they'd make trouble. But we'll win out tonight, and they can go to - . Say, here they come. Now for the time - an' money. Oh, they're jist achin' to give me their wages. They won't forgit old Ned, that's sure. Ha, ha!" and the saloon-keeper rubbed his hands with glee.

The drivers were outside the office now, and were casting furtive glances across the way. Big Jake saw the looks and knew the longing which dwelt in their hearts. He drew forth his pipe, stuck his little finger deliberately into the bowl to see how much tobacco it contained.

"Boys," he began, "have yez anything on fer the night?"

"No," came the somewhat surly response, "unless we go over there."

"Don't go," said Jake. "We've spent too much there in past years. Let's save our money fer them wot needs it at home. Let me tell ye somethin'. Comin' down the road from the boom to-night I felt like seven devils. I was jist longin' to git into that saloon an' have a big drink. But as luck 'ud have it I went into the post office first, an' found this here letter. An' who is it from, d'ye think? From me own little sick lassie at home. Look at the writin', boys. Ain't it fine? An' what a letter it is. She says she's waitin' fer me, an' counts the days until I come. Listen to these words: 'Don't go near the saloon, papa. Come straight home, an' bring the money to pay fer the farm. I pray fer you every day, papa, an' I pray fer all the men on the drive, and fer that poor little boy who got hurt.' Ain't them great words, boys?"

"Ay, ay," came the reply, and into several hearts throbbed a desire to be stronger men, and a few brushed their sleeves across their eyes.

"But that ain't all," Jake continued. "She says that little boy wot got hurt belongs to an old man - a parson - an' his beautiful daughter, who have been good to her. They didn't know where the little boy was, but when they found out they was all upsot, an' left in a hurry, but stopped in to say good-bye to my little Doris. That was two days ago, and they must be up there at Big Sam's now. Boys, let me tell ye this: Anyone who is good to my little sick lass is good to me, an' Jake Purdy isn't a man to fergit; yez know that. Now I have a suggestion to make. Instead of spendin' our hard-earned money with that old wretch, Ned, let's go up in a body to the house an' inquire fer the sick lad. We can't do nuthin', I know, but mebbe it'll please the old man an' his daughter to know that we ain't fergotten the brave little boy. An' come to think further it's no mor'n our duty. That lad saved one of us from death, an' the one that was saved, saved me. Boys, ye can do as yez like, but I'm goin' anyway."

There was no hesitation now among these men. With one accord they turned their backs upon the village, and struck along the road leading out into the country. Old Ned, the saloon-keeper, watched them in amazement. Never before had they done such a thing. What would become of all the whisky in those bottles standing on the shelves?

"The idiots!" he yelled. "What's the matter with 'em?"

Bareheaded he rushed out into the street and lifted up his voice.

"Hi! hi!" he shouted.

The drivers paused and looked around.

"Wait!" panted Ned running up to where they were standing.

"What's wrong, old man?" questioned one.

"Wrong! What's wrong with you? Why are ye leavin' without droppin' in to see me? Surely ye ain't goin' to go away without a friendly call?"

"Look here, Ned," replied Jake, acting as spokesman for the others, "we've made too many friendly calls at your place fer our own good. This year we're goin' to cut it out. So go home an' don't interfere."

Had the saloon-keeper been less excited he would have noticed the warning note in Jake's voice, and the sombre looks of the rest. They were in no mood for interruption at the present time. But Ned was blind to all this.

"Ye fools!" he roared, stamping on the ground in his

H. A. Cody

rage. "Will ye let all that good stuff spile down yonder? Surely ye ain't gone an' jined the temperance gang, an' took the pledge?"

Fiercely Jake turned upon him.

"Ned," and his voice was laden with meaning, "will ye go home an' leave us alone?"

"No, h - if I will, unless ye all come back with me."

Jake's eyes turned suddenly to the right. They rested upon a pond of dirty water several feet deep lying there. Like a flash he reached out and caught the saloon-keeper in both hands, lifted him clear of the ground, carried him wriggling and cursing to the edge, and tossed him in like a ball. With a splash and a yell Ned went under, came up puffing and blowing, and dashing the water from his eyes and ears. A shout of derision went up from the drivers.

"Go home now, Ned," they cried. "You've soaked us fer years with yer stuff, an' you've got soaked now. Good-bye."

With that they continued on their way, leaving the victim to scramble out of the pond and make his way home, beaten and crestfallen.

Along the road the drivers marched, then up the hill leading to Big Sam's abode. It was dim twilight as they stood before the house. The evening was balmy, and the front door stood partly open. For a minute they hesitated, and a whispered conversation ensued.

"You go in, Jake. You've got a tongue fer sich things,"

suggested his companions.

But before a reply could be made there floated out upon the air a sweet voice singing an old familiar hymn. Instinctively every driver pulled off his rough hat, and bowed his shaggy head. It was a woman's voice they heard, low and tender. There was a pleading note in the singer's voice - the cry of a soul for help in trouble.

Little did Nellie realize as she sat by Dan's side this evening, and sang, that she had such attentive listeners. The past two days had been a time of much anxiety. When first she and her father had arrived, Dan did not know them. He was lying upon the bed, his little curly head resting upon the pillow as white as his own white face. Would he ever come out of that stupor? they asked each other time and time again as they sat and watched him. Often he talked, calling aloud for help, and pleading for someone to hurry. Now it was of Tony and again Nellie and Parson John. Occasionally he mentioned his father, and asked why he was so long in coming. The doctor stood by the bedside with an anxious face.

"Do you think he will recover?" Nellie asked.

"I can't say," was the reply. "He has been badly injured. But we should know soon one way or the other. This condition can't go on much longer."

It was hard for Nellie to persuade her father to take any rest. He would insist upon sitting by the bed, and holding Dan's hand.

"Poor, dear boy," he murmured. "Why did you do it?

H. A. Cody

Why did you run such a risk for my sake?"

Once coming quietly into the room Nellie saw her father kneeling by the bedside. His lips were moving in silent prayer. In his heart a deep love had been formed for this little wounded lad. For months past the two had been much together, and the bond of affection had been strongly formed. At length Nellie had persuaded her father to take some rest. He had cast one long, searching look upon the boy's face, and then silently left the room. For some time Nellie sat by Dan's side watching his fitful breathing. One little hand lay outside the quilt. Would it ever work for her again? she wondered. It was a brown hand - the same hand which had reached over and drawn Tony from death. As she sat there the door was quietly pushed open, and Marion stood before her. Her eyes looked towards the bed with a questioning appeal. In her right hand she clutched a little rose. It was the first time she had been in the sick room, and on this evening while her mother was busy she had softly stolen away.

"Give dis to ittle sick boy," she said. "He like pitty woses."

"Come here, dear," Nellie replied, and as the child approached she took the flower, and placed the stem in Dan's doubled-up hand. She did it merely to please Marion, but it thrilled her own heart to behold the little maiden's sweet offering lying in that poor, nerveless fist. "God bless you, darling," she said, drawing Marion to her. "You love the sick boy, don't you?"

"Me love him," came the response, "an' me lore oo. Will Dod make him better?"

"God will do what is best, dearie. You will pray for him, won't you?"

"Me pray for him every night. Will oo sing to Dod to make him better?"

"Why do you wish me to sing?"

"When I'm sick my mamma sings to Dod. I fink He hears better dat way, an' I det better. Will oo sing?"

"If you wish me to, I will."

"Let me det in oor lap den," and Marion, climbing up, made herself perfectly at home.

Nellie was not in a singing mood this evening, but the child's words had touched her. She thought they were alone - just two, to hear. Verse after verses she sang, and as she reached the chorus of the last verse she gave a start of surprise, suddenly ceased, and looked towards the door. A number of men's voices had taken up the chorus, and they were singing, not loud, but as softly as possible:

"Safe in the arms of Jesus,
Safe on His gentle breast,
There by His love o'ershadowed
Sweetly my soul shall rest."

Nellie had put Marion down now, had risen to her feet, and crossed the room to the door. Almost unconsciously the drivers had joined in that chorus. They had forgotten how it would startle the sweet singer, and when they saw Nellie standing in the doorway they were much abashed. They felt like a group of schoolboys caught in some act of mischief, and they longed to get away.

As Nellie looked upon them, a bright smile illumined her face. She surmised the purpose of their visit, and it pleased her.

"Thank you for that chorus," she said, hardly knowing what else to say. "I didn't know you were here."

"Pardon us, miss," Jake replied, stepping forward. "It wasn't fair of us to be standin' here listenin'. But we couldn't help it. An' when ye sang that old hymn it jist melted us down. We come to inquire about the boy. Mebbe ye'd tell us how he's gettin' along."

"There's no change as yet, that we can see," Nellie replied. "But the doctor says it must come soon one way or the other. Would you like to see him? If you come in one at a time, I don't think it will do any harm."

Without a word Jake followed her into the room, and stood with his hat in his hand looking down upon the bed.

"Poor little chap," he whispered. "Ain't it a pity?"

Hardly had he ceased speaking when Dan suddenly opened his eyes and looked about him in a dazed manner.

"Where - where's my rose?" he cried.

Nellie was by his side in an instant.

"Here, Dan," and she lifted up the flower so he could see it. "Hush now, don't speak."

Dan gave a sigh of relief. He looked wearily around, then his eyes slowly closed, and he passed into a gentle sleep. A step was heard in the room, and the doctor stood by the bed.

"When did the change take place?" he asked.

"Just now," Nellie replied in a low voice.

"It is well. The crisis is past. He must have perfect quietness. We'll pull him through now, for sure."

Jake waited to hear no more. He stole from the house, and motioned to his companions. Silently they moved away and strode back to the camp. They were rough men outwardly, this score of river drivers, but a glimpse had been seen beneath the surface. Their hearts had been stirred as never before, and they were not ashamed.

Chapter XXXI

Light at Eventide

It was a bright buoyant day, with scarcely a cloud to be seen. Not a breath of wind stirred the air, and every nimble leaf was still. The river flowed on its way, its glassy surface mirroring the numerous trees along its banks. Across the fields, fresh with the young green grass, came the sweet incense wafted up from countless early flowers.

Several people stood before the Rectory, beneath the shade of a large horse-chestnut tree. Their eyes were turned up the road with an eager, watchful expression. Across the gateway a rude arch had been formed, and upon it the words "Welcome Home" in large white letters had been painted, while evergreens and leaves lavishly decorated the whole. It was Glendow's preparation for the return of their absent Rector and his daughter.

Numerous changes had taken place since the night on which the gold had been found in the safe. The store was now closed and the Farringtons had departed. There had been many threats made by the defeated storekeeper, but they amounted to nothing. Glendow had been aroused, and the one desire which filled all hearts was to have their old Rector back again. They realized as never before the sterling character of the man they had suspected, and what a true friend they had lost. Dan's accident soon reached their ears, and all breathed a prayer of thankfulness when news arrived of his recovery. Nothing short of a reception must take place, and so now more than threescore people, old and young, stood anxiously awaiting the arrival.

"There they come," shouted one, and far up the road a cloud of dust could he seen, and soon a carriage was observed bowling along, containing Parson John, Nellie and Dan.

Their eyes opened wide with amazement as they drew near, saw the cheering crowd, and drove beneath the overhanging arch. Silently they alighted and grasped the numerous outstretched hands. The past was forgotten in the joy of the present, and the shepherd and his flock were once again united.

"It all seems like a wonderful dream," said Parson John to Nellie as they sat that evening together after the others had departed. "We went out as culprits, with only a few to bid us good-bye, and now we come home to the love of our people. Surely the Lord has been good to us, and has led us by ways that we knew not. Truly His ways are not our ways, and He does all things well."

Dan speedily recovered his former strength and his old-time spirit. He was like a new lad. The weight which had pressed upon him so long had been removed. He felt he was no longer a sponger, a useless being. His longing to read and write increased, and as the days passed he made rapid progress. Mr. Westmore loved to have the boy by his side and would often read to him, and Dan would always listen with deep wonder. New fields of knowledge were being gradually opened of which he knew nothing.

"When I grow to be a big man will I know all about those things?" he one day asked, when Mr. Westmore had been reading to him from an interesting book of History.

"That all rests with yourself, Dan," was the reply. "If you want to know, you can. But it will mean hard work. There is no royal road to learning."

"Then I'm going to learn," Dan emphatically responded, and from that day Mr. Westmore began to plan for the boy's future as he had never done before.

One evening about sundown, several weeks later, Nellie and her father were sitting on the veranda. It was a sultry night, and far in the distance faint rumblings of thunder could be heard.

"A storm is coming," Nellie remarked. "I hope Mr. Larkins will get back from the office before it reaches us."

Hardly had she spoken ere a step sounded upon the gravel walk and Mr. Larkins appeared.

"We were just speaking about you," Nellie exclaimed, and now you are here."

"You know the old saying," he laughingly replied.

"Have a seat, do," and Mr. Westmore pushed forward a rustic chair.

"No, thank you, I have some chores to do before the storm breaks. Here is your mail. Several papers and only one letter."

"It's from my boy out west," Mr. Westmore remarked after Mr. Larkins had gone. "We've had little news from him lately. I hope nothing's wrong."

His hand trembled slightly as he opened the letter and unfolded several sheets of paper within. Nellie picked up one of the papers, a daily from the city, and was soon engrossed in its pages. An exclamation from her father caused her to look quickly up. The expression on his face was one of joy. It was that of a man from whom a heavy burden of care has been unexpectedly lifted.

"Nellie, Nellie!" he cried. "Good news from Philip! He's won his case! The mine is ours beyond dispute, and it is far richer than was at first believed. Read it for yourself," and he eagerly thrust the letter into her hand.

Trembling with excitement Nellie did as she was commanded. The first part of the letter told about the long, stern fight which had been made, and of the victory which had been won.

"You little know, father dear," Philip wrote in conclusion, "what this will mean to us all. Upon my suggestion you invested your all in this mine, and at one time it looked as if we would lose everything. But now all that is changed. I am a rich man to-day and you will no longer want for anything. Your investment will be increased a hundredfold, and you will make more in one year than you have made in your whole life. As soon as I get matters in a settled condition I hope to come home for a short visit, and then. I shall be able to tell you everything in detail."

For some time Nellie held the letter silently in her hand. Her father was sitting near with a far-away look in his eyes. Gone were time and place. He was thinking of the day he had bidden Philip good-bye. He saw the mother clasping her only son to her heart, and it was the last good-bye. What hopes and fears had been theirs concerning their absent boy. What struggles had been his out in the great busy world, and how often had his home letters been weighted with despair. Many and many a night had they knelt together and lifted up their voices in prayer on Philip's behalf. Now she was gone. Oh, to have her there by his side to share his joy! A mistiness rose before his eyes, and several tears stole down his furrowed cheeks. Hastily he drew forth his handkerchief and brushed them away. Nellie noticed his embarrassed manner, and surmised the cause. Going over to where he was sitting she put her arms about his neck and gave him a loving kiss.

"You have me, father dear," she said, "and nothing but death can separate us."

"I know it, darling. I know it," was the reply. "I am somewhat unsettled to-night. This news is so sudden. To think that Philip has conquered! Now you shall have many comforts which have been denied you so long."

"Don't say that, father dear. What comforts have been denied me? My whole life has been surrounded by love. We have our little home here, with books and music in the winter, and the sweet flowers and birds in the summer. Does not happiness, father, consist in enjoying the good things around us? Not for my sake am I glad that this good fortune has come, but for yours. If Philip is correct, and we are to have more money than ever before, you will be able to rest and enjoy life to the full."

"Nellie, Nellie! What do you mean? Do I understand you aright? Do you wish me to give up my work?"

"But you need rest, father. You have laboured so long, surely you can afford to let someone else do it now."

"No, no. The Lord needs me yet. There is much work for me to do. Life to me is in ministering to others. During those long days at Morristown, when that cloud overshadowed us, how wretched was my life. Nothing to do - only to sit with folded hands while others waited upon me. I shudder when I think of that time. No, let me be up and doing, and God grant I may die in harness, and not rust out in miserable disuse."

"But you should have an assistant, father," Nellie suggested, "and he can give you great help."

"I have been thinking of that, dear. It seems now as if one great wish of my life is to be granted. I have always longed to give several years to God's service, without being chargeable to any one. Oh, to go among my people, to comfort them, not as a servant, a hireling paid to do such things, but as a shepherd who loves his flock, and whose reward is in doing the Master's work, for the good of others. The people may pay the assistant, but not me. I wish to be free, free for God's service."

H. A. Cody

Footsteps were now heard approaching, and in a minute more Stephen stood before them. The flush of joy that suffused Nellie's face told of the happiness in her heart.

"Welcome, Stephen, my son," said Parson John, reaching out his hand. "Your visit is timely when our cup of joy is full to the brim and running over. We have not seen you for two whole days. Where have you kept yourself?"

"Why, Stephen has been to the city," was Nellie's laughing response. "Didn't I tell you how he had gone with his logs?"

"Dear me, so you did. How stupid of me to forget."

"Yes," said Stephen, "my winter's work is all settled and I have come now to make the first payment on the farm. There it is. Please count it," and the young man placed a bulky envelope into his Rector's hand. "That is a token of my new life, and with God's help it shall continue."

For several minutes Mr. Westmore held the package in his hand without once looking upon it.

"Sit down, Stephen," he at length commanded. "I have something to say - to you - and I feel I can say it now with a clear conscience. Since the day I paid the four thousand dollars for your homestead, people have been wondering where I obtained the money, and they certainly had good reason to wonder. They knew I had invested all I could gather together in that mine in British Columbia, and that I could pay down such an amount was very puzzling. It is only right that you and

Nellie should hear the truth from my own lips. You well know," he continued after a pause, "that your father was a very dear friend of mine. We had grown up as boys together. We knew each other's affairs intimately, and we often discussed the future. Your father made considerable money, and had a fairly large bank account. One day he came to me - only several months before his death - and we had a most serious talk together. He seemed to have some premonition that he would not be much longer upon earth, and was most anxious that I should consent to a plan which he had in his mind. He was fearful lest after his death something should go wrong. He knew what a headstrong lad you were, Stephen, and what a temptation it would be to spend recklessly his hard-earned money. He therefore wished me to act as trustee, with another firm friend who is living in the city, and to place in the bank in our names the sum of six thousand dollars. This was to be left there, unknown to others, until you proved yourself to be a man in every sense of the word. In case of disaster or trouble we were to use the money at our discretion for the welfare of the family and not to allow your mother or sister to come to want. That, in brief, is the substance of the plan. At first I did not feel like undertaking such a responsibility. But your father was so insistent I at last consented. I need hardly tell you the rest, for you know it already. I could not, in justice to your father's express wish, divulge the secret until I was sure that you had taken a firm grip of life. You needed to be tested, to pass through the fire. Now I know you can he depended upon, and so I give you back this money, Keep it; it is yours, and may God bless you. Part of the balance which remained in the bank we used on Nora with such splendid results. The rest shall be handed over to your mother, and I shall

H. A. Cody

thus be relieved of all responsibility. Will that be satisfactory to you?"

Mr. Westmore ceased, and held forth the envelope. Stephen had risen now and was standing erect. His hands remained clasped before him.

"Take it," said the parson.

"No," was the reply, "I cannot."

"You cannot? It is yours!"

"Yes, I know that. But remember, I have undertaken to pay back that four thousand dollars. Through my recklessness I made it necessary to use my dear father's hard-earned money. Not a cent will I touch until the full amount is restored, and if I have my health it shall be done. Do not urge me any more. Put that money where it belongs. It may take me some time to pay all, but not until it is accomplished shall I feel satisfied."

"Stephen, Stephen!" cried the parson, "give me your hand. Now I know that you are in earnest. I shall do as you desire. My heart is full of joy to-night. May God be glorified for all His blessings. I shall away to rest now, for the many wonders of the day have tired me much."

The storm which had been threatening rolled to westward. Far off the moon rose slowly above the horizon. The night was still. Everything betokened peace. On the little veranda sat the two young lovers hand in hand. Heart responded to heart, and time was no more. The present and the future were blended. The rapture of living was theirs, for where love reigns there is life in all its fulness.

H. A. Cody